TO LOVE MERCY

TO LOVE MERCY

Frank S. Joseph

Mid-Atlantic Highlands

Library of Congress Card Catalog Number:
2006920541

Trade Paper ISBN: 0-9744785-3-9

· First Edition, First Printing
Printed in U.S.A.

Cover Design: 1106 Design, Phoenix, AZ
Interior Design: Jennifer Adkins, Grace Associates

Mid-Atlantic Highlands
an imprint of Publishers Place, Inc.
945 Fourth Avenue, Suite 200A
Huntington, WV 25701
www.publishersplace.org

The font used to set the text of this book is Georgia.

For Carol,
Sam and Shawn,
here on earth,

and for
Nate and Dora,
Irwin and Marjorie,
somewhere in heaven.

Author's Note

This novel was born in workshops at the Writer's Center, Bethesda, Maryland, under the wise guidance of Barbara Esstman, Tim Junkin, Ann McLaughlin, John Morris and Carolyn Thorman.

It was nourished along the way by sensitive, supportive critiques from friends and colleagues, including Rick Biehl, Tory Cowles, Vince Crivello, Mike and Marilyn Hollman, Davida Kristy, Joyce McDowell, Judy Thornber, Roberta Weiner and David Yale; and the stalwarts of the Holey Roaders Writers' Group past and present, including Bert Brandenburg, Susan Clark, Solveig Eggerz, Catherine Flanagan, Bob Gibson, Phil Harvey, Art Kerns, Kathy Lorr, Linda Morefield, Leslie Rollins, Wayland Stallard, Pauline Steinhorn, David Stewart and Paul Vamvas.

A half-dozen special people—Lillie Harston-Thomas, Enich Hymon, Harvey Lee, Gladys McKinney, William Williams and the late Bunny Dallas—generously shared their own lives and experiences of growing up and living in Bronzeville; and Jolyn Robichaux assured me, at a critical moment, that I'd gotten Bronzeville right.

I couldn't have reconstructed the Riverview Park of 1948 without the help of Elliot Greene, who misspent huge portions of his childhood there.

For other research assistance and special help, thanks to Harold Lucas of The Black Metropolis Convention & Tourism Council; Jim Grossman of the Newberry Library; the staff of the Chicago Historical

Society; Jack Foster, Miriam Hamilton, Jordan Rolnick-Melechen, Beth Rubin and Marilyn Davenport Smith.

Thanks to John Patrick Grace, my publisher, for deft final edits.

But most thanks go to Carol Jason, my wife, supremely patient and understanding. There would be no book without you.

—Frank S. Joseph

This is a work of fiction, not fact. The events, characters and circumstances in this novel may have been inspired by persons living or dead; but what you read portrayed herein are the pure products of the author's imagination.

The chapter "Dora on the Bus" appeared in slightly different form in Oyez Review and is reprinted by permission of Oyez Review, the literary magazine of the Creative Writing Program at Roosevelt University. Oyez Review, Volume 30, Winter 2002. ©2002.

The quotation in Hebrew in the opening pages is from The Jerusalem Bible. Copyright ©1992 by Koren Publishing Jerusalem Ltd., Jerusalem.

The voices of Timuel D. "Tim" Black, Charles Branham, Junius "Red" Gaten, Marion Hummons, Samuel Stevens and Delores Washington, quoted in the historical Afterword, are excerpted by permission of the Chicago Historical Society from tapes and transcripts of the Douglas-Grand Boulevard Neighborhood Oral History Project of the Chicago Historical Society, 1995.

הִגִּיד לְךָ אָדָם מַה־טּוֹב וּמָה־יְהֹוָה
דּוֹרֵשׁ מִמְּךָ כִּי אִם־עֲשׂוֹת מִשְׁפָּט וְאַהֲבַת
חֶסֶד וְהַצְנֵעַ לֶכֶת עִם־אֱלֹהֶיךָ:

What doth the Lord require of thee?
To do justice, to love mercy,
and to walk humbly with thy God.

Micah 6:8

1
Steve

Tuesday, June 15, 1948

By the time I get back, Dad and Grandpa are standing in the gangway, smoking. They're talking about Earl Caldwell's single, the one that won it, but they look nervous. I know Dad is going to be mad because I took so long with the autograph. But something else is the matter too.

Dad just says Let's get a move on. It's almost midnight.

We'll be OK Grandpa says.

Yeah. When we're in the car with the doors locked. Come on Pop. Come on Steve.

I'm ready to go anyway. I wanted Luke Appling's autograph or even Taffy Wright would of been OK, but when I get to the dugout Appling and Wright are in the showers already and who the heck is left? Then just when I'm turning around I bump into Seerey. Really, he's standing there and I kind of walk right into him. He's fat for a ballplayer. I say Sorry and he says That's OK kiddo do you want me to sign your program and I'm sort of embarrassed because one, I don't have a program with me, and another, I actually didn't. I wanted Appling, not Seerey, who's this new guy from Cleveland that Frank Lane traded for Bob Kennedy and Al Gettel, he's supposed to be a power hitter but he hasn't done much yet and the White Sox are way last, sixteen games out, they're going to need a lot more than Seerey. Though he did get that single in the third. They beat the Yankees nine to eight tonight but it took eleven innings. Rickie says they're crummy and he's going to start rooting for the Cubs.

But now I've been waiting half an hour so I say Sure. Because I think at least I should have someone's autograph for when I get back because it's so late and Dad's going to be mad.

So give me your program kid.

I pretend I don't hear him and reach into my pocket but all I've got on me is the new Appling card. I gave Rickie a Bill Wight for it and then he wanted my old torn Appling card too and I had to promise to buy him ten Mary Janes at the school store and they're a penny each so that's a dime.

I hand the card to Seerey and he writes PAT SEEREY LEFT FIELD BATTING .253. All over Appling's face.

Then I get back and there are Dad and Grandpa all alone. Everyone else is gone home. Well, a colored guy with a push broom. Dad says Did you fall in? I say Huh? and he says Skip it let's just get a move on by the time we drop your grandpa off it'll be one o'clock your mom'll kill us.

I couldn't help it though.

So we're walking along Thirty-Fifth Street and

there's nobody out here either. All I can hear is our shoes. They've got their hands in their pockets and their heads down. Dad's saying Pick it up Pop. Dad calls Grandpa Pop, not Dad, but I call Dad Dad. I guess I could call him Pop. But I never have.

Grandpa says We'll be all right there's attendants. But when we get to the parking lot there aren't any. Just one or two cars left. The Buick is all the way on the far side, over where it's the most dark.

I run ahead and swing around a lamp pole but Dad says Cut it out. I say Why? He says You're making me nervous.

But there's no one else out here.

He says That's why.

I don't get it.

Grandpa says You don't know. The *shochers*.

I still don't get it.

The *shochers*. The *shvartzes*.

Now I get it maybe. Sometimes Grandpa talks those words, I don't know them, but they're bad words or maybe not bad but you've got to say them in Yiddish not English. I don't know if that makes them bad. But it might.

I heard Grandpa say one of them before. Not the other. I never heard the other. They probably both mean the same. I think I know what the one means. *Shvartze*.

Negroes?

He says Yeah Negroes except he says it like knee-grows. What do they teach you in school anyway?

I don't feel so good. My stomach hurts. Maybe it's

just I've got to pee. I should of gone after Seerey ruined the Appling card but I didn't because of how late. I'm sleepy too, even though I stay up this late sometimes reading comics by the hall light and they don't know it unless they catch me but I stuff the comics under the bed when I hear them coming so they don't catch me very often. I'm going to be real sleepy at school tomorrow. Mom almost didn't let me come to the game because of school and she wouldn't of except it's Tuesday and school's out Friday for summer. And I haven't seen a White Sox game yet this year. And maybe because it's my birthday Saturday. I'll be ten. Maybe that's why she let me.

Then out come those kids.

I don't even know where they came from. There wasn't anyone else in the parking lot but us, that's what I thought anyway. Maybe they were hiding. Behind the Buick maybe.

There's about eight of them, seven or eight. I can't tell because it's so dark over there by the fence. But the thing is, they're *kids*, like me. The oldest might be twelve. The girls are as young as me, fifth grade, one of them anyway, and the boys sixth grade, except the tall one might be in seventh.

The tall one says Got a dime? Only it sounds like Gaah dahm because he's colored. They're all colored.

They're all colored at Grandpa's theater too, the Calumet. I guess everyone down here is colored. There aren't any colored on the White Sox though. The Indians just signed Larry Doby but Dad says there won't be any colored on the White Sox ever, not with Chuck Comiskey running it.

The tall kid says Gaah dahm again and he's smiling kind of. His face is pushed close to Dad's. He's about the same size as Dad but skinny. Dad could take him easy. He's real skinny even though he's tall and besides he's just a kid. He doesn't seem scared though. In fact now he's laughing. It's Dad looks scared.

The kids are dancing around us now singing Gaah dahm Gaah dahm Gaah dahm and asking for ice cream. One of them puts out his arms and scoots around us going eeeaaaarrrnnhhhh like an airplane. Another one starts singing Cement Mixer Putty Putty like they sing it on the radio, SEE-ment MIX-uh PUTT-tee PUTT-tee. He sounds like Dora. They all sound like Dora.

Dad shouts Go away and reaches into his pocket. He's got a lot of coins and the keys to the car. He reaches out to the tall kid but then the kid playing airplane bumps into him by accident and he drops all of it. The money and the car keys. The kids start laughing and shouting Money Money Money and scrambling around in the dirt. The girls too.

Then this one kid, he grabs for Grandpa's coat. Little bitty kid.

The kid says Take me back to Comiskey Park old man, buy me some cotton candy. He starts to dance. He jiggles up and down then he reaches for Grandpa's hand. Hey old man you want to dance? Let's you and me dance he says.

I'm standing next to Grandpa so this kid's standing right in front of me. He's got on a checked shirt. His face is thin, almost like a girl's. I look at him and he looks back, right in the eye because he's only a little taller even though he's probably a year older, probably sixth grade. He's got big eyes or maybe it's just because he's skinny they look so big.

Let my grandpa alone.

Aw I'm just playing with him hee hee.

But then I see something, corner of my eye. It's the tall kid. I turn around and he's sneaking up behind Grandpa. He's crouching down like nobody could see him but I see him. He's sticking his hand under Grandpa's jacket.

The little kid sees him too. He starts yelling at the tall one. He calls him Nubby. Get the hell away Nubby we didn't come out here to pick no pockets you're going to get us all arrested you damn fool. He's using cuss words too, the little kid, worse ones than hell and damn.

So what happens next, I've been trying to figure it out exactly but there's some parts I just can't tell because it was so confusing and dark too.

First, Grandpa turns around fast. He must of felt the tall kid reaching into his pocket or maybe he figured it out from the little kid cussing.

The little kid is still holding onto his jacket. I guess he just doesn't have time to let go.

I'm standing right next to Grandpa and he bumps into me, the little kid, and I slip. It's real easy to slip because that parking lot is just gravel and cinders.

I fling my arm out for balance and it hits him. Right in the throat. He goes Gurk because I hit him pretty hard. Real hard. But it was an accident.

Then I don't know, I'm slipping in the gravel, I hear other people slipping and shouting and someone goes Oof. Grandpa.

Dad's yelling Steve, Pop, are you OK? He's helping Grandpa and me up.

The other kids, all of a sudden they're gone. D'sappeared. Except the little one.

He's lying on the ground where Grandpa just got up from. His nose is all squished over to one side of his face. He's bleeding too and his left hand is twisted up underneath him, but his nose. Jeez.

He's out cold.

Dad says to call an ambulance but there aren't any pay phones. Grandpa says Let's just get in the car.

I'm looking at the kid lying on the ground and I can't tell if he's breathing or not. Maybe you can't breathe when your nose is all pushed over like that. He isn't moving at all.

Don't leave him lying there. Please.

You're shivering Dad says. What's the matter Steve you want my jacket?

Then he looks down at the kid. Grandpa looks at the kid too. They look at each other. Finally Grandpa shrugs.

Dad says We're going to have to take him over to Mercy. Come on Pop give me a hand.

Dad gets down on his hands and knees and pushes the gravel around until his keys clink. He gets up and brushes off his pants. He hands me the keys. Steve open the door he says.

He grabs the kid under the shoulders and Grandpa picks him up by the knees. They lug him into the front seat and prop him up then shut the door quick. So he won't fall over.

2
Sass

Got a Dime?

I'm eating my breakfast, my oldest brother Darius comes says Sass get your monkey butt out of my chair, and he gives me a lick so hard my head starts spinning. Where's this chair say it's got your name on it I ask, trying to talk back like he ain't nothing big, like I ain't scared of him, but my head starts hurting something terrible. That was the start of my bad day.

I go to school, teacher's talking about long division, can't understand a thing she says. My head still hurts, Darius gave me such a poke. I get big some day I'll show him what it feels like, sneak into his bed with a two-by-four and lam his fool brains out.

Now I'm lying in this hospital bed, my head hurts worse than it did then. Wonder who brung me here? Last I recall, we were coming up on the white folks, me and Witchie and Sawbuck and Herm and them gals and that damn fool brother of mine Nubby. Nubby thinks he's slick but he's so slow he can't hardly tie his own shoes. Nubby is the reason I'm lying here.

We're out on the sidewalk lagging pennies, Witchie

says, Let's get us some pop. So we go down to the corner, ask old man Levy would he give us a Green River. Levy says Get out of here you no-'count children, you ain't got no money for no Green River nor no Royal Crown neither. Sawbuck, he answers back salty-like. Levy starts yelling at Saw instead of paying attention to me like he should of done. I grab a bottle of Green River out the crate and run out of Levy's store. Sawbuck and Witchie come running out too. Old Levy, he like to bust the screen door trying catch us but we're too fast for his sorry legs. Levy's yelling about the police and shaking his fist, we're laughing and running because we know he ain't going to leave his store for no damn bottle of pop.

We get into the alley, Witchie says Give me some of that pop Sass I'm thirsty from all that running. But we ain't got no opener so Sawbuck runs up to his place and asks his momma for one. She comes out on the porch yelling down at us What kind of trouble you children getting into? But Sawbuck says Oh Momma we're being good go on back inside and he brings down the opener. We pass the bottle around. Sure tasted good while we were panting and laughing and cutting up on old man Levy.

Along comes Mavis and her girlfriends. Mavis says Give me some of that Green River too. Ain't no more girl get your own, that's what Witchie says to her. She says How did you get it? We stole it from Levy's store Witchie says. Oh I'm going tell your momma on you Mavis says, she's such a sissy. You'd best not or I'll tell your momma how you ditched school Thursday and went to the Calumet with Sally Louise and Portia, Witchie says back. So they argue back and forth about who did the worst thing and whose momma'll be giving who a licking, like they do, and me and Sawbuck joke back and forth about their sorry selves, like we do, and along comes Nubby. That's when it started.

Nubby says You ever seen a White Sox game? Of course we ain't seen no White Sox game. We ain't even supposed to cross Wentworth Avenue, how we going to get tickets to see the White Sox? I listen at Bob Elson on WJJD but I don't hardly see how anyone cares about that trash anyhow, he's the most boring white man I ever heard. He says There goes Tony Lupien making a line drive out to deep center field like he's talking about This here fried chicken's getting a little cold. Can't tell if he's calling a baseball game or trying to get some sleep.

Then he talks about that Friendly Bob Adams, Friendly Bob Adams and Beneficial Finance going to make you a loan. Man makes me want to laugh. Down here in Bronzeville, ain't no one making no loans to no body. Ain't hardly no banks and anyway all they want to do is take your money, Poppa says, not make you a loan to buy you a car or nothing. All I seen around here are them currency exchanges to cash folks' checks for a quarter. I ain't seen no Friendly Bob Adams, except on the matchbooks.

I'm going to show you how to get into Comiskey Park Nubby says, standing up big with his chest puffed out. Aw go on you're bragging Mavis tells him, but Nubby says No come on with me I know a way. Them girls start chattering like Nubby is something big but they ought to know him like I do, they'd know the only big thing he is, is a big bag of wind.

Never mind that. They all go running off. Sawbuck and Witchie and Herm, they say Let's go, so what am I going to do? I chuck the Green River bottle against the wall and go running after them. Was a fool to do that.

We get to the ballpark, people are already starting to come out. What did you bring us over here for, Witchie says to Nubby. Even if you sneak us in we ain't going to see no ball game, they'll be finished playing in a few minutes. We're nodding our heads.

Don't you want to see my secret way in, Nubby says.

OK, long as we're here, go ahead and show us your fool way in I say.

Nubby goes up to the ticket box and says to the white man Excuse me my daddy works on the grounds crew and I got to get a message to him. We're ducking behind a souvenir cart giggling so much we can't hardly hear what Nubby says next. What message? I'll see he gets it says the man. Nossir I got to talk to my daddy myself it's real urgent says Nubby. What's your daddy's name, man says. Soames sir, Elbert B. Soames Nubby says back. What's the message, man asks. I'd rather give it to him myself sir it's about my baby brother Nubby says. That gets me hot! What business does he got talking about me? Gets me in trouble with his damn fool plan, I'll see to it he pays the price.

The man gets tired of Nubby's shenanigans. Ain't no Soames works here he says. You're trying to sneak in and see the game. Get your black ass out of here he says. Nubby tries to argue but of course it don't work so he walks back with his head down. He tries to pretend nothing happened but even the girls start making fun of him.

Nubby tells them to shut up. He's getting that look on his face, all hot and righteous, like You can't do that to me don't you know who I am? He's acting like he did last year when the principal expelled him for setting fire to the toilet paper. He'd of been smart, he'd of admitted it and taken his suspension. But no, stupid Nubby's got to go get raucous and try to hit the principal, so they give him a week instead of a day. That's what he's like. He's dumb as a post and the only one don't know it is Nubby.

But them girls went and embarrassed him and now he's got to make himself look good. He says Follow me and tails off down Thirty-Fifth. There's trouble coming sure. Can't count on Nubby when he's acting like this.

First he starts talking about reefer, going to get some reefer. Now I know he's talking big. Nubby ain't never smoked no reefer, him twelve years old, he don't even know what reefer looks like. He hears them winos on the corner talking about it, even they ain't got no reefer nor no money to buy it neither. I tell him that to his face. That gets him madder still. The girls shaming him is bad enough, Nubby don't want to hear no more sass from his baby brother. But that's why they call me Sass and I ain't ashamed of the name.

We get to State Street, Nubby says Let's get us

some Karmelkorn. Karmelkorn shop is right next to the Calumet so folks can get Karmelkorn to bring inside the movie. Sawbuck asks Nubby does he have any money? Of course Nubby ain't got no money. Anyone got money? Portia has a few dimes. Now I know Sawbuck's got some money because he always has it but he don't never share it. Sawbuck says Naw I ain't got no money neither like I knew he would. Come on Saw we know you got it give us some of that money of yours Witchie says and sticks his hand into Saw's pocket. Saw and Witchie start hitting each other and horsing around but I know they ain't really mad so I tell them Come on that ain't getting us no Karmelkorn and they cut it out.

Where are we going to get money? Everyone starts jabbering. Blessed if I know. Ain't no one out here going to give it to us.

Colored folks ain't got no money anyhow says one of Mavis's girlfriends, little buck-toothed gal name of Sarah.

But that was exactly the wrong thing to say. That's it, Nubby says, let's go back to the ballpark and find us someone who *does* have some money.

We all know what Nubby is talking about, don't have to ask. Whoopee they start yelling and Let's go and This gonna be fun! Stuff like that.

Oooh I can't be robbing no white folks says Mavis.

Ain't said nothing about robbing no one you little goody-goody, Witchie says. We're going to ask them nice and polite for some money for Karmelkorn.

Yeah, we're going to ask them for a loan, Sawbuck says.

Yeah, Friendly Bob Adams is going to make us a loan, Witchie says, and *everyone* thinks that's funny. They all start laughing and singing and carrying on, skipping back Thirty-Fifth Street toward that old parking lot.

We get there, we see the three white folks. One's an old man and he's so short he's as short as us. Another's a kid like me. Third one, he's about Nubby's size, must be the kid's daddy. He's the only one could hurt us if he tried. Ain't no one else around and there's more of us than there are of them. Nubby says This is going to be easy.

Witchie says Shush up you all they're going to hear us so we all pipe down and try to walk like Indians, though I'm thinking the white folks are going to hear us stirring up the gravel for sure.

But they must not be listening. The one who's the daddy, wearing a suit, when he notices us, his face looks like he's just seen his own ghost.

Nubby goes up to him, asks him for a dime. Crazy Witchie starts dancing around singing Got a dime! Got a dime! Got a dime! Sawbuck puts out his arms and scoots around them like he's an airplane. Girls are giggling and sort of hanging back but they're excited too.

The father, he reaches into his pocket and holds out his hand to Nubby but Nubby don't take the money. Nubby seems to care more about trying to make a fool of this poor white man. Maybe Nubby still is thinking about them girls making a fool of him. But Nubby seems to forget, there's polices all around the ballpark to protect white folks. One of them comes up, sees what we're doing, he'll take his nightstick upside our heads and haul us off to the Bridewell. See can our mommas get us out of *that*.

Then Sawbuck bumps into the guy, the daddy, and knocks the money out of his hand. Everybody goes scrambling around in the dirt like chickens.

I'm horsing around with the old man but I'm thinking, this is all starting to look crazy. What are we out here for, to get money for Karmelkorn or to scare these white folks? Nubby is acting like the leader but he ain't got no damn plan. And these fools, they're cutting up like it's a party. We got what we wanted, couple of dimes, better cut and run right now.

But then stupid Nubby comes up behind the old man and tries to pick his pocket. I yell at Nubby to stop before he gets us in some kind of worse trouble. The old man slips and I'm still holding onto him. I must of slipped too. Then something hits me in the throat, real hard. Danged if I can remember what happens after that.

◆   ◆   ◆   ◆   ◆   ◆   ◆

Woman wants to know my name and where I live. Jesse Owens Trimble ma'am. I live at Thirty-Sixth and Wabash.

She asks what's the address. What's she talking about? I told her I live at Thirty-Sixth and Wabash. No son I mean what's the number of your building? White woman calling me son, I ain't her son. But my chest and head and nose and wrist hurt so bad I don't feel like sassing her right then. I don't know no number ma'am, it's the second building from the corner ma'am. Which apartment? On the top on the left, the one at the back ma'am.

What're your momma's and poppa's names? Mister and Missus Trimble ma'am. Yes yes she says like my teacher does when she's talking to the dumb ones. But what's their first names? My poppa is James and my momma is Mattie ma'am. I keep calling her ma'am, maybe she'll stop asking so many questions.

But she don't stop. What were you doing out there at Sox Park? Why are you asking? Don't you go giving me your smart talk, I'm from the police she says. You can't be no police, you're a gal I tell her. I'm from the Juvenile Division, they got plenty of gal polices down there she says. She pulls out a shiny badge and waves it in my face. Got a big old nose like a rubber ball and hair coming out of her nostrils.

Don't you go telling my momma and poppa I did something I say to her. Poppa sees me in here, he'll take his belt to me, I'll be hurting a lot worse than I am now.

Why, what did you do, she says. Breath smells like a hot dog.

Nothing, and I try to raise my right hand up out the covers. This white woman thinks I'm going to tell on my friends, she's crazy.

The white folks already told us what you did.

What'd they say?

Never mind what they said, you tell me your story.

Didn't do nothing to them.

Then how did you get injured?

I don't know ma'am.

That's the truth anyway.

All right she says, you won't talk to me, I'll bring your momma and poppa in here and have them ask you a few questions.

I start crying then. It was so stupid, wish I could of stopped myself, but I couldn't. The thought of Momma weeping and praying over me, I just got scared. I squeeze my eyes tight together to stop the tears coming out but it don't work. This white policewoman is sitting there, face like a rock.

What you want to know I blubber.

That's more like it she says. She's got a mean smile now. Tell me everything that happened in the parking lot.

Well I may be crying but I ain't lost my mind. Got to tell this woman a story so I don't go to jail. I'm thinking harder than I ever thought in my life. Then I recollect something.

Was a little white boy out there, he might of hit me in the throat.

Policewoman looks like I hit *her* in the throat. You accusing that white boy of assaulting you child? I can tell she's fixing to say Nigger child but she don't.

Yes'm. Last thing I recall. Us kids, we were just having fun out there. We weren't going to do nothing to hurt the white folks. We danced around them for fun. We knew we were scaring them but we didn't plan on hurting them. We were just hoping they'd give us some money to make us go away. Then that kid flang out his arm and socked me in the throat. It hurts to swallow ma'am.

Lord God Almighty, I went and told this wicked white policewoman the truth. About the dumbest thing I could do I imagine. But then she says OK young man, you excuse me for a few minutes, I'm going to talk to the doctors. Then she comes back and says, Your doctors were wondering how you hurt your throat. Maybe your story checks out.

◆ ◆ ◆ ◆ ◆ ◆ ◆

I fall asleep then. Have me a dream about Poppa. Poppa is coming out of his church with Sister Amelia and fat old Sister Ruth, one on each arm. These here gals are angels he says. They've come down from heaven whilst I was preaching my sermon and they've whispered in my ear about you, boy. They say you are trying the Lord's patience with your evil ways.

Yes sinful child, Ruth says, the Lord's sent us here to punish you for picking on them white folks. Then Ruth and Amelia turn red like the devil. They breathe fire on me. I'm crying and bawling, Poppa is praying over me like he does when he's trying to cure some old lady's arthritis, but he don't tell Ruth and Amelia to stop, no no. He keeps on yelling and preaching and signifying, Yes sisters purify this child, drive the devil out of him, make him whole and clean in Jesus's name!

Then Amelia pulls this big old bit brace out of her purse, just like ones the carpenters use, and she starts drilling away at the right side of my head screaming Come out evil thoughts come out of this child's head come out come out! She's shouting right into my ear, and that drill is going right into my brain, my head feels like it's about to explode. I wake up. My head still feels like it's about to explode.

White boy is sitting by my bed. Must be the kid from the parking lot. I just stare at him.

Boy is nine or ten I judge, younger than me a year maybe. Just a plain old white kid. Got straight brown hair. Kind of small for his age. Looks like he don't spend too much time outdoors.

Kid wants to say something to me but he don't say nothing at first. Just sits there twisting his hands in his lap. Then he asks Am I hurt.

Of course I'm hurt. My head is pounding like it's got a streetcar running through it. What's this white boy care to know that for? I ain't nothing to him except trouble maybe.

He says he was afraid I died. Look at this stranger white boy, talking like he's my momma or my poppa and Momma and Poppa ain't even showed up yet.

I don't want to talk to this kid so I don't say nothing, just stare at him. Kid gets nervous, can't keep himself still.

I'm sorry I hurt you he says.

That's it. I can't keep quiet now. Ask him what's he talking about.

Says he hit me in the throat. But he didn't mean to.

So it's true. I can't believe this kid, him no bigger than one of them gals.

How did you do it?

Says I was standing in his way. Says he really wasn't trying to hurt me. Says he just got scared. Says it was an accident.

What happened after that?

You were unconscious. We brought you here.

Bring a colored kid to a hospital? Tell him the hospital folks must of been laughing when he walked in.

White kid looks at me like he don't understand what I'm saying. Asks me my name.

Sass.

Is that your real name?

Real enough. What's it to you? That shuts him up for a minute.

Wants to know where I go to school. Tell him Raymond Elementary.

Asks what grade. Sixth grade. Why you asking me all these questions?

Boy says he don't know. He's got a sad look on his face. For a moment I think about asking him where he goes to school too. But this is all so crazy it don't make a lick of sense. First we try to get these white folks to give us money. Then the white folks carry me to the hospital. Then this white boy shows up talking like he's trying to be my friend. I ain't got no white friends. Only white folks I ever talk to are in stores, unless you count that policewoman.

What do you want from me, I ask him.

I don't know that either he says, and he starts to cry.

3
Steve

These People

I hate Miss Ford. One time, Steve Kasten did something she didn't like, so you know what she does? She grabs him and pulls him up out of his seat. By his hair.

Now she's got the map of Britain up. I hate that pointer of hers too. She hits her desk with it when she thinks we're sleeping but we're not asleep and she knows it. Maxine Hamel says her hair is gray, not red. She saw her in the beauty shop getting it dyed.

Here comes a train. I know without looking because the glass in the windows goes glglglglgl and you can feel it in the chairseat. I hope it's a freight.

One, two, three four. Erie Lackawanna, Soo Line, Grand Trunk Western.

Fourteen, fifteen, sixteen …

What does Grand Trunk Western mean? Why does the Illinois Central let Grand Trunk Western cars on its tracks? How many freight cars can a steam engine pull? I counted ninety-eight once. Then the streamliners started showing up and they go *fast* man, the passenger trains anyway. Mom and Dad rode to Florida on an Illinois Central streamliner, the Green Diamond or maybe it was the Panama Limited. They ate steaks and slept overnight in a room like a broom closet Mom says. Next day they were in Miami. They should of taken me.

The IC puts the streamliner engines back-to-back to pull the freights. I counted one freight, it was a hundred and twenty cars. The steam engines can't even pull a hundred. They can make the windows rattle but they can't even pull a hundred.

Seventy-seven, seventy-eight, seventy-nine, and it's gone.

That kid. When Grandpa got up off him, I didn't even think he was breathing. I don't think I hit him that hard though. Not really.

It was just supposed to be a ballgame. Dad even came home from work early.

We picked Grandpa up in front of the Calumet and he was right on time like always, six on the nose. He's standing next to a guy shining shoes on an orange crate. And a woman singing hymns and shaking a tambourine. And two guys in undershirts yelling at each other, something about a bet. Mom says you've got to keep the car doors locked but I really like going down there. It's not anything like Hyde Park.

You can't miss Grandpa. He's got on that straw fedora he wears to keep the sun off because he's so bald, and a vest and a tie. His shoes are shiny. Wingtips Dad calls them. And of course he's the only white person on the sidewalk.

We drive to the ballpark past guys standing out in

front of their houses, waving at us to park in their driveways for a buck. Dad says he doesn't do that because you never know. He goes to the lot on Thirty-Fifth instead. It's a two-block walk to the ballpark but Dad says he'd rather pay them a buck than let the Comiskeys hang him out to dry, whatever that means.

Grandpa has the tickets already. Right along the first base line.

The hot dog guy comes along. Dad gets one with mustard for me and one plain for Grandpa because of his heartburn. Then they treat each other to Meister Braus from the Hey Cold Beer Here guy. Peanuts too and a Coke for me. At the seventh-inning stretch, Grandpa and I go out to the bathroom and he buys me a White Sox cap on the way back. When old Mister Arthritis, Earl Caldwell, finally taps out that single that puts Taffy Wright across, Grandpa lifts his empty beer cup to the guy in the next seat. Even though he doesn't know him.

That's when I ask to go get Wright's autograph.

Dad says no it's past eleven. I'd of dropped it except Grandpa says Come on let the kid go I'll square it with Jean. As if you had any clout with my old lady Dad says and gives Grandpa a wink like it's a joke between them.

I wish I hadn't though.

The kid is totally limp. They have to pick him up like a sack of potatoes. His mouth is hanging half open and there's spit running down his chin.

I'm sitting in the back seat right behind him, looking right at the back of his head. His hair is cut right down to his scalp, real short but it's still curly. Little tiny curls. My hair is so straight.

Then Dad swings out of the parking lot, kind of hard. The kid's head slides against the passenger-side window and leaves a smear of blood.

◆ ◆ ◆ ◆ ◆ ◆ ◆

Two guys come out with a wheeled cart. Dad goes inside with them and the kid. Grandpa and I are sitting in the back seat in the dark.

I ask Grandpa what's going to happen.

He turns and looks at me the way he does, like an owl. Right in the eyes because actually he isn't much taller than me, even though I'm ten and he's sixty-five.

Kid shouldn't of been out there he says.

He's so small Grandpa. He might even be younger than me.

Don't matter Grandpa says. They're punks all of them. Kid in the theater the other day, we caught him slicing up his seat with a pocket knife, doing it just for fun. Kid your age. Just another punk. Mack run him out of there.

Didn't you call the police?

What for? Happens all the time. Business I'm in. He gives a little snort. Got to deal with these people, they don't respect my property so what am I going to do? Wasn't like getting robbed.

Getting robbed?

Couple of guys stuck us up just last week he says.

Grandpa! Were you hurt?

Nah he says. They put a .38 in Mattie's face and

she gave them the cash. Eighty-five dollars. Second time this year. Jesus he says. He looks disgusted.

Did she have a gun of her own?

He gives me a look like Are you kidding? But if I'd been there I could of saved her. Break the glass, knock those guys out, a left and a right.

Was she OK?

She's used to it he says. She called the cops but they ran off. Couple of *shvartzes*.

But Mattie's colored too.

Yeah so what he says. You think they cared?

Mom says colored and white are all the same. She says if a colored steals it's just because he doesn't have as much as you, not because he's colored. She says they need to be treated fairer so they can get jobs and get more money. Then they won't go around robbing people.

Your mother says a lot of things he says. Your mother ain't down here with them every day like I am he says. You ever think about why they ain't got no jobs, no money? Maybe if they started behaving like civilized people they would. He coughs and wipes his nose.

They're different from us he says and now he sounds sort of different too. You ought to see what I see in that theater he says. Kids— like you only colored— coming in without their mothers, dumping the popcorn on the floor and the Coke too, Mack got to clean it up and I got to pay him to do it. That's all there is down here, *verstehe*? No white, just colored. So I know them. You're growing up now. You got to get to know them too.

I do, I do so know them. Rosetta Beamis. She's colored. I go to school with her. She can hit a baseball farther than I can.

You been to her house? She been to yours? He's looking at me funny now, not exactly mad, but sort of.

Grandpa why do you work there every day? Why don't you buy the Piccadilly on Hyde Park Boulevard? Nobody comes there with guns.

The Pic? You going to loan me a million bucks? And who'd buy my theater from me?

Maybe Mack?

Mack ain't got a pot to piss in he says. These people don't want to own businesses anyway.

These people. Negroes. Colored. *Shochers. Shvartzes.* It's suffocating in here. Why the heck is Dad still in there anyway?

◆　　◆　　◆　　◆　　◆　　◆　　◆

But then Dad comes out like nothing's the matter. He doesn't say anything, just puts the car into reverse and starts backing out.

Dad are we just going to leave?

We have to get home he says. Your mother must be going nuts.

But what if the kid dies?

Son he isn't going to die he says. He just has a broken nose.

No Dad. Look at the car seat, and I point to the blood on the seat and the window.

Oh all right he says. We'll just ask them how he's

doing. Then promise you'll quit worrying for Christ's sake. He parks it again and we go inside. Grandpa too.

Dad goes up to this woman at the desk. She's behind a cash register, the kind with the glass window. She's wearing those clown glasses that swoop up in the corners. There's a pencil sticking out of her hair bun. Mongol No. 2.

Who's that child they just brought in Dad asks her. I don't know why he's whispering.

We are trying to find that out sir. Didn't he come in with you?

Yes but we aren't his family Dad says.

Yes sir. That's obvious sir and she goes heh-heh. How did he happen to be with you?

There was an accident at the ballpark Dad says.

What sort of accident sir?

Grandpa shakes his head and frowns at Dad.

Dad goes Uh. Why do you want to know?

You'll need to make a report to the police she says.

Can't we skip that?

Oh no sir she says and sits up real straight. Every accident case there's got to be a police report. I'll call them myself. She picks the phone and begins dialing. It shouldn't take long before one comes by she says. They're in and out of here all night. You can just have a seat over there.

So we sit down in these red leatherette chairs with a bunch of other people who are mostly snoring. There's a copy of Collier's from last October. *A sonic boom splits the desert dawn as Captain Chuck Yeager becomes the first man to shatter the sound barrier in his top-secret Bell X-1 rocket plane.*

The kid is bleeding and unconscious. The kid has a broken nose. Why are Dad and Grandpa still talking about the White Sox?

Then I hear the woman, Over there Seamus, them, and this young cop comes over to us. He sits down and pulls out a Big Chief notebook, same as mine in school. He has freckles.

Just tell me what happened please. He sounds like Pat O'Brien in *Fighting Father Dunne.*

Dad tells him how those kids asked us for money. I'm thinking please Dad don't say anything about the kid's throat because I'll go to jail but the cop isn't paying any attention to me. He's asking Dad and Grandpa something. Fell on him how?

One of them was trying to pick his pocket Dad says and points to Grandpa. Tall kid, almost my size.

That was the kid you brought in?

No Dad says. I don't know what happened to the tall kid. Disappeared with the others. The kid we brought in was one of the little ones. Somehow he fell and my father here landed on him. We were protecting ourselves. Dad clears his throat. Really officer it was just an accident.

We'll have to get his story when he comes out of Examining the cop says.

But he's a—. Dad is sort of stammering.

A child?

Ah, yeah, a child and a, uh—.

The woman behind the cash register pipes up. He's colored Seamus.

The policeman stops writing and scratches at his freckles with his pencil hand. He looks at Grandpa, then Dad, then me, then Dad again.

He's been hurt. I have to investigate. At least take you down to the station. He says it like an apology.

On account of some little colored punks? Grandpa's face is getting red.

Dad goes Shush to Grandpa. Officer this isn't fair he says to the cop. You don't even know who this child is. Where are his parents?

Where is his family Cynthia?

He's only been in Examining fifteen minutes the woman says. We don't know anything about him yet. Let me see if I can bring someone out.

She presses a buzzer and out comes another woman. This one is all in white—white cap, white jumper, white-polished shoes.

He's colored she says. About eleven years old. He's conscious now but still a little dazed. His breathing and vital signs appear OK. Looks like a concussion. Broken nose. A good deal of blood from cuts and abrasions on the back of his head. Some difficulty breathing. He injured his throat though I can't imagine how.

That's it. Now I'm going to jail for sure.

Do you know the boy's identity the policeman asks her. He's not paying attention. He must not be a very good cop.

No idea she says.

Are you going to keep him?

Of course she says to the cop. He's in no shape to leave. Besides we have no place to send him.

I better call my sergeant. But the cop doesn't go to the phone. He looks at Grandpa and Dad. Maybe that's not such a good idea he says. Excuse me he says and goes over to the desk.

Cynthia can I see the child?

Sure he's in D over there, and she waves her hand toward the room marked *D*.

The policeman goes inside. *The sleek aerodynamic X-1, loaded with a witch's brew of volatile fuel and liquid oxygen, nestles inside the bomb bay of a four-engine B-29 roaring through the darkened sky. Inside, the boyish Yeager, just twenty-four years old, sits hunched over in the cramped cockpit in pitch darkness, waiting for the moment when the bay doors explode open, the X-1 tumbles out at twenty thousand feet, and the rocket motors' six-thousand-pound thrust snaps his head back like a rag doll's.*

The policeman comes out and he's frowning. He looks at Dad. Please get into your car sir he says and follow me down to the station.

4
Steve

What Salt Is

The police station is real crummy. I can't use the toilet because the last guy didn't flush it. I try to but the doo-doo just goes around in circles. Someone put a cake of mothballs in the urinal too.

They're fingerprinting a guy. I ask if I can get fingerprinted too but the policeman tells me to go sit down.

They ask Dad and Grandpa a lot of questions. They say they have to because someone has been seriously injured. They say they'll go to the hospital and ask the kid questions too.

They say they might have to charge Grandpa with Salt. Grandpa says that's a lot of crap and they'd just better try. Dad tells him to hush up and they argue some. Then the police tell us we can go home for now.

I ask Dad about the Salt but he says he doesn't know what I'm talking about. He says it's too late at night for silly questions and turns on the car radio. WBBM, Bing Crosby and Jo Stafford.

When we get home, Mom's in her nightgown, still

up. Her eyes are all red. She says Go to bed right now honey you've got to wake up for school in just a few hours, but then she asks what happened so I know we're going to be up a little while.

I ask if Grandpa is going to jail but Dad says Don't worry, your grandpa is one tough customer.

Mom says Are they going to file charges? Dad says Even if they did a judge would throw it out because he's, and Mom says, Colored, and Dad says, Yeah.

Are you OK baby? Those bad boys didn't do anything to you did they honey?

I'm thinking about the kid lying on the ground.

No Mom. I'm OK.

You sure they didn't hurt you? She looks at my face for cuts.

No Mom really. I'm OK.

What's the matter then? Why are you sniffling?

Dad says He's had a long night Jean.

Oh honey you're crying tell me what they really did to you she says. She goes to hug me. She doesn't get it.

They didn't hurt me at all Mom. I hurt one of them.

She stops hugging. She looks real surprised. So does Dad.

I hit that little kid in the throat. That's why he fell down. It was real dark. I couldn't see him standing there. I didn't mean to hurt him. It was an accident.

She says, Good.

No Mom. I hit him hard. Real hard. Dad will he be OK?

Sure, and Dad musses my hair. Maybe you saved my life. Hey no tears now.

Yes my brave boy Mom says. Brave boys don't cry like that.

But I can't stop.

◆   ◆   ◆   ◆   ◆   ◆   ◆

Next day at recess Rickie wants to know what happened.

He says Were you scared?

Sure.

Was your dad scared?

I think so. I'm pretty sure.

Were they all colored?

Yeah all of them.

You scared of coloreds?

Are you?

I think my dad is.

Why? He say so?

No but I think he doesn't like them. He calls them niggers or *shvartzes*. It's like he calls some white people he doesn't like polacks or sometimes dagoes.

You know what a kike is?

No what's a kike?

I don't know he says but Coach called me a stupid kike yesterday after I broke the sink in the boys' bathroom.

I thought he said Mike.

Why would he call me Mike? My name's Rickie.

Do you know what Salt is?

Salt? Sure.

No not like on food. It's something the police do.

All right. What's Salt?

It's got something to do with going to jail. What if my grandpa goes to jail Rick?

Boy. I never knew anyone who went to jail.

Come on. It's my grandpa not some crook.

Then why is he going to jail?

I didn't say he is going to jail. Might go to jail.

Well why would he might go to jail for?

Hurting the colored kid you dummy. Knocking him out. Breaking his nose. Salt.

Didn't the colored kid try to hurt your grandpa?

He didn't though. Nobody got hurt except him. Nobody got hurt except the little colored kid.

They should send those other kids to jail Rickie says. They could go to the kid in the hospital and make him tell who they are then go to those kids' houses and put them in handcuffs. Then he starts singing DUM-da-DUM-da-DUM-DU-DUM, like on *The FBI In Peace And War*.

You didn't see the kid. You didn't see how his nose was pushed over. You didn't see how his head was bleeding.

Oh he'll get better Rickie says. Remember when Harry Weinstein fell off the jungle gym and he was bleeding all over and they had to call an ambulance? They took him to Michael Reese. He had to have fourteen stitches. But he's OK now. You can still see where the stitches were. Ask him to let you look under his hair.

But what if they send my grandpa to jail?

They'll feed him bread and water every day. He won't come out until you're in eighth grade probably.

Yah yah you're just making that up.

That's what my mom says. They only feed you bread and water. You got to sit in a little cell all day with bars on it and three times a day a guard comes by and sticks a metal tray through a little slot and it's got a glass of water and a slice of white bread. That's what she says. Just one slice. Wonder Bread maybe. No butter or anything.

How do you know he won't get out until I'm in eighth grade?

Just guessing he says. But you know that guy, Leopold Loeb I think his name was, he killed that little kid, he'll never get out of jail my mom says.

Rickie. It was me. I did it. It was my fault.

Now Rickie looks like Mom and Dad did when I said it. Real surprised.

But you said your grandpa fell on him and broke his nose.

Yeah. But the reason the kid fell was, I hit him in the throat. I was swinging my arm around. I didn't know he was next to me. I knocked him backwards and then my grandpa fell on him.

You mean you were the one stopped all those kids from hurting you and your dad and your grandpa?

It was an accident. I didn't mean to do anything.

So then dummy Rickie says, Jeez Steve that's keen.

Why is it keen?

Because you were kind of the hero.

I tell him I don't feel like a hero.

Bet your dad and your grandpa think you are.

He doesn't get it either.

Rickie I say.

Yeah?

I need to go to the hospital and see if that little kid is OK.

Mercy Hospital

The bus I know goes down Hyde Park Boulevard, Drexel and South Park Way. I've taken it lots of times with Mom and Beth. I don't remember it going past Mercy Hospital though.

Maybe the Illinois Central? I don't know. I've never taken it by myself. It only stops once or twice between here and downtown. And it costs fifty cents for grownups, a quarter for kids. The bus is just a dime for kids.

There's a streetcar goes past school, just across Lake Park Avenue.

There's a streetcar goes in front of the Calumet too. Mmm.

I went on a streetcar once. Mongie, that's my other grandma, moved into an apartment hotel after Bunga died. It's called the Sutherland I think. Mom took me to see her. I was five. I remember there was a lot of clanging and noise. A guy with a brass shield on his hat. He gave Mom a crummy little piece of paper with a lot of lines and circles and boxes on it, and letters and numbers inside the boxes. He had a special punch that made holes in it like triangles or stars. It's a transfer she said. Looked like a ticket to Mars.

That streetcar was same as the one across from school. It went to the Sutherland Hotel where Mongie lived. Forty-Seventh Street and Drexel Boulevard.

Yeah.

Me and Mom got off at Forty-Seventh and Drexel and the streetcar kept on going. It went across Forty-Seventh heading west. Yeah, had to stay on Forty-Seventh because there are no streetcar tracks on Drexel.

Maybe that streetcar keeps on going west until it gets to State Street. Maybe it's the same streetcar that goes in front of the Calumet. Goes to Thirty-Fifth and State.

Maybe.

If I can get to the Calumet on the streetcar, I can ask someone how to get from there to Mercy Hospital.

The bus is a nickel for kids so maybe the streetcar is too. So what have I got on me? Five quarters, two Roosevelt dimes, three nickels including a buffalo nickel, one lead penny and four copper ones—.

Sorry Miss Ford. No ma'am I didn't want to give them to the other kids. I'll put them away. Yes ma'am right now.

If I'm home by six, Mom will think I was playing in Farmer's Field.

Wonder if Rickie wants to come with?

There's the bell. Finally.

Would you look where you're going? Jeez my mom just bought me these shoes.

Yeah I know which way I live Miss Smarty-Pants.
I'm just going this way because I got to go to, uh, the
school store. For candy. Then I'll go home.

Yeah you too. See you tomorrow.

Here it comes. Boy does it ever go slow.

Do you go to Mercy Hospital?

Change on Cermak to the 21 bus east. Ten cents
please. Sit right up front and I'll call your stop so you
don't miss it. Here kid take your transfer too. Give it to
the next driver and you won't have to pay another fare.

Thanks.

Ticket to Mars.

◆   ◆   ◆   ◆   ◆   ◆   ◆

There goes the George F. Harding Museum.
Middle ages. Armor suits. Halberds and pikes. The
guide said they hung the prisoners from those things
with iron hooks. While they were still alive. Yikes.

There goes the Blackstone Library. I'm not supposed to walk any farther than the library. Maybe I
should of asked Rickie to come.

We must be to Forty-Seventh now. There's Powers
Cafeteria where I went with Mom one time. Franks and
beans. The woman behind the counter had a hairnet on
and gravy all over her uniform. She called me *hon*.
There were cops and firemen in the line too, big guys. I
don't think they shaved that day. Or bathed.

There goes Mister Quinn's store, the one with the
beer-barrel sign. I played with Patsy Quinn on the Old
Block when I was five. She had four brothers and two
sisters. Mom said that's because they're Catholics and

that explains that. So I didn't ask what she meant.

There goes the Ken Theater. They had a twenty-five-cartoon special last month. She made me go with her to buy shoes instead.

Magazine store. Wire racks out in front. *The Daily News. The Herald-American.*

Tresses 'n' Curls, that one must be a hairdresser.

Tavern. Another tavern. The neon in the first one says Fox Head 400. The other, the neon says Heileman's Old Style.

Another one. Fox Deluxe. Is Fox Deluxe beer same as Fox Head 400 beer? Or are they different? I like the Hamm's commercial with the Indian tom-toms. *FROM the land-of-sky-blue-wa-a-ters, FROM the land-of-pines, lofty-balsams, COMES the beer-refreshing, HAMM'S the beer-refreshing*, then the tom-toms, *boo-doo-doo-DOOM.*

Boo-doo-doo-DOOM.

There goes Joe's Barber Shop where Dad took me for my first haircut. Joe's hair is all slicked down. Wildroot he says and sings it like they do on the radio, *Ya better get Wildroot Cream Oil Charley.* He combs the Wildroot into my hair until it looks almost like his, slick and shiny. Dad is standing there singing *Shave-and-a-haircut six bits.* Dad bought me some Wildroot from Joe. Mom made me stop using it after a week on account of the grease spots on the pillow. But Dad and I still sing it in the car. *Shave-and-a-haircut six bits.* Wonder what six bits are.

There goes the Catholic church. Our Lady of Sorrows. That's where Patsy Quinn goes, with Jesus over the door. He looks so sad. Mary too. She always has tears in her eyes. They should look happy. Aren't they supposed to be helping Christians get into heaven?

No statues in Sinai Temple. No stained glass either. Just the ark and the Torah, written by hand. One man labored twenty years to write that Torah. That's what Dr. Mann told us in Sunday School. That's how he talks. One long piece of parchment. All in Hebrew, going the wrong direction. Maybe he used a straight pen. And a bottle of Parker Quink.

Oh gee. There goes the Sutherland Hotel.

◆   ◆   ◆   ◆   ◆   ◆   ◆

Now we're the other side of Drexel, still on Forty-Seventh. I don't think I've ever been here before.

It looks crummy. Like we crossed a line.

These people look crummy too. That guy who just got on, he has coal dust and grease all over his face and his shirt. The kids don't look so good either. Holes in that one's knickers. Her saddle shoes are scuffed. And that woman across the aisle, she needs to pull up her stockings.

Oh. She's asleep.

Checks Cashed—Money Orders. Currency exchange. Red neon green neon. We've got them on Fifty-Third Street too.

Fried fish. I can hardly see in the window on account of all the grease but everyone inside looks like they're colored.

So's everyone out on the street.

So's everyone on the bus except the driver and—.

Maybe that's why that guy is looking at me.

Oh what was that one? Big red neon cross and a sign—.

BE SAVED SINNER

It's got letters on the window too, black and gold, what's it say?

Glory Life in Jesus Church
Rev. James B. Trimble Pastor

Jeez, it's a church. In a store. With a neon sign.

Oh my gosh, I did it. There's the Calumet. We're at Thirty-Fifth.

Mister do I get off now?

Nah you got to stay on to Cermak. That's Twenty-Second Street. Just hold your shirt on.

Jeez this streetcar goes slow.

Cermak Road, CERR-mak, change for the Number 21.

Now.

Which corner's the bus on Mister?

That one. Don't forget your transfer.

Thanks. See here it is.

Oh yeah? Better look in your pocket.

For what?

The other half you tore off.

◆　　◆　　◆　　◆　　◆　　◆　　◆

Excuse me. Could you please—.

Excuse—.

S-sir, does the bus stop for—.

Ma'am I'm waiting for a bus to go to, I mean, does the bus to Mercy Hospital stop—.

Excuse me. Ma'am? Do you know where Mercy Hospital is?

Yes child. Just get on this bus and get off in six or eight blocks. Just get off when I get off.

Are you going there too?

Yes and I'm late for work. Where is that all-fired bus?

Are you a nurse?

No child I just sweep and clean. Them nuns run things over at Mercy. I just sweep and clean.

It's the Number 21 right?

Right and here it comes. Just get on child. Come on. Climb on up quick now before he decides to go off without you.

Mister I got this transfer on the streetcar and I put it in my pocket and then I guess it tore off but it was an accident I got both halves and I really—.

Oh. OK. Thanks Mister.

Sit down right there child. Right across the aisle from me. That's right, just sit yourself down. Now you just keep an eye on me. When I get up you get up OK?

Thank you.

That's all right honey. Wish this blame bus would move a little faster. What you doing down in this neighborhood without your momma?

I'm going to visit a fr—. Uh. I'm going to visit someone.

By yourself?

Sure. I ride the bus all the time.

If I make my voice deep I'll sound more grown up.

To Mercy? Where do you live child?

Mmmmmmmm. Around here.

Oh child I don't think they taught you how to lie yet.

Maybe she isn't laughing at me, maybe she just thinks it's funny what I said. Yes because look at her face now.

Tell me the truth. I ain't going to harm you. Are you trying to run away? I can spare you a dime to call home.

I'm not running away.

Where do you really live then?

Madison Park.

Where's that?

Do you know where Hyde Park Boulevard is?

Certainly do. So you live in Hyde Park. I expect you're Jewish too.

Y—. No I'm—. Uh.

But look at her. She's still smiling. Maybe she's just talking, making conversation.

Yes ma'am.

Well child I certainly can't make you out. You're white, you're Jewish, you're from Hyde Park, you say you got a friend who's sick at Mercy, but about the only white folks I see at Mercy are them Catholics from over in Canaryville. The Hyde Park Jews, they all go to Reese. Who's your friend?

Just a kid.

What's his name?

I don't know—I mean. Um.

Is he Jewish?

No he's a—he's colored.

Oh my land.

Is something wrong with that?

Never mind. Tell me this one thing. How do you purpose to get past the front desk? They don't let in no little children by themselves. Don't even matter it's your momma is dying in there. Them nuns got rules.

I—uh, I—I didn't think about that.

So you ain't never been to this hospital before?

No.

And you're going to visit a colored child, you don't know his name?

No. No ma'am. I'm sorry ma'am.

You don't know who he is, you don't know nothing about visiting no Mercy Hospital, but you're going anyway, you think you can find him. Have I got that right?

Yes. Ma'am.

All right child. Get off the bus. I'll see what I can do for you.

♦　　♦　　♦　　♦　　♦　　♦　　♦

This hospital doesn't look anything like Michael Reese. There's a Mary statue right at the front door where you walk in, painted pink and green. Big as a real grown-up.

Do we have to check in over where it says *Reception*?

Just give me your hand child. Just give me your hand and walk on. You going to be fine.

Thanks.

OK child you see this one coming down the hall?

She's the Mother Superior. Just look her in the eye. Look her smack in the eye and say Afternoon sister.

Afternoon sister.

That's good honey. Very good. I reckon God must be telling them nuns to leave you alone.

The sign says *Children's Ward*. This is it right?

Right. Just walk on through these double doors here. These are charity patients mostly. You see your friend?

I'm not sure I— no, that's— he's a little—.

Would you recognize him?

Yeah. Sure. Uh, maybe.

Come child, let's just you and me walk through this ward together. Ain't no nuns in here right now. You look to the right and to the left. Take your time. We'll go as slow as you please.

That's him.

I thought maybe so. I worked a little late last night. They brought him in at the end of my shift. Had a concussion and a broken nose. You know how it happened?

Yes.

Thought you might.

Thank you.

All right, that's all right. Ain't nothing to thank. Good luck to you child. I'm going to my work now. You can turn loose of my hand.

◆   ◆   ◆   ◆   ◆   ◆   ◆

He's small, smaller than I thought, and thin, with a thin face, almost like a girl's, only I can't see his nose

on account of the adhesive tape and the bandages.
   I think he's asleep.
   Oh you're awake.
   I didn't mean to hurt you. Did you mean to hurt us? How come your mom lets you go out late at night? Have you ever been to my grandpa's theater? Do you listen to Captain Midnight? What's your favorite, Wheaties or Cheerios?
   Are you OK?
   What a dumb thing to ask.
   Why? Who are you?
   My name is Steve. *I'm the boy from the parking lot. The one who hit you in the throat. But it was an accident. Grandpa says kids like you slice up the theater seats for fun. He calls you Yiddish names in return, some kind of a fair trade. People like you ride street-cars, shovel coal, wear uniforms, clean hospitals, smile. You came in a gang way past bedtime and asked us for money. If it'd been me, I'd be punished. Dad was afraid but Grandpa, old as he is, was not. Who am I? Who are you?*
   What you doing here?
   I came to see you.
   I don't understand.
   I was in the parking lot.
   So?
   So, I wanted to see if you were OK.
   This ain't making no sense.
   What's your name?
   What's it to you?
   Want some gum? I've got Doublemint.

Give it here.

You can't open it. Your arm's strapped down.

Let me try.

Unh-unh. Even if you did you still couldn't get the tinfoil off the waxed paper. You need two hands.

You going to keep the tinfoil?

Well uh—. You want it?

Sure.

OK. Here.

Thanks.

What's your name?

Sass.

Is that your real name?

Real enough. What's it to you?

Where do you go to school?

Raymond Elementary.

What grade are you in?

Sixth grade. Why you asking me all these questions?

I don't know.

What you want from me?

I don't know that either.

What you crying for?

I'm not crying.

Yes you are. Ain't you the one ought to be crying. I'm the one in the hospital.

Does it hurt?

Hurt? My head is pounding like a drum.

What else?

Broke my nose. Scratched my head up. They said I got a brain concussion from being knocked out. They got my arm tied down too but I think it's OK now. And my throat hurts.

You know, we brought you here.

You what?

We brought you here. We had to. You were unconscious. My dad would of called for help but there weren't
any telephones. You were bleeding. Your nose was all
smashed over—.

Lord have mercy.

Well we couldn't leave you lying there.

Them hospital folks must of been laughing when
you walked in.

Laughing?

Bunch of white folks bringing in a colored boy? I'll
say.

No they weren't laughing. They just took you into
one of those rooms and my dad and my grandpa talked
to a policeman for a while, then we had to go to a police
station. They asked them some more questions then we
went home. But my grandpa might have to go back to
the police station or something, maybe a court. I didn't
understand that part real well.

They say anything about my momma or my poppa?

No. Where are they?

I don't know.

Now it's you who's crying.

No I ain't.

Yes you are.

What happened to them others?

You mean the kids you were with? They left. Ran
away. Right when you got hurt.

Them's my friends. Some friends.

How come you were out there?

Wouldn't you like to know.

When will you get out of the hospital?

How do I know? I don't even know how long I been in here. Only people come to see me are nuns. I ain't even seen Momma.

Maybe your mom and dad don't know you're here.

I told them nuns to tell them.

Don't cry.

I ain't crying I told you.

I could call them. Tell them you're here. I have a dime.

We ain't got no phone. Besides why would you want to do that?

If I were in the hospital and my mom didn't know where I was, I'd be pretty scared.

Just shut up. I ain't scared of nothing.

Where do you live?

Thirty-Sixth and Wabash.

It's not far is it? I could go over there.

Hah! What's Momma going to think, little white boy comes knocking on her door, tells her I'm at Mercy? She'd faint is what she'd do.

How do I get to Thirty-Sixth and Wabash?

Boy I believe you're crazy.

Uh oh what's that?

Nun.

I better go.

Yeah you better go. You better go home.

Maybe I'll come back again.

You better not. You ain't got no business with me. You come back here, you're going to get both of us in trouble. And I'm in trouble already.

Well maybe I could come to your house after you get out.

Now I know you're crazy. Get on out of here.

Don't you even want to know my name?

No I don't.

It's Steve.

Go away. And stop looking like that.

Like what?

Like someone just kicked your dog.

All right I'll go. I got to be home soon anyway. I'm sorry.

Sorry? What you got to be sorry about?

Sorry I— I don't know. I guess I shouldn't of come.

So— you just going to go?

Huh?

Nothing.

What?

What's your last name?

It's Feinberg. Steve Feinberg. I live at Thirteen-Fifty-Six Madison Park. What's yours?

Trimble. Jesse Owens Trimble.

But your nickname is Sass.

Yeah. That's right.

OK. Well. Goodbye.

Yeah.

Aren't you going to say goodbye too?

I done said it.

No. All you said was Yeah.

Yeah.

OK. Well so long. I'll see you.

I don't think so.

6
Dora

Dora on the Bus

*T*hese children. Their momma lets them be too free. How's she expect me to raise them right when she don't give me no support?

Bus coming.

No it ain't mine. Number Four, goes up Cottage Grove. I'll be out here waiting another ten fifteen minutes in the rain. Oh Lord my hip does hurt, it's so cold at six o'clock in the morning, don't matter it's June.

My boy Joseph. Lord. Wonder how he's doing.

How are you, sister? Oh, fine fine. Yes I'm going to work too if the good Lord lets me get there in this weather.

I feel it more each day. Alive these fifty-seven years—maybe fifty-eight, ain't sure. Standing out here in this cold and wet every morning, of course I'm going to feel it. Momma had the rheumatism too, passed while I was a young gal.

These children. That boy Steve, he minds pretty good, but that girl Beth, she gives me trouble trouble.

Her momma is the problem. I know that. Ain't I raised three sets of white folks' children already?

This momma, she don't like me. I can tell it easy. Oh yes she acts like there ain't nothing wrong between us, like I ain't colored or something. Shoot. She's got eyes don't she?

She comes up to me says, Dora, when you make the beds could you please make them with hos-pi-tul corners? She says it like that, hos-pi-tul. Here I'll show you what I mean she says. Then she lifts up the sheet and the cover like I'm some child she's showing her how to put on her drawers for the first time. Here Dora, first you lift these sheets up, then you tuck this one under, then you fold the top part over and tuck it in tight, like this. After you get done, the end of the bed will look like this. *She's so proud she's grinning across her face. I've been making beds that way when she was still a little baby, long time before I ever seen no hos-pi-tul. But I don't say nothing.*

I ain't saying she's bad. She just don't respect me and she's trying to pretend ain't nothing wrong. That don't work. Folks, they know how other folks feel. Can't hide it you know. Can't no one really.

Well some of them can too. Dora you fool, don't you know, old as you are, there are some bad *people in this world.*

Man comes up to me when I got off that train from Sunflower Mississippi, Nineteen Hundred and Nineteen in the year of the Lord praise Jesus, don't know a soul, getting off that train and I am so scared. My darling boy in jail, my poor man don't know where

I've gone.

I look up, see the light coming in from up three stories in the air like them big churches in Italy I seen pictures in the National Geographic *one time. Sound of them steam trains* whisss! whisss! whisss! *Be hundreds, maybe thousands of people all around, hurrying this way and that, some white some colored. Country folk. I was dizzy.*

And this here gent *comes up. He's wearing shiny shoes and one of them hats with a snap brim. He swoops it off now and makes me a kind of a bow, real stylish. No one ever did that to Dora Barfield. Then he says Excuse me young lady you look like you could use a ride somewhere.*

Well he told the truth anyway. I was feeling so alone I let him take my bag and walk me out of that big old station to his car.

Car's shiny like his shoes, a Packard with one of them convertible tops. He says Go on in don't be scared I ain't going bite you. Man don't know it but I ain't never been carried around by nothing bigger than a mule.

So he says What's your name child? Dora! That's a mighty fine name. And you are a mighty pretty young lady. I am guessing you come to Chicago from the South, from the state of Mississippi, am I right? Yes sir. He goes chattering on. I say yessir nossir but I'm thinking, What's going to become of me? Why did I leave my boy in jail? Leave my man without telling him a word? What am I going to do in this city, ain't got no friends nor no kinfolk neither?

Man says his name is Herbert. Says he owns a funeral parlor on South Indiana Avenue. Says he likes to help people coming up from Mississippi because no one did that for him when he came up from Mississippi himself ten years ago. Says Chicago's been mighty good to him. Lots of colored folks up here now, some of them getting good jobs in the steel mills and the stockyards what with the World War and all, getting some money for a change. They go out on State Street, go into them taverns at night, get a little drunk and pull out a straight razor, why child, some of them bound to die sure as you're born heh heh. That's what he says. Strange I can recall it now, I'm feeling so scared riding around in his big old car, looking out the window at the cars and the people, so many of them like I never seen before in my life, seemed.

He drives to a mission, the Church of Gospel Spirit in Eternal Life, had a cross in the window and some candles burning in jars. Parks the car in front. Says to me Go talk to the Reverend Martha inside, she'll help you find work and some place to stay. But before you go how about giving me a kiss for all I've done for you. Then he grabs me and pulls me down, starts yanking and pulling at me, telling me how much he loves me and how pretty I am.

After he gets done with me he drives off. I look around, my pocketbook is still in his car with all the money I took from the jar.

I can't bear this no more. What he did to me was bad enough. But I just lay there on that seat, didn't say nothing, let him do what he wanted. Jesus help me to forget this.

Bus coming now. Be good to get on that bus, my feet so cold and wet. Hope the heat is working.

Morning sir. Yes sir got my dimes right here. Thank you sir.

Got to sir them too, they ain't nothing but bus drivers.

Well the heat is working anyway. Get warm these next twenty minutes. Hope it's just twenty minutes, this weather.

Look at that. That poor man trying to haul them groceries into that shop, got no more sense than a jackrabbit, using that little old cart. Hey you you're going to drop that all over the sidewalk. Now ain't that something? He done it too. Wish I could've told him so he heard it, poor fool. He ain't listening to me neither. Nobody goes listening to Dora. Not that momma, not them children, nobody.

They don't listen, they don't learn. Be lots of things I've found out since I was a little girl in Sunflower Mississippi, things some folks might want to learn. Things folks ought to know, they go staying up here in Chicago, half of them don't even use their heads for nothing besides a hat-rack. I swear.

Don't blame some of them though. Sometimes I don't understand things here neither. Chicago ain't nothing like Sunflower Mississippi.

Wasn't no more than a few weeks after I got here they had that terrible riot. Heard them screaming nigger this and nigger that, then I seen a hundred men coming right down the middle of State Street, clubs in their hands, no police to stop them. At least in Mississippi the white folks stayed to their own side of the tracks. They weren't after me though. They were looking for men and boys. Pack of dogs, too scared to hunt alone.

You put some hurtful sinners on this Earth Lord, that was Your mysterious will. Best not to think about that no more. Life is hard enough. Sometimes I think I'm better off in this cold city working for white folks. Least I get good food, work in a clean place, ain't nobody trying to hurt me no more. Nor mess with my lady stuff neither. You do yourself harm thinking about that old time, Dora Barfield. It's Nineteen Forty-Eight, not Nineteen Nineteen.

My boy. Locked up in Parchman down there. Lord that child's been in that penitentiary since he was a boy himself. He'll be an old man when he gets out if he ever does. I believe I'll never see my Joseph again. Locked in that jail 'til he dies—.

Stop that sniffling. You're a grown woman. Someone sees you on this bus wiping your eyes, be thinking you're crazy or something.

Lord I am grown too. Look at me Big old woman, look like that raggedy-headed old woman on the Aunt Jemima box, sure enough do. Even wear one of them handkerchiefs on my own head sometimes. Bless me if I know why they go putting that picture on that box.

We are in white folks' neighborhood now, yes! Look at them nice apartment buildings, all clean, got grass growing in front in summer-time and them little four-o'clocks pretty in front all pink and white. Not like Twenty-Ninth and Prairie, trash on the side-walks and trashy people too. Some good church-going folks, sure. But the others, why did You put some of them on this Earth?

Took that boy and his sister out and picked them four-o'clocks for the seeds. The children squeezed on the flowers and the nuts fell out in their little hands. They laughed and laughed! Steve says Dora they look just like them nuts of pepper in my momma's pepper-mill. Gives me a chuckle just thinking about it.

They're good children. I know it. I get frustrated with them Lord but they're good in their hearts. Chil-dren are children. If they ever knew what it was like when I was coming up though, maybe they'd try to be some better.

That boy, he's sweet, but the child's got to grow up into the man. Ain't right to go too easy on him. His momma, she goes too easy on him. Me, I got to hold him to his task. That's my job, even though she goes to fighting me.

Thinking about the time that boy nearly died. Least I thought so then.

I hear that glass a-breaking. Pack of children downstairs running away. Then a scream and a knocking on the door, like to broke it down. Steve is standing there heaving and crying, poor thing, the blood just covering his chest. I see it now, that white white shirt of his, all red and wet.

What happened to you child? He don't say noth-ing, can't talk, just keeps on bawling and holding his wrist. I see he ain't stabbed in the heart but it's his wrist that's a-bleeding so. Thank You Jesus I say. But then I think, suppose he is dying? Knew a man once who died from bleeding at the wrist.

Finally he stops crying and starts telling me the story, how that pack of wild Indians is running after him trying to kill him with a knife. So he runs and he gets through the outer door downstairs, them evil children running and screaming after him. But he can't find his key to get through the door inside, it's locked. So he pushes his hand splang! right through the glass.

Hush child I say. Them children were teasing you. Ain't no real knife, must be a rubber knife. I act strong to him but my heart is pounding. I open the tap and the water washes off that bright blood. Now I can see glass sparkling in the cut. Lord child hold still while I get it out. Yes child I know you're scared but you got to be brave now because this here glass got to come out, every bit of it out. Then I take off his belt and wrap it tight around his arm to stop the bleeding.

And then I take that boy to my bosom and hold him. He's crying still and the blood goes trailing down my apron, his little body shaking. I'm crying too now, tears burning my eyes, thinking how cruel children are ... thinking about my Joseph on that dusty street twenty-nine, thirty years ago, looking up at me with no understanding in his eyes ... thinking how a woman can love a child, a white child, though it ain't her own.

Maybe I saved Steve's life that day. But it don't

matter now. God will judge me for my sins alone.

I recall the sheriff taking my Joseph away. Him playing out in that dusty street, wasn't even a street actually, couldn't call it that, more just an old dusty road with big holes, Joseph out there with that little gal, that little Rusty, yes, folks called her Rusty because she had that red hair and that yellow skin.

She was a pretty thing though I hate to say it. All them yellow gals, we thought they all were pretty back then. Even the little ones, long as they had them freckles and that red hair.

Wish I could've killed that little gal right then. Just eleven years old but I'd've killed her sure if I'd've known what was going to happen to my Joseph.

Dora. Stop that. God will be punishing you. Lord forgive me for these thoughts. I do love You above all others Lord and I fear the fires of Hell. Oh Jesus I fear them please oh sweet Lord be merciful unto me. I am a sinful woman. I am a sinful woman. Oh Lord I know You will punish me for my sins because You must, for I have sinned and the Lord punishes all sinners. I fear the fires of Hell for Eternity for these sins I have committed against You. I feel the flames now.

Sitting in that dirty jail. Bugs everywhere. He'll never be able to tell me what it's like in there. Even if he knew where I was he might not tell me, such a good boy. Probably be afraid for his momma, she'd have a stroke or something if he told her the truth. But the Lord loves the truth. The truth shall make ye free, that's what the Scripture says. I love the truth and I love the Lord, praise Jesus.

I dream they're lynching my Joseph. Crowd of white men yelling and screaming and shaking their fists. My boy screaming and crying. Stand him up on a hay bale under a big tree, loop that rope over a branch, him just eleven years old, me standing like a stump, can't do nothing but look.

Saw a lynching once. Of course it wasn't an eleven-year-old though I heard they lynched a boy thirteen over in Jasper County. Man they lynched was a big man, bigger than any of the white men done the lynching. How they strung him up, must've been hard. I couldn't do nothing. Nothing but look. Wish now I hadn't.

Was a day in my life, I was just a little gal, couldn't've been no older than that Rusty gal or my Joseph. My Daddy took me to see a fair. I put ribbons in my hair, bright yellow they were. I was a pretty thing that day, little gal wearing ribbons, dressed so fine. I felt the love of the world when we walked to that fair, my Daddy and me.

Daddy bought me a soda-pop. Ain't never had one before. I laughed out loud when the bubbles burst in my mouth. Daddy laughed too, he's so tickled with me.

My Daddy put me on the merry-go-round, big old horse with a high mane of hair, was plaster. Merry-go-round starts turning, music starts playing, toodle-ee-oodle-ee-oo, that horse starts going up and down to the time of the music. I felt like I was in heaven with God and the angels. Never been a time like that.

Now here I am on this bus, got nothing better to do than think about Sunflower Mississippi. Go on you fool, them times are gone thirty years now. Why even bother your head with them? It's Nineteen Hundred and Forty-Eight and you are living in Chicago Illinois now, living in another world. Your son is still in prison most likely. Your husband's gone Lord knows where. Expect he's down in Mississippi still wondering what happened to Dora Barfield.

Lord Jesus I can't carry this load no longer. Jesus help me to carry this load. In Your glorious name I pray to You. Please Lord help me bear this load like You bore Your cross on Calvary.

I think of You carrying Your cross when they lynched You Lord. When I think of Your young life taken from You I cry and cannot stop. That cross on Your shoulders, them white folks tormenting You as You walk. You must've been thinking how You can't bear it no more. You didn't bear it much longer neither.

You were just thirty-three years old. My Joseph, he'd be thirty-nine, forty years old now if he's still alive. You're more lucky than him.

Dora Barfield! The Lord will be frowning on you for your sinful thoughts. Oh Jesus forgive me for my sins. You are God's son. I'm just an ignorant old woman on this bus, looking out at this rain and slop in this awful place that ain't my home.

'Tis my home, though sometimes it feels more like Hell.

That yellow Rusty gal, she and Joseph went up on them railroad tracks. They were just being children, doing what children do. Lord I did things when I was a child too. This Steve I'm taking care of, he'll be doing things too, he gets a little older. Don't matter he's white, children still are children. Least while they're children. They grow up, they start being something else, some of them. Lots of them. Colored ones too, 'deed I say so. Some say the white folks hate the colored but what about the colored folks who hate the white? Tell the truth!

Lord when I saw that child's dead bleeding body, it was pitiful. I'd have picked him up and held him in my arms, white as he was, and not cared whether I was in Sunflower Mississippi or Chicago Illinois. But I dast not even cry out. My Joseph, he's standing there, blood on his own clothes, and that little Rusty gal, she's got blood on her own self too. My heart wanted to fly out of my body.

The sheriff's deputies, they come lickety-split. Told me You go along gal. Ain't no call for you to come with us. These nigger children killed that white boy. You know they are going to jail. You'd best hope they don't hang for it.

How am I going to say? How could I say? I couldn't say nothing. My throat felt like was somebody choking it shut. Couldn't no words come out. I just stood there like a post. Momma! Momma! Joseph was screaming Momma. I couldn't speak. Like I was watching that lynching again.

Don't know what happened to that Rusty gal but they took my boy straight away. They gave him a trial but it don't mean nothing. Over in a day.

Jesus forgive me. After they arrested him I lay in my bed them five days. They tried to drag me to the trial but I wouldn't go. Deputy said they might make me take the stand against my own son. Said if I didn't they might throw me in jail too. I'd've gone to jail seven lifetimes to save my Joseph. But I couldn't face some white judge using big words, making me say something I didn't mean to. Send my own baby to the gallows. When they took him off to Parchman I was lying there still.

Finally got out of bed, pried up the floorboards with a clawhammer, took all the money out the jar and got on the Illinois Central midnight of that same day. Didn't say nothing to nobody. Never spoke to my husband, never spoke to my preacher. Never spoke to my baby again. More to answer for Jesus.

Should have stayed in Sunflower you cowardly woman. Found some city lawyer to help Joseph tell what he seen. Endured your pain like Jesus endured them thorns. Look at the pain I caused my baby. Look at the pain I've made for myself ever since.

Got on the train instead. Colored folks them days, all they could talk about was Chicago Chicago Chicago. They were going to Chicago like it was the Promised Land. Wanted to go to the Promised Land myself.

Traveled a night and a day and a night again. White men on the other side of that curtain playing cards, smoking cigars, spitting, taking the Lord's name in vain. Like to make me sick but I couldn't say nothing. Pullman porters on the other side of the curtain with the white men, colored standing up in the Jim Crow in the dark.

Swaying back and forth. Mothers with little babies crying at their breast, didn't matter, we were all standing up. Nobody slept. Least the others had their families. Asked why I didn't have no one with me. Couldn't tell them the truth.

Got off at last, all I seen was trash in the gutters, coal dust in the air, snow on the ground. First snow I ever seen and it's black with coal dust. Promised Land hunh! More like Hades.

I wrote to my baby. Wrote it to Parchman Work Farm, Parchman Mississippi, Mister Joseph Barfield. That's all the address I had. Asked him to forgive me. Told him I'd be back for him some day.

Didn't get no answer to that letter nor the next one nor the next one after that. Wrote him every day for a year, didn't get no answers to no letters at all. Never heard from my boy again. That's how the Lord is punishing me for my sins. That's the Lord's will.

We pay for our sins for eternity. The Bible says it and now I know it's true. I'd be glad to die if I could forget my sins forever, but I never can. That's the Hell the Lord has prepared for me.

Oh Jesus Lord, before I die, lift up Your sweet face and tell me what my boy really did.

Gal sitting over there. Looks like I know her. She's looking at me too.

Face so familiar. Must be someone I know. Can't place her.

Oh Lord.

She seen me? She recognized me? She gets off this bus I'll never learn her secret. Get up and speak to her you fool.

Girl I'd say. You girl! You know who I am. You were with my son Joseph when that white child died. Don't you lie. Tell me what happened on that day. Release me!

If I do that she'd be saying, Your son killed that boy. He picked up a big old rock and stove in that white child's head. She'd be saying, I don't know why he did it, he always was doing crazy things.

No! She'd say, I did it! I killed that white boy my own self. And you know why old lady? That child tried to kill your son, that's why! He picked up that big old rock, said, Nigger child I'm going to bash in your head now, and quick as he did it I pushed him back and he fell into that old gully, hit his own fool head on a stone and died right there.

But maybe she'd say, That white boy was our friend, we were playing along them railroad tracks just as nice as you please. He and Joseph go up along the edge of a big old ditch together and they dare each other to jump across. Joseph jumps first and he makes it to the other side but that white boy cotches his foot and falls to the bottom, hits his head and dies on the spot. What else for would I be crying my eyes out when we came back you stupid old woman?

Wait. Suppose she says, Must be some mistake, I ain't never been no farther south than Harvey Illinois. You're thinking about someone else old woman. I don't know you, don't know your son neither. She'd be saying, Get away from me, don't bother me on this bus.

I will speak to you girl. I must know. I must speak to you and know the truth at last. I must get up out of this seat and speak to you. I'll be putting my hands around your throat and choking your life away lest you tell me the truth. The fires of Hell do not make me afraid because I am in Hell now.

She's getting off the bus. She's gone.

Turn back! Can't you see my face? Can't you see my suffering? If you'd stepped forward then, my Joseph might be in my arms right now. The Lord knows your sins though. The Lord will be punishing you like He is punishing me.

No Lord. Can't blame no one but myself.

Goodbye ladies. I ain't ashamed of crying, not no more. You can think what you want. I carry my pain where I go, and it don't go away on no bus.

7
Steve

Steve and Dora

I wake up and it's still dark outside. I start getting
ready for school then I remember it's Saturday, so I
push my face back into the pillow and pull the covers
up nice and warm. It's way too early— five-twenty-nine
on the Baby Ben. Janitor Pete hasn't even turned on
the steam yet. But then I hear it, clank clank clank then
hissss, and a car down in the alley. No, too noisy.
Maybe a truck.

That's when I remember. It's my birthday. Party
this afternoon. Now it's hard to get back to sleep.

I turn on the Philco, it warms up half a minute and
on comes Happy Hank. *Hi kids wake up and smile, It's
Happy Hank and I'll be here for a while.*

I turn it off. I'm too old for Happy Hank. I'm ten
today.

Ten is way better than nine. Marv Lerman is ten
and he can ride a two-wheeler no hands. Mom prom-
ises I'm getting a raise in my allowance when I'm ten.
And she's going to let me walk to Stineway's Drug Store
by myself.

On Wednesday I went a lot farther than Stineway's.

I never told her. I never told anyone—not even Rickie. I show up late for dinner and she starts to yell so I lie. I say I stopped to help a little girl get a kitty out of a tree. Aw honey you've got such a sweet heart she says. Looked her right in the eye. It was easy.

I wonder how long before his parents showed up at the hospital.

Why didn't they come right away? Will his nose heal straight? Alan Parker got hit with the baseball bat and his never did.

Oh man I'm never going to get back to sleep now. Where are my slippers?

I brush my teeth and go into the kitchen for a glass of milk. The milkman leaves it by the back door in half-a-gallon bottles so they're pretty heavy, but Dora puts them on the bottom shelf of the fridge so I can lift them out. I'm pretty strong for my age Mom says.

Pour the cream off into the pitcher like she says. The milk tastes like Ipana Toothpaste.

Dora's in the dining room sleeping on the roll-away. I can hear her snoring through the kitchen door.

I could wake her up. She could make some break-fast. Or I could wake Beth. That might be a good idea. Dad just showed me how to play gin rummy. I could teach her. But she'll just want to play Fish or War or Old Maid. Let her sleep.

I pick up the Captain Marvel comic book from last night. I don't like Captain Marvel as much as Superman. No one does. But the great thing is when he shouts *Shazam!* and the god on the cloud hits him with a lightning bolt—now that is neat, that's why I keep buying Captain Marvels. What if I had super-powers?

That colored kid. Wonder if I'll ever see him again. *Maybe Dora would make me some toast.*

I tiptoe into the dining room.

Dora?

Man can she ever snore.

Dora?

She says What for you turning on that light child?

Dora would you make me some breakfast?

What time is it?

It's before six.

It ain't light yet child she says. What you waking me up for?

I have to tell you something.

What you got can't wait 'til I wake up? But she's moving under the covers now, like a whale coming up for air. She's bigger than Coach and he's six feet.

I sit down on the bed next to her. She puts her arm on my shoulder and I snuggle in. She's still nice and warm from being asleep.

I have to ask her.

Dora have you ever been to my grandpa's movie theater?

I don't go to no movies child she says. I'm here or I'm in church. Ain't got time for such foolishness.

Do you know where my grandpa's theater is?

Didn't even know your granddaddy owned a theater. He never told me that. It ain't my business what your granddaddy owns.

I ask where she lives.

I live at Twenty-Ninth and Prairie. She says it like Puh-RAY-rie.

Why are you so full of questions child, here it is still the middle of the night?

I don't know I say. I ask if she's ever been to Mercy Hospital.

Surely have she says. Was sick with the pneumonia in Forty-Four and went to Mercy. Had a wen taken off my head another time. Looky here, and she puts her head down to show me where it was.

Is Twenty-Ninth and Prairie near Thirty-Sixth and Wabash?

Not too far. What for you want to know about Thirty-Sixth and Wabash?

I don't know what to say so I say Dora would you make me some toast?

All right child she says, you turn the other way while I put my robe on and get me some slippers on my feet. The springs creak when she gets up.

She tears the cellophane from a new loaf of Holsum Bread and puts two slices into the toaster.

You care for eggs and bacon too?

No just toast. With grape jelly.

She doesn't say anything for a minute, just butters the toast. *I hope she isn't going to get mad at me.*

Dora. Did you ever go somewhere you weren't supposed to go?

Yes child yes and she sighs. She's going to say something else but she stops herself.

Where was it? Tell me about it.

Never mind about me. That was a long time ago,

long time before you were born. In Sunflower she says.

What's Sunflower?

Where I came up. Down in Mississippi.

Did you get in trouble for it?

I'm still in trouble.

What kind of trouble?

She doesn't say anything, just starts brushing crumbs off the counter. She's got a look on her face, it's sad or angry, I can't tell which.

Is it a secret?

Yes she says. Yes it is.

Will you tell it to me some time?

I doubt it. Doubt it very much.

I did too.

You did what child?

Went somewhere I wasn't supposed to go. It's a secret too.

Mmmm she grunts.

I'll tell you my secret if you tell me yours.

She walks over to the table, slides back a chair and sits down across from me. Then she reaches out and takes my hand.

No no child she says, kind of whispering. Some secrets are too deep to tell.

Her eyes are brown and filmy. Her hands are twice as big as mine. They're full of creases across the knuckles, but the skin on the back of her hands is smooth and loose. I can see the bones underneath. The skin on the back of her hands is lighter than the skin on her face, and the skin on the palms of her hands is as white as mine.

Look at my hands. Pink, stubby, short little fingers. I'm about as much like her as a cocker spaniel is like a wolf.

How long have you been working for us Dora?

Since you were six, seven maybe. Was six because I helped with your seventh birthday party too. This'll be the fourth birthday of yours I've been here. You plan on helping me put up the party decorations later on?

Sure.

Hope you help me clean up the mess afterward too. She smiles at me.

Dora tell me your secret.

It don't work that way child she says. I'm a grownup. Grownups don't got to tell children their secrets. Unless they choose to.

Yeah I say. But what if I guessed?

Can't guess this child.

Bet I could if I tried. Is it about your son?

She puts her hand in front of her mouth like she's trying to stop the words from coming out.

How'd you know I had a son?

You said so once. His name is Joseph. He's in Mississippi. Where you're from.

Yes yes. Yes he is. She looks real unhappy now.

Do you ever see him?

Can't see him. She blows her nose and turns her head so I can't see her face.

Is that the secret?

Yes it is. Part of it.

She's still turned away and blowing her nose. I ask if she's OK but she doesn't answer.

Dora. Did you know we were in an accident Tuesday night?

What you mean accident?

Not really an accident. Well. My grandpa and my dad took me to a White Sox game and after the game, when we were going to the car, some colored kids—I mean, some Negroes—they were, mmmmmm, Negro kids. I think there might have been about eight of them, maybe more. They tried to get money from us. They didn't stick us up, just sort of danced around and teased us and asked us for money.

How old were these children?

My age. A little older. The oldest was twelve maybe.

She rocks her whole body back and forth. It's a long time before she says anything.

I seen no-'count children like that she says at last. Lots of times.

It was late. Real late. Way past my bedtime.

And you were by the ballpark?

That's right. In a parking lot near Grandpa's theater.

Where's that theater of his?

It's about four blocks away. On State Street. It's at Thirty-Fifth and State.

I seen that theater, walked past it on the way from church. They call it the Calumet. Ain't no place for you late at night. No white folks down in Bronzeville late at night anyhow. Even colored folks, they don't go out on them streets late at night if they have a lick of sense. I don't myself and I don't live no more than a mile away.

Do you want to know what happened next?

She frowns. Don't know as I do child.

It was dark and somehow one of the little colored kids—Negro kids—got hurt. My grandpa fell on him. *And I hit him in the throat.*

Your granddaddy fell on a colored child? Her eyes get wide.

Yeah. He broke his nose.

Child I must not be understanding you. How did this thing happen?

He fell on the kid. He fell backward. It was an accident. The kid was pulling on his suit jacket and he fell. I don't know. It was real confusing. Dark too.

She's holding my hand and looking into my eyes. We just sit there for a few moments, looking at each other that way, then I feel something inside opening up like a trap door. I start talking again, almost whispering, and my voice is a little shaky.

Dora?

Yes?

After school? On Wednesday? I went to visit the colored, I mean the Negro, boy.

You went?

By myself.

Lord have mercy! It sounds like someone punched her in the stomach.

Child you are in the way of trouble. She grabs my toast plate and puts it in the sink. She sets it down so hard I think she's going to break it.

I know it I say and put my head down.

Does your momma know you went by yourself?

No. Please don't tell her.

I can't promise that she says.

Please.

She doesn't say anything, then she sighs. All right. If she don't ask me I won't tell her. But if she does, the Lord says I must.

I know I say. *Then I just can't stop.*

I went down there on the streetcar.

Child it's best you don't tell me no more of this story.

Dora I've got to tell you.

No you don't child. And I don't got to hear it. She's mad now.

He was in Mercy Hospital.

So that's why you asked me about Mercy she says with her hands on her hips.

Yes.

Tell me no more child. You're going to get me in trouble too.

No no Dora! How would you get in trouble?

I can't explain. You're just a little child. There are things you don't understand.

Dora. He lives at Thirty-Sixth and Wabash. I want to see him again.

She shakes her finger in my face. Go take off those pajamas and get dressed. Right now. Scat! She marches out of the kitchen into the dining room. She swings the door so hard it bangs against the wall.

I'm still sitting at the kitchen table so I close my eyes but it doesn't work. I see those kids dancing around in the parking lot again. I see that kid, Sass, lying in that hospital bed with his face full of bandages.

I can't think.

Dora?

She's standing in front of the dining-room mirror running a bristle brush through her hair. It's gray and black, shiny. Dixie Peach.

Thought I told you to get dressed she says.

Dora, some day would you take me to Thirty-Sixth and Wabash?

I don't want to hear no more about this she says, trying to look into the mirror instead of at me. No more, hear? She brushes faster.

Are you mad at me?

I'll *be* getting mad at you, you don't stop this crazy talk.

I've already gone there once. I could go again by myself.

She gives me a look because I never talk back to her like that. Well, not much.

Go on some streetcar by yourself? Rather take you.

Good. So when can we go?

Shush up child she says. Didn't say I *would* take you.

But why not Dora?

That colored child ain't going to want to be seeing you again.

I know she's right. It feels bad when she says it though.

And why would you want to be seeing him anyway?

I don't know I say. What I'm thinking about is what Grandpa said. *Different from us.* And he said something else too. I know them he said. He said, I know them, and you got to get to know them too. *Yes.*

You and that colored child ain't got nothing to say to each other. She's sticking bobby pins in her hair now, pretending she isn't paying me any attention.

Maybe we do.

She drops the hairbrush. Her voice is shaking again. Child you are searching out more trouble than you ever found in your life. I know what I am saying. My boy Joseph—.

Go on.

Never mind. Just listen at what Dora Barfield tells you.

What were you going to say about Joseph?

Never mind! She's sticking in a bobby pin and pressing her tongue hard against the side of her lip.

Did Joseph get in trouble too?

More trouble than you can dream of. And all on account of a white child.

What happened?

He's in jail.

What did he do?

Nothing. He didn't do nothing, my poor baby. She's still futzing with the bobby pin but she can't position it because her hands are shaking.

What happened?

I never told a soul about this. Don't know why I'm telling you. She takes out some Kleenex and blows her nose.

Is he all right?

They took him away. Took him away from me. I

can't see her face because she's trying to turn the other way but I can hear her voice, shaking.

But Dora—.

No buts. She turns back and her face is all tight now. Just stay here with your own friends. Don't go looking to make friends with no colored child down on South Wabash Avenue.

But Dora. Nobody's going to put me in jail.

You don't never know she says.

What happened to your son?

I said all I'm going to say about my son. Go along out of here. I got to put on my clothes.

◆   ◆   ◆   ◆   ◆   ◆   ◆

I try to talk to her again but she won't talk to me all morning. I try to help arrange the party stuff but she just shoos me away. It's one o'clock, time for the party to start, and I still can't get her to talk to me.

So the doorbell rings and it's Rickie, first as usual. He hands me this box covered in white tissue paper and Scotch tape. The cardboard is showing through the edges where the tissue paper doesn't cover. I wrapped it myself he says.

Then Beth comes out of her bedroom. She's got on her pink tutu from ballet class, she's smudged lipstick and rouge all over her face, and she has my Wildroot on her hair.

She kisses Rickie.

Poor Rick doesn't know what to do but I do. I'll kill her.

Get away you baby I shout at her. This is *my* party.

Then I call for Mom to get her out of there before she spoils everything.

Just a minute honey Mom yells from the kitchen. I'm mixing the punch.

Beth sticks out her tongue at me. I can be here she says. Mommy said yesterday that I could. You can't kick me out.

Rickie laughs so I've got to beat her up now. But she runs the opposite way, smack into Dora.

Girl you're going to make me drop this here cake Dora says. She looks down at Beth and I think she's even more disgusted than I am. But Beth isn't paying any attention. She jumps up and hides behind Dora's skirt.

Stop this foolishness now the both of you Dora says and holds out her palm, but it's too late. I slam right into her full force.

She barely notices. I said she was big, didn't I? She stoops down, grabs my arm with one hand and slides the cake off onto the table with the other. Then she reaches the other hand behind her and grabs Beth who's wriggling like a fish. She drags both of us back into the kitchen.

Miz Feinberg ma'am these children are acting up she says. Can you talk sense to them please? I got to get this party ready. Other children will be coming any minute. Then she lets go of us and goes back into the dining room. The door swings shut behind her.

We're yelling at each other, she started it did not, that stuff. Mom looks at me, then at Beth, then at the ceiling.

I *so* wanted this to be a nice day she says and sighs. Beth go to your room.

Mo-o-o-mmmy you said I could be at the party Beth says and starts to cry. It makes the eye liner drip black down her cheeks.

Oh honey don't cry Mom says. All right you can stay but you two must stop fighting now or I'll have a nervous breakdown.

Rickie's watching all this.

Mom she's just a pest my friends hate her she'll spoil everything!

Mom goes Hmm. Beth dear maybe it *would* be better if you went over to Betty's and played for a few hours.

But Mommy she says. You promised.

Stevie I *did* promise her Mom says. She's looking from one of us to the other again. When we talk at once her head goes back and forth like she's watching ping-pong.

The dining room door swings open and Dora comes back into the kitchen with a dishrag in her hand. You girl she says to Beth, I need you to help me set the table. You, she says to me, go on out and be with your guests.

Mom looks relieved. She goes back to futzing with the punch.

◆   ◆   ◆   ◆   ◆   ◆   ◆

After Musical Chairs, Beth gets bored and asks Dora for her ice cream early, then goes back to her room to play with her dolls. Mom's in her room too, reading a novel by Alberto Moravia. Dad's on the phone. Rickie and the others have gone home.

Dora is sweeping cake crumbs off the dining room table but she holds up her hand even before I've had a chance to say anything.

I know what you're fixing to say she says. Don't ask me again about my Joseph. It ain't your business and I ain't going to tell you. Shouldn't of said nothing in the first place.

Then she drops her voice, so Dad can't hear from the next room I guess. But child please *please* listen to what I'm telling you she says. Colored folks and white folks will be together in heaven some day, it says so in the Bible. But until that day of glory we are living here on this Earth. We got to be careful, all of us. Things can happen, you don't even know how. One minute you're OK, next minute bang! Someone smites you on the cheek, don't even say hello. White folks, colored folks, they're the same. Some you can trust, some you can't. You don't know which is which.

And folks don't *like* it when the colored and the white get too friendly. Folks make you pay a price. White or colored, they make you pay a mighty high price.

I don't say anything back to her, just nod. This is the second time I've heard it— first from Grandpa, now from Dora. I just go into my bedroom and lay down, stick my face into the pillow. Trying not to think.

8
Sass

Jesse Owens Trimble

I'm still wondering about Momma and Poppa when they show up about seven at night. Momma is weeping and wailing, Poppa looks like he's fixing to take his belt to me. Poppa is sitting there in that rickety little chair the white boy sat in, slapping on his knee and hollering about what a no-'count child I am. Momma goes trying to shush him, waving her little hands in the air. I'd been hoping they'd come but now I'm wishing they'd go away.

How they found out, that police lady came over in the afternoon and told them. Momma was at work still but Poppa was home because he works early shift. Wonder if that nasty woman told them we tried to get the white folks to give us money? Poppa's bound to go cuckoo, kicking at the chairs and pounding on the icebox like he does.

Momma and Poppa want to take me home right then. Nun says no, he's still recovering, suppose he gets a blood clot, whatever that is. Momma says she don't care about no blood clot, she wants her baby back at

84

home. Momma and Poppa argue back and forth with the nun, finally the nun just shrugs and tells them they been warned. They get me back into my clothes and hustle me out. Was kind of hard to put my shirt on with my arm hurting still. I told that nun I didn't want no sling but she made me take one anyway.

We walk home up Wabash. It's a long way. I'm feeling kind of dizzy but I don't say nothing. Get to the building, old Herm is standing on the corner. He shouts Hey Sass hurt your head? I say to him You damn coward why'd you leave me out there? He just laughs and winks at me.

Up in the apartment I look around for Nubby but he ain't there. I swear I'll kill him when I see him. Darius is gone too, probably out with his buddies or them slut gals he hangs around with. Were me, I'd be ashamed to be seen with one of them skanky things.

Poppa don't say nothing on the walk, but I know it's coming and I know when. It's coming now. We get inside, he picks up the first thing comes to hand. It's a copy of *The Defender* lying on the table, lucky for me. Can't do me much harm with no newspaper.

He goes waving it around in the air like he's fixing to hit the light bulb. Then he goes whap! on my good arm. Goes shouting What trouble you been in?

He gives me another lick with the newspaper. It don't hurt much. Not like when he socked me on my eleventh birthday for saying I didn't have to mind him no more. Man's strong, working in them steel mills every day.

Momma tells him stop, can't you see the boy is

injured already. That just gets him arguing with her. Pretty soon he goes slapping the newspaper on her instead of on me. I hate it when he hits Momma but I dast not say nothing. He'll just start hitting on the both of us at once.

Nubby walks in then and a good thing too. Poppa asks where he's been. Soon Poppa's arguing with him instead of me and Momma.

My head starts to hurting real bad just then. I go into Momma's bedroom and lie down on the bed.

Momma follows me in. She pokes her finger under my bandage like she's fixing to unwind it off my head.

She opens the jar of Vaseline, starts rubbing some on my back. She starts singing that old song she used to sing when I was little, *Hush little baby, don't say a word, Momma's going to buy you a mockingbird ...* My back don't hurt but it feels so good I don't tell her to stop. I lie there and close my eyes.

Honey what were you doing out there? She's talking and rubbing at the same time.

Oh Momma we weren't doing nothing. Just playing.

Playing what baby? She keeps her voice low and soothing, just rubbing away.

Nothing Momma. I'm feeling good now, ready to fall back to sleep.

She wants to know how did I get hurt.

I don't remember, Momma. It's partly the truth. I don't recall falling and hitting my head and breaking my nose. I did recollect about the white kid hitting me in the throat when I talked to that gal from the police but Momma don't need to know about that. Nor about the white kid coming to the hospital neither.

She asks who was I out there with.

Herm. Sawbuck. Witchie. Some of them others. Wish I could tell her about Nubby too. He deserves to get in trouble more than me. But if I did she'd start to crying and carrying on so I don't.

But then she starts getting upset. She gets that mean low tone in her voice like she does. She calls me Satan's child, tells me I'm going to Hell for all eternity if I keep on hanging out on the street bringing shame on the family. Don't she and Poppa work hard to put food on the table and Jesus in our hearts? She ain't looking for no answer. Almost rather have Poppa beating on me.

But I must look pretty bad because all of a sudden she starts crying again and hugging and kissing on me, saying she's sorry and she shouldn't of yelled at her poor injured baby. She fans her hand at me to cool me down. She starts fanning so hard I wonder she might hit me in the eye. I try to tell her to stop but I get a little dizzy. Must of gone to sleep then because next thing I know I'm waking up and it's the morning after.

◆　　◆　　◆　　◆　　◆　　◆　　◆

I ain't eaten no supper the night before nor lunch neither. Ain't never been so hungry. I go to the icebox to see what we've got and there's Nubby sitting at the table. Just looking at him makes me want to kick him in the face.

I call him a damn stupid idiot for getting us in

trouble. He just grins at me. Don't say nothing—just stares and grins.

Get rid of that smile fool.

Make me he says back and hits at me. I can't get in a fight with him, me with bandages on my face and one arm still bad, though I surely would if I could. So I duck and call out for Momma. Nubby tells me to shut up, don't wake them or they'll come out and beat on the both of us.

You know the police are going to come for you I say to him. They'll be arresting you, don't matter you're still a little kid.

How are they going to do that? Who's going to tell them about me? Ain't going to be you surely. He gives me a look like I never seen. First time I ever been scared of him.

What if I do?

I'll kill you. I'll kill you dead. I'll take one of Momma's knives while you're sleeping.

Hah you wouldn't dare. But I'm thinking he would.

Then Momma and Poppa walk out in their pajamas. They tell us to get dressed. Say Nubby's got to go off to school. Nubby gives me one more of them looks and goes off to put on his school clothes.

◆　　◆　　◆　　◆　　◆　　◆　　◆

You know how sometimes you get a feeling about something? You just sort of know what's going to happen next even though you don't really know? I heard that knock on the door, I knew it was the police.

Policeman walks in, shows his badge, asks to sit

down. Big fat white man and his uniform don't fit right. Got a red face from climbing the stairs.

Says he's Officer Mallory, are you the Trimbles? Poppa says yes. Momma don't say nothing. She looks scared.

This Jesse? He jerks his head toward me. Poppa nods.

Can I talk to him? Poppa nods again.

Policeman looks at me now, makes his face all friendly. Starts out calling me son like the police lady did. Maybe they tell them to do that in police school.

There's some things ain't clear to us down at the police he says. I want you to answer honest, OK son?

OK sure I say. Like fun.

You take any money from those white folks?

Nossir I surely didn't sir.

You try to?

We were just asking would they give us some money. I didn't try to take nothing from them sir.

How'd that white man fall on you?

I give him a look like he's crazy. What's this policeman talking about?

Man says he fell on you. Man comes down to the station, makes a report, says he fell on you. Broke your nose, cracked your skull.

Tell him I didn't know that. I surely didn't neither.

He gets a cold look. You lie to me boy I'm taking you down to the station.

I ain't lying sir. Nobody told me how it happened and I don't recall it.

Well here's something else. Man says he fell on you because he lost his balance. Thinks someone might of pulled him backwards. Someone who might of been trying to pick his pocket. It couldn't of been you could it?

Nossir. Should be telling him about Nubby right now. Damn.

Who else was out there with you? Give me their names.

Only one who knows is Momma. I look at her from the corner of my eye. She looks even scareder than before. But she shakes her head no, makes me a sign, like. I believe Momma is telling me to lie.

Tell the policeman I don't know their names.

Policeman laughs but ain't nothing funny. You ever hear of Montefiore boy?

Yessir.

I send you to Montefiore you'll be one sorry kid. They don't like no coloreds at Montefiore.

Nossir.

So give me them names now.

Told you I don't know who they were sir. Bunch of kids I never saw. They were a lot bigger than me sir. First they asked me for money. Told them I ain't got none and they threatened to beat me up. Said I had to go along with them and find some white folks who'd give us money. I was scared of them. I had to go along sir.

Policeman makes a sneer, says That's the biggest bunch of bullcrap I ever heard. Says to Momma, Ma'am would you please give me the names and addresses of some of this boy's friends?

Don't tell him nothing Momma I'm thinking. I try to signal it to her with my eyes. This here policeman goes talking to one of the girls, they're bound to blabber everything. Even Herm or Witchie might.

But then Poppa speaks up. Asks are there any charges against me or not.

Policeman gets a disgusted look like Poppa went and found out something he wasn't supposed to know. Says there ain't.

You say the white folks ain't pressed no charges?

That's right.

Well then what's this all about?

We're just trying to get to the bottom of what happened. Your son is injured you know.

You ain't asking about his injuries though Poppa says. You're asking whether he committed some crime. But you ain't got no complaint filed, am I right?

You wising off to me?

I'm wondering that my own self right about then. Momma is the one usually sticks up for me but now she's so scared she's shaking. Poppa is the one to be tearing me down but now he's standing up to this white policeman. And all their talk about tell the truth and shame the Devil? First time it matters, the both of them go telling me to shut up. Glory be.

Now Poppa says to the policeman, I ain't trying to wise off to nobody officer but if there ain't no charges what are you doing here?

Policeman looks like a balloon with the air going out. He gets a sour look and says OK but we ain't done with this. I'll be asking around the neighborhood. We're going to talk to the white family some more. Suppose the white folks decide to bring some charges after all. You'd best hope they don't.

He gets up, puts on his police hat and heads toward the door. He didn't say hello when he came in and he don't say goodbye when he goes out.

♦   ♦   ♦   ♦   ♦   ♦   ♦

Soon as the door closes Poppa is on his feet. He's so mad he like to blow up. Momma tugs on his arm and tells him calm down James. That only gets him madder. He pushes her away and grabs me by the shirt.

Boy he says, I broke the Lord's commandment for your benefit but you'd better don't break it to me. I want the truth. You tell me everything that happened out there Tuesday night.

So I tell him enough that he ain't going to ask for no more. I say it was me and Witchie and Herm and Sawbuck but I leave out about the gals and Nubby. I say we weren't trying to do the white folks no harm. We just asked for change I say. I leave out the part about Nubby coming up behind the old man and trying to pick his pocket. And I leave out about the little white kid socking me in the throat. I say it's all the truth, cross my heart and hope to die.

None of that cross my heart he says. You swear it on this, and he takes the Holy Bible down off the shelf.

I put my hurt hand on the Bible and my good hand in the air and swear. Done so much lying already, ain't one more going to hurt.

But I'm thinking, Got to talk to my friends fast. Even talk to Nubby if I got to.

After school's out I jump out the back window and

cut over to Witchie's. Ask him what happened after I got hurt.

Witch says he ain't seen what happened. Was too dark. All he knows is everybody ran after I went down.

Well how'd I go down?

Says looked to him like the old man fell on me but he wasn't waiting around to find out.

You're some friend.

Shoot Sass he says, what could we of done? We'd stuck around, they'd of called the police on us for sure. Were you, you'd of run too.

We go out on the street and find Herm. Herm says same as Witchie.

Swear to it I tell them. Put your hands on your hearts and swear. We got to tell the same story or else we're all of us in trouble.

Herm says ain't nothing to tell. Says, we were just playing, didn't take no money. Even Nubby. Says, they should arrest Nubby before they arrest you. Or that old man in the straw hat. For falling on you and putting you in the hospital.

Get some sense Witchie says. They ain't going to arrest no white man for falling on some colored kid.

Herm asks am I going to tell on Nubby.

No I ain't. Don't you tell on him neither.

Why not? Was Nubby's idea.

Just don't, that's all.

When'd you start protecting Nubby when Nubby ain't never done it for you?

He's my brother. But I'm thinking, best if Nubby never even finds out about the police. They start asking

him questions, Nubby'll get everyone in trouble, dumb
as he is. He might even tell the police it was me reached
for the old man's wallet, just to get even. No, much as
I'd like to see him in trouble, I got to keep him out of it.

◆　　◆　　◆　　◆　　◆　　◆　　◆

I come home and Momma gives me two aspirin
and a glass of water. I go lie down in the bedroom, shut
the door. Got another one of them headaches.

I'm feeling awful tired too, want to be sleeping. My
mind starts to wandering.

I think about Poppa and the policeman, how he
stopped me from talking. Said it was for me he did it. I
don't recall much else he ever did for me. Now he
finally goes and does something and what is it? Telling
me not to bear witness to what I know.

Momma too. She knows I was with Witchie and
Sawbuck and them all but she gives me a sign not to tell
the policeman. You don't tell the truth when you know
it, that's same as a lie. Bible says so.

I lied my own self. Lied to the policeman because I
had to. Lied to Poppa. Lied and lied. Didn't feel bad
about none of it neither.

I think about that hospital. I'm in bed, don't know
a soul, wake up and there's that little white boy sitting
on that chair. Steve, his name was.

Don't know how he got there. Don't know why he
came. He's the last person I ever thought I'd see.

Wonder if he got a licking for coming to the hospital. Were me, Poppa'd of taken his belt to me for sure.

But maybe that boy's daddy don't give him no lickings. Maybe he just takes his son to White Sox games and buys him ice cream. Some daddies do that I guess. That's what old Ozzie does on Ozzie and Harriet. Ozzie is always giving things to his boys. He'll be telling David or Rickie on the radio, Go down to the soda fountain and buy yourself a treat. But first you got to mow the lawn. Wonder what it would be like to have a lawn. That Rickie, he argues when Ozzie says to mow it. But I'd mow one if I had one.

That white family brought me to the hospital. Policeman said it. White boy said it too. I never heard of such a thing, white family picking up a colored child and dragging him to the hospital. They'd of called the police maybe. Have an ambulance come. But he said they brought me. In their car.

I don't recall any of that. Must of been unconscious. Wonder if it was one of them big old DeSotos with whitewall tires and Fluid Drive. I like them DeSotos. Maybe I rode in one and didn't know it.

Let's see what else do I recall. Us kids trying to scare the white folks. There were a lot of us and just three of them. But they shouldn't of been scared of us. We couldn't of hurt them even if we wanted to. We're just little kids. There'd of been any polices around when it all happened, they'd of marched us off to jail. Us, not the whites.

I recall the little white boy being out there all right. Boy looked scared of us too. But he had no call to be scared of me. He ain't but a little smaller than me. If we'd of been in a fair fight, I don't know who'd of won.

Then the white boy comes looking for me in the hospital. If that don't beat all. Couldn't say what he wanted, just sat there looking at me with cow eyes. Like he's trying to solve a mystery. Like I'm the mystery.

I recall the old man too, man who must of fallen on me. Tried to get him to dance. Little old guy but he wasn't scared, not at all. I'm hanging onto his jacket, he's just staring at me with them cold blue eyes.

His jacket felt like wool.

Wool is nice. Poppa's got one pair of wool pants, what he wears when he's preaching. They're black. Goes with his suit coat, it's black wool too.

Sometimes Poppa wears his gray silk tie with that suit. One time, he didn't know it, I took that tie and tried to tie it around my own neck. I was just little. I recall standing in front of the mirror, trying to tie it so I'd look like Poppa. Tried and tried. Never could get it right. But the way that silk felt on my hands, I still remember it. It felt smoother than anything I ever touched. I want a tie like that when I get older.

Poppa looks real good when he wears that tie, them wool pants, that jacket. He'll be up in front of the congregation singing hymns to Jesus, he looks like he has the Holy Spirit inside of him.

That little old white man out there had on a suit and a tie. And a vest and a straw hat too. Might of had on spats, even. Was very old-fashioned-looking.

Old man reminds me of someone, now that I think of it. Looks like someone I might of seen somewheres. Ain't possible though. Only white folks I ever see are the teachers and the principal ... the man who collects the rent ... and that old white guy that Momma works for, guy who owns the Calumet. Couldn't possibly be him.

9
Joseph

Selassie and the Ant

Man I got to get up it's eleven o'clock at night it's eleven leven leven not seven seven seven got to wake my head get out of bed go earn some bread. Start at midnight. Middle of the night got to do it right. Folks counting on me.

Get up up up go to work work work can't be no jerk can't sleep can't shirk— shirt ... where's my shirt?

Here. Ooofff, smells a little. That's all right. Lots of smelly folks out on State Street. Smelly damn shirt. How long since I washed clothes?

Ain't no time for laundry now. Got to put on my shirt, put on my pants, put on my shoes, do a little dance. Wish I had me a radio to dance to.

I can hear the news from Africa though. Don't need no radio. Plays in my head. Tunes of pleasure, worlds of treasure, who can ever take their measure. Read it in some book. Book of Days I count the ways O let me count the many ways I've walked in state down State for I am great. The great Selassie, god of Addis and Asmara.

He had them braids, Selassie. I could do that. Let's just see can I twist my hair up a little in back. Wonder how he makes them stay in place like he does.

Lordy I'm still so sleepy. Turn on this here hot plate, make me some coffee, maybe that'll wake me up.

What's that, little bug? Ant on the hot plate.

Little black ant. Little Black Sambo. Simbo Sambo Jimbo Jambo, little ant don't give a damn-bo. Bug is black but he don't give a damn. Ain't that something?

Come on up here. I ain't going to hurt you. Just crawl onto this here piece of newspaper. See, I ain't turned on the hot plate yet, all on account of you. Going to tell you my story, ant. Going to tell you about me and the Man in the Moon.

What you like to eat, ant? Put you in this here jar where you'll be safe, be my friend. Only friend I got.

To Do Justice

*W*e go over to Grandpa and Grandma's house that night. Dora comes with, to clean up. She's got the left-over birthday cake in a paper bag.

I said house but it isn't, it's really a hotel. It's called The Standish. There's a desk and a switchboard and a woman named Mary who runs it. Last time Beth asked could she plug the cord into Grandpa's phone and Mary let her. This time Dick lets me run the elevator. I don't let go of the handle in time though. We go past the fifth floor but only just a little. He says Let go and he takes the handle. He makes it go real slow until it's back at the floor, then he opens the accordion doors for us. See he says it's a little trickier than you thought, that's why they pay me to do it. Beth laughs and I sock her and Mom says Stop it you two and we get off.

After dinner we're in the living room, Grandpa and me and Mom and Dad and Beth. Grandma and Dora are in the kitchenette cleaning up.

Grandpa is talking about the Calumet, which if I owned it, boy, I wouldn't even go see the White Sox.

Movies all the time.

They give me candy free. Sometimes Mattie lets me work the ticket thing. You know how the cashier hits a key and a ticket pops out? Underneath the chrome ticket thing there's this big roll of tickets. There's already a line of little holes that's been punched between each ticket. When the ticket pops out, all Mattie has to do is tear it along that line of little holes. The ticket tears right off. She punches the 1 key and this sprocket turns the roll a little so just one ticket comes out. When she presses the 2 key the roll moves out two tickets. I know. Mattie let me look underneath.

The projection booth is my favorite though.

You go up these wind-y iron stairs. The door is iron too. They're all enameled red for danger— the stairs, the door.

After George lights the arc they lock him in from the outside. Mack comes up the steps and slams down an iron bar so he can't get out. It's in case the arc catches the film on fire. That way, Grandpa says, the fire stays inside the booth and only the projectionist dies.

George says they stopped using nitrate film after the war so he doesn't worry about fires any more except if they play some real old movie. But the fire marshal still makes them lock the doors from outside.

George starts cranking the carbon rods apart. There's this big crack and buzz. Shut your eyes or you'll go blind he says but I look anyway. It's orange at first like a candle flame, then it goes white then bluish-white. Then you really *do* have to close your eyes. Even after you can still see it. Green and yellow and orange with your eyes closed.

Just look at it through the red glass George says. No you can't light it he says. Much too dangerous for you honey he says. Besides I'd lose my license.

◆　　◆　　◆　　◆　　◆　　◆　　◆

The theater has been in the family since the silents Grandpa is saying. It was Uncle Lou's but Lou didn't have kids so Grandma got it and of course she wasn't going to run it so I did. Nineteen and Seventeen he says. Was just starting to turn colored.

But I'm still thinking about the colors from the arc when you close your eyes. What colors Grandpa?

The *colored*. They were just starting to come in to the South Side he says. Theater was a nice place then, not like it is now. We showed silent movies, Chaplin, Clara Bow, Rin Tin Tin. Was a beautiful neighborhood before the World War, the first one. South Prairie Avenue where the Marshall Fields lived, we went down those streets when your Grandma and I were first married. We'd walk by the Pullman house, it went for half a city block. Had two footmen in uniform outside, only thing they had to do was to wait for the boss to come home from work.

Then after the war the *shocher*s come up from Mississippi on the Illinois Central he says.

Dad says *Colored* Pop.

Grandpa waves. Yeah colored, that's what I meant. You'd go by Twelfth Street Station and there'd be hundreds of them coming out onto Michigan Avenue carrying cardboard suitcases. First they moved into those tenements used to be on Grand Boulevard by the Regal Theater where the colored stage shows are now. Then they moved in near the Calumet too, off of State Street, east and south of the ballpark. They can't move west and north into Bridgeport and Canaryville because the Irish'll kill them. But there were other places where the whites just skedaddled.

Dad says, Like us?

Yeah Grandpa says, we moved with all the others. The Jews left Grand Boulevard overnight— went to Hyde Park and Englewood on the South Side, and Albany Park and West Ridge on the North Side. We went to Englewood, Fifty-Eighth and Michigan.

I remember it Dad says. Nice little apartment.

Yeah Grandpa says. Pretty soon it's the Depression and the *shvartzes* are south to Forty-Seventh Street. The Pullmans and the Marshall Fields decide they'd rather live someplace else. So the rich ones leave Prairie Avenue and their mansions get turned into tenement houses. Such beautiful buildings. Now there's laundry hanging from the windows. Those footmen have to go find jobs someplace else. Grandpa shakes his head like there's a fly buzzing in it.

Do you hate the colored Grandpa?

Mom gets all upset. Of course he doesn't darling.

I want to tell her about the parking lot, how I thought they were going to leave the kid lying on the ground. But Grandpa starts talking again.

How could I hate them? I'm with them every day he says. They're like everyone else. There's good ones there's bad ones. George Sullivan, finest man in the world, a fine man, been working for me thirty years, since he was fourteen years old, sweeping out the theater, selling the drinks. Now he's the projectionist, he's in the union, makes a lot of money, never had an accident in the booth thank God. It's a dangerous job, the arc, a man could get killed up there. I trust George as much as I trust anyone I know. Damn fine man.

Mattie too he says. Best cashier I ever had. Got an adding-machine in her head. Never misses a day and she's always got a smile. It's like he's talking to himself.

Mack too, Pop. He's been with you a long time Dad says.

Yeah. Hired him twenty years ago. Sweet guy. Got his head in the clouds a little. Talks to me about poetry, damned if I know why. I don't read no poetry. But that's what he likes to talk about. You know he's got a college degree?

You're kidding Dad says.

Yeah. Studied to be an engineer at some colored college in Atlanta or somewhere.

Dad says, Now he's an usher.

Grandpa says Yeah, how many colored engineers you know? Dad nods.

But some of those others. His face gets a little red. Did I tell you what happened last week?

Couple of them are sitting in the middle together drinking Richard's Wild Irish Rose out of brown paper bags. It's a matinee. We've got a Hopalong Cassidy on the screen. Hoppy's in trouble. One of the *shochers* pulls a gun out of his pants, yells Here Hoppy I'll help you, and shoots three holes in the screen.

You should see Beth's face.

You don't believe it? It's the God's truth he says to her and holds up his right hand. Man shot three holes in the screen.

What happened? What happened? I tell her to shut up, let him tell it.

We ran him out of there he says. Me and Mack, we go down where these guys are sitting. Middle guy is still waving his pistol in the air and shouting at the screen. Everybody around him is running out into the aisles and down under the seats. I'm behind Mack, me being white I've got to let Mack handle this. Mack's real diplomatic you know? He says Excuse me sir, he calls him sir, there's no shooting guns allowed in this theater.

Grandpa starts laughing.

Kind of funny huh? 'No shooting guns allowed in this theater.'

He's laughing pretty hard. He has to stop talking for a second.

Well. George cuts the arc and turns on the house lights. Then he turns on the radio so it's playing through the loudspeakers and we're standing in the middle of the theater with the lights on listening to *Our Gal Sunday*.

He's laughing so hard now he's crying. He pulls a white handkerchief out of his vest pocket and wipes his eyes.

We're the only ones left in the place. Mack says to these guys Please follow me. He's wearing his usher uniform so he looks official. They follow him. Maybe they thought he was a cop. They come out into the lobby and George is waiting. He's been watching from up in the booth so he knows which one has the gun. George sneaks up behind the guy and grabs him in a half-nelson while Mack cold-cocks him. The guy's friends are looking at each other like, What are we doing here? They make a break for the doors so they get away. But Mattie's called the cops and they come in swinging their billy-clubs. They give this guy a few more pops for good luck then they take him away.

Dad's laughing too. We're all, except Mom.

I fail to see the humor she says and she shoots Dad one of her looks. What about these children? What are they going to think?

Oh, Mom it was funny Beth says.

It *was* funny. But what if the guy who shot the holes in the screen was the guy who stuck Mattie up too? Maybe everyone down there has guns. Even those kids in the parking lot.

Maybe Mom's right.

Now she's saying, We try to teach these children tolerance and then they hear stories about coloreds with guns acting like savages and—

—and they're not Dad cuts in. He nods at her then at Grandpa. Right Pop?

Don't get holy on me Grandpa says. What about that time in Grant Park?

Never mind about that Pop.

Go on. Tell your children. Tell your wife.

Dad looks at Mom and shrugs. *You* know he says

to her. That time at Soldier Field. It was nothing. They just stuck me up is all. And roughed me up a little.

Beth looks a little scared. Who? she says.

I don't know, Dad says, couple of guys. Couple of colored. I was coming out of a Bears game, got in my car, these two guys were hiding in the back seat. They took my money and one of them hit me with something, a pistol I guess. Didn't get hurt though.

And what did they say to you? Grandpa's got this little smile on his face. I think they're going to have a fight. I could go to the bathroom now. Maybe I will.

Oh come on Pop let it alone.

They called him a goddamn white son of a bitch. He folds his arms when he says it. He's still got that little smile.

Pop I said *drop it*.

You want your kids to know what they're like? *That's* what they're like.

Well *they* are not "like" that or "like" anything and your grandfather ought to be ashamed of himself Mom says. *They* are just like *us*. There are good ones and bad ones—your grandfather said so himself. Those ones who held up your father were bad ones but there are good ones too.

Dora sticks her head out from the kitchenette. Missus Feinberg, I'm reminding you like you asked. Don't forget to take your pills after dinner.

Mom I'm going to the bathroom.

No sit down honey just for a minute. Listen to me. I want you children to know about brotherhood and tolerance. Racial prejudice is the worst thing in our society. I find it disgusting.

Here they are ma'am. Dora comes out with a bottle in one hand and a glass of water in the other.

You children ever hear the word "stereotype"?

No Mom.

A stereotype is like a mistaken picture in your mind. It's a picture you have about a certain kind of people. You think every one of them is like the stereotype, like the picture, like that false picture, but it isn't so. Every one is unique, a unique individual, just like you and me.

Dora's still standing there holding the bottle.

Can you children think of a stereotype of a Negro? Can you Beth?

Shirley Temple and the tap dancer?

Good darling. His name is Robinson, Bill Robinson. He is a real person, not a stereotype.

Bojangles I say.

Well yes honey she says, but I'm afraid nicknames like that just add to the stereotype. He's one of the most talented entertainers in America. I want you to call him Mister Robinson.

Ma'am your pills Dora says.

Mom looks up like she just saw her. She unscrews the cap, shakes out a pill, slips the bottle into her purse, then reaches over for the water glass. She swallows then hands it back to Dora. Dora stands looking at the half-full glass. Then she nods though I didn't hear Mom say anything. She goes Yes'm and heads back to the kitchenette.

Grandma comes out with the Black Cows. We run

back to the dining room. Beth likes to turn hers into mish-mosh soup with the straw but that's disgusting. It's better to eat some ice cream, then drink some root beer, then moosh them together in your mouth.

◆　　◆　　◆　　◆　　◆　　◆　　◆

Grandpa starts dealing Five Hundred Rummy. I notice it for the first time, that little spot near his thumb. What's that?

Tattoo he says.

A little blue spot? What kind of tattoo is that?

I stopped the guy. He stuck the needle in and I lost my nerve.

Dad says Where was that Pop? Slobodky?

Naw he says I was here already. Nineteen years old.

What's Slobodky Grandpa?

Slobody he says.

Slobodky Slobody Dad says, and he laughs like it was funny.

Tell us Grandpa. I put down my cards. I love these stories.

Where I come from. Russia.

Lithuania Pop?

Russia, Lithuania, what's the difference? The Russians had horses, the *litvaks* walked.

How come you don't have an accent Grandpa? I'm thinking about Harry Levin's grandma. She's from Poland and you can't understand a word she says.

I don't know. I ain't got one is all.

What was it like in that place, I can't remember

how you said it.

Slobody. Not a pot to piss in. I remember sitting in a whatchamacallit he says, had an ox pulling it—oxcart —me and my brother Yosl, that's your Uncle Joe, and Meir, your uncle Meyer. Going over the border to Germany or they called it East Prussia then. Was probably your age Steve. Year or two later we were here.

Mom says What about your father and mother?

I don't remember much he says. I was twelve when we got here, they were both dead soon after. Couldn't stay there though he says. Goddamn Russians setting fire to the houses he says. Wasn't any time to sit around like we are now.

What else Grandpa?

There was one thing he says. He puts his cards down.

My own grandfather. He prayed a lot, my grandfather. Very religious man. Read the Talmud with a group of men. I remember them sitting around a wooden table, smoking and talking, eating apricots out of a bowl. Wearing *tallis* and *yarmulkes* like in *shul* only they had on dirty work clothes instead of good clothes. And arguing at the top of their lungs. About Maimonides I think.

He laughs a little. He's staring out the window. Just staring, not looking at anything in particular.

Anyway my grandfather worked with metal, what you might call a jeweler today, only we were so poor in those days I don't remember any diamonds or rubies. Might have been some though. He made pretty things, my grandfather.

One time we were sitting together, him and me. We

were under a tree looking out over a hill. There were cows grazing down below and some goats. I could smell his pipe. I remember that smell even today, what they call Turkish tobacco. Very strong smell but sweet too. He says 'Natan,' that was my name then, Natan, not Nathan like it is now, 'Natan, you know the prophets?'

I didn't know what he was talking about. I was just a boy, maybe seven years old. No I said, what's the prophets?

'The prophets were them people in Torah times' he says. 'They were the wisest of the wise. They gave the people the lessons to get back on the line when they were going off, worshiping them golden calves and whatnot. And the wisest of the prophets was the Prophet Micah.'

I asked my grandfather why.

'Because the Prophet Micah said the wisest thing in the Bible.' He leans over so I can smell the tobacco smell real good and takes my arm. 'You'll hear people arguing for the rest of your life. What does this mean, what does that mean? But the Prophet Micah said it all in two sentences:

'What doth the Lord require of thee? To do justice, to love mercy, and to walk humbly with thy God.'

Grandpa's looking straight at me now like there's no one else in the room.

And I've remembered that Steve he says. I don't go to *shul*, you know that. You don't have to go to no *shul* to be a good Jew. That's what my grandfather was saying to me that day.

And then my grandfather reaches in his pocket

and hands me this thing he made out of silver. Beautiful little thing. Kind of oval but not exactly, with rounded sides, kind of an uneven shape actually. He had engraved those words from Micah all by hand. Raised letters, all by hand. Very small, but you could read them if you could read Hebrew, which I could not do then or now. But my grandfather could.

I've carried that thing with me all my life Grandpa says. Some day I'll give it to you Steve.

Could I see it now Grandpa?

Sure. I got it right here he says. I carry it always. He reaches into his vest and fumbles around.

It's here somewhere he says. He pokes into the vest pocket on the other side. Maybe it's in my pants he says. He pushes himself out of the chair and jiggles inside his pants pockets.

Must of left it in my jacket he says. Just a minute. He goes into the bedroom. We can hear him calling from there, Maaartha where the hell is my suit jacket? Then Grandma goes into the bedroom. I can hear them arguing. Then he shouts goddamn it where's that silver thing of my granddad's? It ain't in these pockets. Where'd you put it? Then she says something and he says goddamn it again.

He comes back into the dining room. His face is bright red.

It's them goddamn little *shochers* he says. One of them punks must of stole it in the parking lot.

What are you talking about Pop? Dad's got this expression on his face. Real worried.

At Comiskey Park the other night, them little

niggers—.

I look into the kitchenette. Dora's putting away some glasses. She's about six feet away. Maybe she didn't hear.

Mom and Dad are shouting now too. Pop! Pop! Calm down for Christ's sake. Let's look for it. It's got to be here.

But Grandpa's mad like I've never seen him. I've always got it with me he's yelling. If I send a suit to the cleaners, first thing I do is take the damn thing out and put it on the dresser. The dresser! He shoots back into the bedroom.

I can hear him yanking out dresser drawers and shouting. I run in to the bedroom and he's got a drawer open so far it's almost falling out of the dresser. He's sweeping the underwear and socks from one side to the other and grunting. Grandma's yelling at him Nate stop messing everything up but he isn't paying her any attention at all.

He slams the drawer shut, runs out to the living room and picks up the phone. I'm calling the police, goddamn it, get them to find those kids. Find that one was in the hospital, make him tell who the others were. Slap all their black asses in jail until they cough it up.

Dad says Pop calm down. We'll find your silver thing. I'm sure it's here.

No it's not he says. I even went through that other suit I was wearing.

OK. OK. Calm down please Pop. I promise you I'll take care of it. We'll go back to the police. I'll go down there, we'll go down there together, we'll take Steve if you want. We'll go in the morning OK? But for God's sake relax. It's Saturday night. We can't do a goddamn thing about it now. Let the kids finish their root beer.

◆　　◆　　◆　　◆　　◆　　◆　　◆

The next morning is Sunday. After breakfast, me and Dad pick Grandpa up in the Buick and drive to the police station where they made the first report. They ask for the same officer but the sergeant says he's off duty. He sits us down with another policeman in a uniform. He has a clipboard and a pad.

Grandpa tries to describe the silver thing. He makes a shape with his hands.

The policeman asks how big it was.

Oh, small, pretty small, this big, Grandpa says.

Do you have a picture of it?

No I ain't got no picture of it. How would I have a picture?

How about you draw me a picture of it?

I ain't no artist.

Suit yourself. Going to make it harder for us to find. The policeman yawns.

Give me your pencil and a clean sheet of paper. I'll draw you a goddamn picture. Grandpa draws this funny shape, it doesn't look like much of anything. The pencil lines are smudgy too.

That's it? The policeman smiles a little.

Well it had lots of lettering on it but I can't draw that, Grandpa says.

Our stolen-property guys are going to have a tough time with this.

Grandpa adds some words on the sheet and draws an arrow from the words to the picture. The words say: 'Lots of little letters written in Jewish on top.' The policeman smiles again.

And it was sterling silver Mister Feinberg?

Not sterling Grandpa says. Not sterling, not plate. Pure silver, soft enough that you could put a mark in it with your fingernail.

OK the policeman says. He pulls the sheet off the clipboard and drops it into a folder. We'll look into it.

We'll look into it? That's all?

It ain't a murder Mister Feinberg. And it happened four or five days ago.

Well what are you going to do?

Oh I guess we'll talk to the Trimble kid again the policeman says. Other than that I don't know.

You grill that kid Grandpa says. His face is red again. You make him tell what he did with it. Search his home. Threaten his parents. Goddamn it I'm a tax-paying citizen of the City of Chicago. I pay you people enough money every week I deserve something. You know that cop, Two-Gun Pete they call him, Silvester something-or-another, works State Street? I pay that guy off once a week to keep things nice around my theater. Must of given that son-of-a-bitch ten thousand dollars in his life. Now for the first time I want something and the goddamn police department says It ain't no murder Mister Feinberg.

He's imitating the policeman. Making fun of him.

Well I'll tell you something mister—now he's shaking his finger in the policeman's face—I want a detective on this case. I want action. I want that little *shocher* in jail.

We'll do what we can, Mister Feinberg. The policeman puts the folder in a drawer and sticks out his hand. Grandpa doesn't shake.

◆　　◆　　◆　　◆　　◆　　◆　　◆

After we leave the police station we drive past blocks and blocks where it's all colored. I never noticed before.

There are lots more people on the streets. They're sitting out on the fire escapes too.

One place we go past, there's furniture out on the sidewalk and clothes. A woman is sitting on the pile of clothes holding two little kids. She's crying.

The buildings look crummy.

If Grandpa has them arrest that kid, Sass, he'll go to jail. Just like Dora's son. Nothing but Wonder Bread and water for years maybe.

11
Dora

Talking to Jesus

Lord these children left a mess. Birthday-cake frosting on the chair, forks on the floor. Here's a cup of soda pop on the credenza, didn't even put a napkin underneath, left a white ring. Cake frosting gone and sunk into the chair cushion already. Never going to get this stain out. Better show it to Miz Feinberg. Not now though. They're fixing to go off to Miz Martha and Mister Nate and I got to go with them an hour or two. Can't do it tomorrow neither. It's Sunday, I'll be in church praying in Your holy name. Just have to wait 'til Monday.

White folks don't teach their children to be neat. I swear Lord. Every family I worked for. Steve and Beth too. They just throw off their clothes and leave them on the bedroom floor like little pigs. I tell them to pick up but might as well be talking to myself. Can't no Dora teach them how to do right. Got to come from the mother and she don't do it. I pray for her Lord. Mend her ways before she spoils them any more.

I tried to teach my Joseph how to do, You know I

116

did. Joseph did right too mostly speaking. Always respected me, always respected his daddy. Did his chores, even helped the old neighbor lady do hers. Went and picked turnips for her when she was too stiff to bend over. Was just seven years old. Wasn't scarcely big enough to pull them turnips out of the ground.

Maybe I'll go to the market tonight, get me some turnips myself. Cook the greens up with a little vinegar and bacon, be mighty tasty. Then I'll go over to the church if it ain't too late. Reverend Trimble asked would I help mimeograph some new hymns for services tomorrow. Glad to do it.

He's Your servant, Reverend Trimble. He's a good man too. Has a temper though. Man of God ought to learn to control his own self. But I shouldn't judge him. Judge not lest ye be judged, You said it Yourself.

The Reverend got a hard life like the rest of us colored, working out there in Gary Indiana five days a week, then he comes to church and preaches most every night and Sundays too. Don't know how he does it, getting up at three, driving out to Gary in Jeter's rattly old Chevrolet with Jeter and Morris and them others, it's pitch black nighttime outside. Maybe he sleeps in the back seat.

He told me what it's like working in them blast furnaces. Says, Sister Dora it's so hot there the sweat just pours off my face like a river. Don't matter it's winter and fifteen below, when they open that furnace door it's like the fires of Hell. I asked him not to say Hell in front of me and he apologized but I shouldn't of said nothing. He wasn't cursing.

Them boys of his, Lord. They ain't coming along so well. That oldest, Darius, he don't even come to church no more. Used to be the best boy in my Sunday School class. Prayed to God all the time just like his poppa showed him. Now I see him hanging out on State Street with no-'count hoodlums. Stopped going to Phillips too. What's he expect to amount to, no high school? Be lucky to get a job in the steel mills his own self.

His brother Isaiah, one they call Nubby, I couldn't do nothing with him at all. I tried to teach him Your word but he just wanted to shout and cut up in class. Had to repeat fifth grade his momma says.

Now I got little Jesse in Sunday School. He's the one I worry about most. Child's got more brains than the other two put together. And when he smiles he lights up my heart. But look how he's behaving lately with that smart-aleck talk, him just eleven years old. He tried to give me that sass of his but I put him in his place. Had to. It was for his own good. He goes down that path with his brothers, it'd be me would have to answer to You. But he's bound to if he don't straighten up soon.

Well I done about the best I can with this cushion. Have to let it dry to see if I got all that stain. Monday. Can't be bothered with it no more now. It's six o'clock. Find my hat and bag, go over to them grandparents' place a while, then go on home. Tomorrow is Your day Lord and I got plenty to do.

◆   ◆   ◆   ◆   ◆   ◆   ◆

Thank You Jesus. Them Sunday School children went easy on me today. Even little Jesse didn't act up. Poor child, wearing them bandages on his nose. Wonder how he got his self hurt. Children get in such mischief these days.

Miz Trimble looked very nice this morning, didn't You think? Very nice. That camellia on her bosom was lovely and it had a beautiful smell. I used to think she was forty-five, forty-six years old but her oldest one Darius ain't even eighteen yet I don't think. I could be wrong ten years. She might've been a beauty. She's very pretty still. Her hair ain't got no gray in it though I believe she earned a gray hair or two, working every day and raising three boys too.

Pity she's got to leave on Sundays in the middle of praising Your glorious name. It's on account of that job of hers. She's cashier at some movie theater or other. Got to go open up the business, even on Sundays. It's a sin against Your name to show movie pictures on the Sabbath. Colored folks out on State Street ought to be in church praising You, every last one of them. Glad I got a job leaves me my Sundays to do that.

Now I'll just sit back and listen to the choir. I pray for the light of Your grace to shine on me today. Hallelujah.

◆　　◆　　◆　　◆　　◆　　◆　　◆

Wish the Reverend ain't preached about Joseph and his brothers Lord. Puts me in mind of my boy Joseph.

Joseph's brothers sold him into slavery. I ain't no better than those sinners. I might as well have sold my own child into slavery. What's my baby but a slave, in jail down there?

Gran was born a slave rest her soul. Took care of white folks' children too just like me. Wonder what she thought about them. She might hate their folks Lord but how's she going to help loving a baby child?

I told Joseph I'd see him again but it must be when we meet in heaven. I know that now. I'll never get back to Sunflower. Ain't got no money for train fare, ain't got no people there no more, can't leave my job. Besides how would I find him? He might be in jail still, he might not. He might be in Mississippi, he might not. He might be living next door to me right here in Chicago. I might meet up with him on State Street and not even know who he was.

◆　　◆　　◆　　◆　　◆　　◆　　◆

Where's my purse? I'll go out, get a few things from the grocery, go on home early.

'Bye sister, 'bye Reverend. 'Bye Sister Monty Lou. Your choir gals made a joyful noise to the Lord today.

Mighty nice sunny day. Lots of folks out here.

Give me a copy of *The Defender*, would you young man? Here's a dime.

Lord look at this. Joe Louis going to fight in New York City. Jersey Joe Walcott. Heavyweight title. Hope Louis wins. Man makes folks proud to be colored. Makes me proud too though pride is a sin against Your name. But ought to be some better way for colored folks to get ahead than beating up on other colored folks, don't You think? White folks too, that German, Schmeling. The white folks just going to try to get even, that's how they are. Wish Joe Louis was a preacher or a teacher or a doctor, not some boxer. Still he's a good man, Joe Louis.

That other boxer was a hero to the colored too, Jack Johnson. Had a beautiful big old house down on South Wabash Avenue back in the old days. Three stories and a porch, nice as any white man. Nicer. That was a sinful man though, Jack Johnson. Gallivanting down State Street with a white woman on his arm, trying to show folks the world couldn't knock him down a peg. Folks in Bronzeville went crazy for Jack Johnson Lord. Heard one man say Give it to them in the ring, Mister Jack, then give it to them again in the crib. But it was a disrespect to colored women everywhere, what Jack Johnson did. Don't know why other colored folks didn't see it the same way.

Look at these lettuces out here on the sidewalk. Got lettuce, kale, potatoes, yams, some carrots. Carrots look pretty good. Never did get no turnips last night.

Excuse me, young man you got any turnips today? Inside?

These look pretty fresh. I'll take a bunch of them. I'd like some salt pork too. Ain't got no salt pork today? Bacon will be fine. Give me some of that Oscar Mayer. Some dried beans too, ones they call navy beans. I used to eat them black-eyed peas but I believe they gave me gas on the stomach. Little pot of navy beans and molasses tastes mighty good you know and they're very easy to digest. Got to boil them a minute in the first water then throw it off and boil them again until they get soft. That way it takes the dirt and poison out of them and they don't give you no gas. You ought to try them some time young man.

I'm sorry young man, wasn't paying attention. I saw someone across street I know. Look over yonder. See that little boy with the bandages on his face, front of that movie theater? He's the son of our pastor Reverend Trimble, Glory Life in Jesus Church. Don't know which church you go to, young man, but you ought to come by Glory Life in Jesus and hear Reverend Trimble preach some day. We got a mighty fine choir too, best in Bronzeville. Ain't no shame in storefront churches young man. Jesus ain't too proud to come into no storefront. Jesus lives in the heart of every man, He goeth through every door.

Who's Jesse talking to Lord? Must be Mattie. That theater must be the one where she works. Just across and down the block from church. Glad it ain't no long walk for her.

Says the Calumet on the sign. Didn't someone just tell me about the Calumet Theater, or ask me about the Calumet Theater, or something? Who was it? Blessed if I can recall.

I got the money right here in my purse young man. Here, I'll count it out— one, two, and thirty-five cents, even. I'm going to give you five pennies if you don't mind because I don't like to carry them around.

Believe I'll just cross the street and say hello to them. Then I'll go on home.

How you doing Sister Mattie? I was in that food shop across the street and I saw you and Jesse so I thought I'd wish you a blessed Sabbath day. Jesse, don't you forget to read your Bible lessons this week. We're studying the Gospel of St. Matthew, Miz Trimble. Jesse's a mighty good student, he surely is. Reads out loud from the Bible to the whole class. Reads as good as any high school student. Maybe you'll be a preacher yourself someday, eh Jesse? Well I got to be getting along now.

It's so nice, believe I'll walk rather than take the bus. These groceries ain't too heavy. Go over to the drugstore then walk home. Look at all this traffic crossing State Street Lord. Didn't even used to be a stoplight at Thirty-Fifth when I first come up from Sunflower. Had a policeman in the middle directing traffic.

Wonder if I got to be back at church tonight for the ladies' meeting. Miz Trimble, she'll know. Cross back and ask her soon as this light changes.

Is that a white child? Standing off to the side talking to Jesse? Sure looks like it from here.

Looky there Lord. That white child, he's whispering in Jesse's ear now. How can that be? What's he doing down here?

Oops. Drat. Durn bag tore. Turnips and beans and bacon all over the sidewalk. Oh land, now I'll have to carry them loose in my arms. Where'd those boys disappear to? Look away for one second and they're gone.

Sister Mattie, is the ladies' meeting tonight? At

seven? Thank you kindly. Excuse me, my groceries spilled. I'm going to have to go back to that food shop and fetch another paper bag unless you got something I can carry them in. Why that's mighty kind. Yes it's a little too big but it'll work just fine.

Let me ask you something Mattie. Was Jesse just now talking to a white child? Over to that side, over there? No. I didn't think he knew any white children.

Well maybe I didn't see nothing neither. I was all the way across the street and my eyes ain't so young any more. Maybe I imagined it. 'Bye now. Thanks for the paper sack.

My oh my. Maybe I imagined it Lord but I don't think so.

Oh well. Time to go home. Fix a little lunch, read this Defender, *then read my Bible a while. Then I'll come back to church tonight to praise Your name. Walk then too if it's still nice out like this.*

On Monday, let's see, got to take Steve to the doctor's office after school. Usually she's the one takes him but she's busy with some meeting or other so I guess I got to do it.

Steve. Calumet Theater. Wait a minute. It was Steve was the one talking about that theater. The Calumet. He said his granddaddy owns it. Owns that Calumet Theater.

So that white child ... I didn't imagine it. That white child might have been Steve. Must have been. And that Calumet Theater, it must be the same theater that Mister Nate owns.

Oh Lord Jesus give me strength.

Steve said he went down to Mercy Hospital to visit some colored child with a broken nose. Jesse Trimble got a broken nose. So the child in the hospital must have been Jesse. Steve must have been visiting Jesse Trimble.

Wait. I got to sit down on this here streetcar bench. Help me Lord. Help me gather up my thoughts.

What else did Steve tell me? Said he and Mister Charles and Mister Nate were in a parking lot after some ball game. Said a bunch of colored boys and girls came up and asked them for money. Said he hit one of them by accident, hit him in the throat somehow, then Mister Nate fell on him. Believe that's what he said. Then they carry that child to Mercy Hospital. Then next day, Steve takes the streetcar by himself to Mercy. To visit that child.

Lord that child's got to be Jesse Trimble. My preacher's son. Sure as I'm born.

And his mother Mattie, why, she's working for Mister Nate. Right there, across street in that Calumet Theater.

Lord, tell me what I must do. I know—I'll march right back to that theater and tell Mattie ... what? That Jesse's been talking with Steve? So what? Steve ain't nothing to her.

Wait a minute. She's bound to know Steve, working for his granddaddy and all. Wonder did Jesse tell her about Steve coming to visit him at Mercy? Wonder does she know... it was her own son Jesse in that parking lot with Mister Nate and Mister Charles and Steve ...

What am I going to do? Oh Lordy Lordy Lord.

If she don't know about that parking lot, I can't be the one to tell her. I ain't supposed to know it myself. I'd just be making trouble.

I know. I'll tell Mister Nate. Yes. If Steve is down here then Mister Nate's got to be down here too, right inside that theater. Mister Charles too more than likely. I'll go right back across street and tell them that Steve and Jesse— oh no. Oh Lord this is complicated.

Now Dora Barfield you just calm yourself down. Let's see. What would I be telling Mister Nate? That the child from the parking lot is the son of his cashier? Mister Nate would fire Mattie for sure. Tell Mister Charles that Steve went down to Mercy to visit Jesse? By his own self? He'd fire me and have a heart attack too.

Best do nothing right now. Just walk on home and think this over. Don't go doing something foolish, ain't that right Jesus? Don't go opening my mouth until I know what's going to come out of it. I go saying the wrong thing, Lord, it'll just make trouble for them. And for me too.

12
Steve

Steve and Sass

Grandpa opens the glass theater doors and knocks on the door of the box office. Morning Mister Feinberg Mattie says through the wall.

She clicks open the door. It scrapes every time. I don't think Grandpa fixes things around here very often.

Oh good morning to you too Mister Charles. Then she sees me. Stevie! How you doing baby?

Fine Mattie. Mattie and George are the ones I like best down here.

Nice to see you honey she says. She likes me too. You going to watch the movie today? I think we got Randolph Scott in some Western.

Could I Dad?

I don't think so son he says. We'll be going home in a half-hour.

Grandpa unlocks his office and he and Dad go in though it's so small they can both barely fit. I'm out in the lobby by the popcorn. They've got Milk Duds! Popcorn too though people can bring in Karmelkorn from next door. The lobby smells like popcorn and Lysol.

And pee.

So I look out the glass doors and there he is.

I know it's him because of the bandages on his face. He's standing in front of the box office with his head bent, talking through the slot.

Why would he be talking to Mattie?

I hold my breath and sneak toward the glass doors. I crack one open and whisper *Hey.*

He doesn't notice at first. He starts to turn away. Then he says something to Mattie. *OK Momma I'll see you tonight.* The hairs go up on the back of my neck when he says *Momma.*

I squeeze through the theater door. He still doesn't see me. *Good.* I press my back against the outside doors and scooch toward the wall on the other side. Then I scrunch into the corner and wait.

He walks right past me.

I sneak up behind him until I'm so close I can whisper right into his ear. *You're in trouble.*

He spins around and goes Whuhnh-h-h like he got his breath knocked out.

Sssshhhh. Don't run away.

I grab onto his arm. He tries to shake me off but I grab even tighter.

The police are coming to put you in jail. For stealing my grandpa's thing.

What thing? He shakes even harder but I'm stronger than he thinks.

My grandpa had this silver thing. He can't find it. He thinks you took it. This time I'm not whispering.

I didn't take no thing he says. Let loose of me.

You have to prove it.

I ain't got to prove nothing he says. What are you doing here? How'd you find me?

This is my grandpa's theater.

What theater? What are you talking about?

This theater. The Calumet.

Your granddaddy owns the Calumet? Come on.

No really.

Naw he says, you're kidding, and he looks at my face for the first time. Your granddaddy don't own it. You're just making it up.

I'm not. Honest I'm not.

So then my momma works for your granddaddy. That's funny he says but he doesn't laugh. He just stares at me with his mouth open.

Yeah funny but I don't laugh either. Listen I'm not kidding. You are really in trouble unless we find that thing of his.

What is it? He pushes my hand off his arm.

I don't know I say. I never saw it. It's silver. It's worth a lot of money. His own grandpa made it for him. He went to the police and told them to arrest you. You and your friends— all of you.

Aw you're just trying to scare me he says.

No! No! I went too. I saw the policeman write it down.

He backs away. I ain't got your granddaddy's silver thing.

Well maybe one of your friends stole it.

They didn't steal nothing. None of us did. You didn't go to no police neither. You're lying. He starts to run so what can I do? I jump on him and we both hit the sidewalk.

He shouts Careful! Can't you see I got bandages on? You're going to sprain my wrist again.

We're lying on the sidewalk looking at each other. My leg hurts so I look down and there's a rip in my corduroys. My knee is scraped so bad it's bleeding through my pants.

Ooohhhh look what you did. He holds up his right hand. It's bloody like my knee.

I'm sorry. I didn't mean to hurt you—. I almost say *again*.

Look at my hand! He wipes it on his chest which is dumb because now he's got blood on his shirt too.

I try to get up. My leg's on fire. He tries to get up but he's got a sling on one arm and his other hand is bleeding, so he just squirms on the sidewalk like a crab. I hold out my arm to help him up but he just waves me away. Finally he gets to his feet somehow.

I ain't going nowhere with you he says.

If you don't you're going to jail for sure I say. All they give you is Wonder Bread and water. I don't think he buys that so I say, And they won't let your mom come to see you.

You're full of it. I'm going on home. You go back with your granddaddy. But he's still standing there.

Does he really own the Calumet?

Yeah. I get to see movies for free. Popcorn too. You want to see movies for free?

He laughs. He ain't going to let me in there he says. They kick us out already when we make too much noise.

Well I'd ask Mattie to let you in free. She's my friend.

You crazy? She don't even let me in free and she's my *momma*. He starts walking up State Street but not very fast. Actually he's kind of limping.

Want to see free movies? *All your life?*

You're crazy and dumb too he says, walking away.

Really. If you help find his thing, I'll ask Grandpa to let you in free.

Oh yeah he says, your granddaddy'd really do that.

I would. I'd say Grandpa this is my friend uh uh Jesse—.

Sass.

—uh Sass and he helped find your silver thing and uh he's a great kid and uh you got to let him come in to the theater free for the rest of his life. I'd ask him that.

You would not.

Would too and I take a deep breath. And I'd ask him to let in your friends too.

For life?

Um. Sure.

Cross your heart he says.

I say Cross my heart and hope to die because that's how the Christian kids say it.

And Jesus and the angels?

And Jesus and the angels. When I say that one I get a funny feeling in my stomach.

What's this thing look like?

I think it's about this big and it's shaped like this—. I make a shape with my hands but really I don't know what it looks like except what Grandpa said.

It's pure silver and it's got letters in Hebrew.

What's Hebrew?

What they write on the Ten Commandments.

You mean *Thou shalt not steal?* Stuff like that? That's English.

No, I mean on the stones, what Moses brought down from the mountain, you know, *Hebrew.*

Never heard of it he says and folds his arms. That just smears more blood on his shirt.

Well let's just look for a silver thing with funny-looking letters you can't read.

Where are we going to look he says.

The parking lot.

Right now?

Yeah.

Why don't you go by yourself he says. So I have to admit I don't know how to get there.

Oh shoot he says, it's just a couple blocks.

Which way?

That way. Man you *are* dumb. Well come on let's go.

13
Joseph

The Emperor

Got me my keys right here. Dozens. Loop them on my belt, weigh a pound.

Got every store on State Street, palm of my hand. Some fool come up to me, ask for my money, I'll give it to him and smile, say, Mister just don't take these here keys.

Now get me my flashlight and I'll be all set to go on out. Flashlight and keys hanging down to my knees, I ain't no tease, I'm ready prepared, steady not scared.

Go out and get me a bite to eat first. Get me a hamburger with ketchup on it, ketchup so I can catch up, catch up with a robber, latch him up, latch him in the hatch. Latch him in the booby hatch. Yeah, him, not me.

There's robbers out on State Street, burglars and thieves. Thieves and burglars, robbers too, but I'm the man takes care of you. I'm proud to be that man. Proud of my pride, pride of lions, Lion of Judah, Tarzan of the Jungle, bongo bongo bongo I don't want to leave the Congo but they ain't getting me. Spear me one of them lions first. The postman rings twice but Selassie spears first, the Emperor Ras Tafari hurls his deadly spear first. I stride down State Street with my hunting party. Crowds make way.Would of speared you too, Marcus, but you got your spear into me before I ever had a chance. Dirty man.

Dirty prison man hurt a baby was the plan. You didn't want none of my food like them others. Not in the mood for food. You took my butt and made me a slut so why not take all of me. Can't do that dirty thing no more though. Tie you up in one of them Parchman dungeons. Orders from the Emperor on high.

You got you some hamburgers tonight? Give me one with ketchup on it, lots of ketchup. Catch it up with ketchup.

White Sox vs. Senators

Poppa says he ever catches me going across Wentworth he'll give me a licking I won't forget but I done it lots of times. Heck, just the other night at that parking lot. And this time I ain't getting in no trouble for sure. I got a white boy with me.

We come up on the parking lot again and it's all different than it was at night. They're playing an organ inside the ballpark, and the crowd's yelling and shouting and carrying on so loud we can hear it all the way out here. White Sox against the Senators. The lot's full of cars.

The white boy, he looks around like he ain't never been here before, though he just was. Where'd we park he says.

I point to the far end. You were over there. We start walking but the cars are jammed so tight together we got to squeeze between them sideways.

He stops and looks under one. I just stand there with my hands on my hips.

I don't see it he says.

Why don't you look under that one instead? He says OK and goes down on all fours. He's so dumb he don't even know I'm sassing him.

He scoots over to the next car. It ain't there either he says.

How many cars you plan to look under?

All of them I guess. Come on and help me he says.

I can't be crawling around no parking lot and I point to my sling. I got one hand still hurts and now this other one is bleeding too.

We'll never find it he says. We'll have to come back when no one's here.

Oh sure. Your momma's going to let you come down here some night and crawl around on your belly for a few hours.

Hey he says to me, *you're* the one in trouble. You better start looking too.

I ain't looking for nothing.

Well then let's go ask the parking-lot guy he says, so we go over to the booth and knock on the glass. Guy inside is hunched over his portable radio listening to the game and smoking a White Owl.

Mister. Mister.

He holds up his finger and goes sssh. Quiet, Appling is up.

The white boy, Steve Whatsisname, shouts out Mister! We got to talk to you.

Man turns down the radio. Whaddya want? He looks disgusted.

Did you find a little silver thing out here last week? Whaddya talking about?

Did you find a little thing shaped kind of like this and old Steve makes that shape again with his hands. It has Hebrew lettering on it he says. And it's silver. Pure silver.

Man says Are you nuts?

No really mister. My grandpa lost it in this parking lot.

Man says When was that?

Last Tuesday.

Man says Oh that's rich. Naw no silver thing. Just a suitcase full of dollar bills. Oh yeah, and a bag of gold coins someone left last time Cleveland was in town.

Hey mister.

Yeah? Man looks over at me.

How come they hired a jackass to work in the parking lot?

Man says Huh?

I'm sorry. You ain't no jackass. It's your momma is one.

Man drops his cigar and tries to get out but the door sticks, good thing. I give a whoop and start zigzagging through the cars. But old Steve stands there like he's growing tree roots. Man finally unsticks the door and goes grabbing for Steve's shirt. At last Steve wakes up, starts to run too.

I'm about five cars ahead of him and he don't look too fast to me. I push it, maybe he ain't never going to see me again.

But then I look back at him instead of where I'm going, like I should of, and trip. He catches up with me and I'm lying across someone's fender.

Aw I thought I'd lost you.

Why'd you say that to that guy?

Why'd *he* say that stuff about dollar bills and gold coins?

But we shouldn't of wasted time arguing because now the man catches up. He grabs at my shirt. I'm trying to shake my arm loose from him but I can't get free, when what do you know? Steve goes and kicks the guy in the shins.

He shouts at me, *Run.*

The man lets loose of me and grabs at his own ankle. What the hell he calls after Steve, why you helping that smart-mouth little shine? But I'm running too now. Man's hop-skipping after us shouting, *Punks.*

We make it to the sidewalk, Steve grabs my hand and runs into the street, out to the center line. Cars zooming by us both directions. There's a little break and Steve heads to the other side. Like to yank my arm out of its socket.

Come on.

There's a bus pulling up. *Get on* and Steve pushes me inside. Bus driver slams shut the doors and swings out into traffic. That old parking-lot guy is standing across the street all red in his face, still waving his arms and shouting at us.

◆   ◆   ◆   ◆   ◆   ◆   ◆

Steve reaches into his pants for a dime and hands it to the driver. Driver gives me a cold look. What about you bud?

I shrug. What the heck am I doing on this bus

anyway?

Give him your dime Steve says.

Ain't got no dime.

Steve fishes into his pocket and pulls out two nickels, gives them to the driver. We plop down in a seat up front.

You got blood on your pants I tell him.

You got blood on your shirt he says back.

I look down and sure enough. It's all over the front of my shirt, and it's been there long enough so it's turning brown.

Oh man look at me. I got to get home.

Steve gets up. Is this where you live?

Sit back down boy I tell him. I can't get off this bus now.

What do you mean?

Can't get off. We're past Wentworth Avenue. We're in Bridgeport.

What's wrong with that?

Can't cross Wentworth. They'll kill me.

Who'll kill you?

Who do you think? The paddies.

He gives me a dumb look. I slap my forehead.

The Irish, fool.

Which Irish? Why would they kill you?

I swear you're about the stupidest person on this bus. Because I'm colored, that's why. Or maybe you didn't notice.

Just because you're colored?

I don't say nothing back to him, just give him a look.

Well when will it be safe for you to get off he wants to know.

I don't know I tell him. I ain't never been on no bus.

His eyes go wide open. You're kidding he says.

No I ain't.

How do you get downtown he says.

Ain't never been downtown. You been downtown?

You never been to the Oriental Theater? Never been to Marshall Field's? Jeez, and he shuts up. Get some peace and quiet for a few minutes anyway.

We go past gas stations, hot-dog stands, houses with them gray asphalt shingles, feels like miles. I look out at the folks on the street.

He must be looking too because he says, They're still white.

We must still be in Bridgeport he says.

They're white everywhere except in Bronzeville I tell him.

In where?

Bronzeville. Where I live. Where the Calumet is. Where all the colored are.

He wants to know why they call it Bronzeville.

They call it the Black Belt too.

He says no there must be some coloreds who don't live there. Says, I go to school with coloreds.

How many?

He says Uh one. But I like her.

I tell him, Well she must live in Bronzeville.

Is this really the first time you been on a bus?

I said it was.

So then it's the first time you ever been outside of whaddyacallit … Bronzeville?

So?

So. Just thinking. He don't say nothing for a few more moments, then, So. So you ain't never been to the Museum of Science and Industry?

Naw. I heard of it but I didn't go. We were going with my class but they didn't have no way to take us there.

It's really keen he says. They got the biggest electric train set you ever saw. It's about a block long.

You mean, like the El?

No he says. *Toy* trains.

Toy trains. Bet that'd be fun.

You don't have a train set?

Me? Didn't know there was such a thing 'til you said it.

You play baseball? He's just running his mouth now.

Yeah. Sure.

What position?

What do you mean, position?

Second base? Third base? I play second usually.

I donno, we just play. Getting tired of this.

You got a glove he says.

Naw I say, ain't got no glove. Ain't got no electric train. Ain't got no big old red Buick. Ain't got no silver thing that just makes trouble for other people.

What's the matter with you he says.

I'm getting a headache. And I got to get home.

Oh gosh I do too he says and now he looks real

worried. Where *are* we?

I don't recognize nothing out the window. Ain't but a few houses and stores now, with vacant lots and fields full of weeds between them.

Rumbling sound, kind of faint. Let's get off he says.

The bus shoots out a cloud of blue smoke and moves away from us and we're standing on the curb. The rumbling gets real loud now so I look up, see this huge airplane go smack over our heads, so close we can see a big eagle on its tail, blue and red. I can even read what it says on the side. Eastern Airlines Route of the DC-6's. It keeps on coming down and down until it crosses a chain-link fence on the other side of the street. Hits the ground like a feather pillow. Little puffs of smoke where the wheels touch.

Steve's scratching his head. Where are we?

Tell him I don't know.

We cross and walk past the fence toward the buildings. Middle one got a tower on it with a big light on top going around and around, green then white then green again. Sign hanging over the front door says

Welcome To
CHICAGO MUNICIPAL AIRPORT
and below it
World's Busiest Airport

I look over at him. You ever been here?

Naw he says. Let's go in. Maybe you can call your momma.

Can't.

What do you mean he says.

I ain't got no money. And we ain't got no phone neither.

Holy cow he says. How do you talk to your friends?

I see my friends every day.

Well what if you wanted to talk to uh, your cousin?

My cousins, they're all in Alabama. I ain't never seen a one of them.

Well I'll call my dad he says. He'll come out and get us.

He'll come out and get *you*. He ain't going to get *me*. He's going to put *me* in *jail*. Remember?

Oh gosh he says. What are we going to do?

Get on the bus and go back.

He reaches into his pocket, pulls out a few more coins.

OK. I got enough.

I ain't never been to no airport neither I say. I guess I'm grinning a little because he gives me a smile back and we head on inside together.

It's full of men in suits and ties. They're either running around like they're hot stuff or they're standing in line looking bored. Got leather Samsonite bags piled next to them with their initials stamped in gold. Cigarette smoke everywhere. All white here too.

Look I'm going to call home anyway he says. I got to tell my parents I'm OK.

I point to a pay phone. He lifts it off the hook and drops in his dime. Stands there a minute or two with the phone squeezed to his face. Starts shifting from foot to foot. Starts looking worried. Then he starts looking *real* worried. Then he hangs up.

Ain't no one there he says. We're sunk. I don't

know how to get home from here.

Oh don't worry so much I tell him. We can get back on that same bus. You go back to your granddaddy and he'll take you home from his theater. I just live around the corner.

Yeah yeah he says. Give me a minute to think. Way he looks though, ain't much thinking going on.

He wants to know what time it is. I point to the clock on the wall, says two-thirty.

My dad and my grandpa are going to be calling the police. What am I going to do? Eyes are bugging out now.

Why would they go calling the police? You're just gone an hour and a half. My momma don't worry about me unless I miss dinner.

Yeah but I was down at the theater he says. I wasn't even supposed to go outside onto the sidewalk.

They think someone going to kidnap you?

No. It's just— it isn't safe my dad says.

Ain't safe? I been walking around there all my life and nothing's happened to *me* yet.

Maybe it's not safe for white kids he says.

Wouldn't know. You're the first one I seen on State Street, ever.

He looks like he's thinking about that, then he turns around and walks toward the middle of the terminal.

Where you going?

Let's watch the airplanes for a few minutes he says.

We follow a sign, ***Observation Deck***, up some winding stairs and come out on the roof. That green-and-white light is right smack above us, turning and turning. We can see the whole airport from up here.

There's a real big airplane right down in front of us, got a guy in coveralls yanking on the propeller until it catches. It does and a big cloud of smoke shoots out the back. That guy jumps back fast so he don't get hit. Plane's got four engines and three tails. It's a Lockheed Super Constellation. I know. I seen one in a newsreel.

I have no idea how to get home he says.

Why don't you shut up just a minute. I'm having fun.

But he keeps talking like I ain't even opened my mouth. We'll have to go back to the theater like you say he says. But couldn't we stop at the parking lot first? Please?

I ain't going back to that parking lot I tell him, no sir. Police coming for me, they're just going to have to come.

Well maybe I can sneak away tomorrow and we can go back then he says. I'll get on the streetcar again. We can meet in front of the theater.

You stand there on State Street two minutes, someone'll be calling the police, white boy like you. And if you're standing in front of the Calumet, my momma'll see you sure, and I make my voice to sound like hers. *What you doing out there Stevie honey?*

That's too much for him. Let's just go back then he groans, so we walk back down them spiral stairs.

There's a bus pulls up when we get to the corner. Steve hands the bus driver two more of his dimes and we sit back down again, but it looks same as it did before and it wasn't too interesting then. Next thing I know, he's snoring. So I close my own eyes too.

Maxwell Street

I wake up and look out the window. We're some-where but I don't know where.

I look over at the white boy. He's snoring away. I should wake him but I don't. Figure I'll just look out the window some more. This is starting to be fun.

We go past some kind of factory. I know it's a factory because it's got them slanty window things on the roofs like in my social studies book. Lots of men coming out the gates when we go past. Most white, some colored too.

We go past a big store, got lots of cars behind a plate glass window. New ones. Got shiny chrome all over. Big green one in front looks mighty pretty. Sign says Kaiser Frazer. Never seen cars inside a store before. Ain't no colored in there, least none I can see.

I'm kind of hungry.

Steve, he yawns and turns over. Hey I say to him. Wake up.

Oh man he says I had me a bad dream. First I'm back in the police station and my grandpa is arguing with the policeman but hc isn't talking, he's spitting poison darts. Next I'm back in the hospital and this nun walks past me and raises her arms but she's not a nun, she's a big black buzzard. Then I'm back in the parking lot reaching under a car but I'm not lying on gravel, it's broken glass. I can see that silver thing under the car. I reach and reach but the more I reach the farther away it gets—.

He snaps out of it. Where are we he says.

Tell him I don't know.

He gets that worried look of his, makes him look like my grandmomma. Starts talking again about getting home.

Don't be a crybaby I say. Let's get off this bus and get something to eat.

He likes that, says he's hungry too.

We ask the driver where we are. At Cicero and Roosevelt Road. Where's that? You're on the West Side. Are we anywhere near Bronzeville? He ain't never heard of no Bronzeville. Are we near Hyde Park Steve asks. Bus driver starts to laugh, says we're so far from Hyde Park it'll take us all day to get back there. Steve gets that grandmomma look again.

Steve asks how to get back. Man says, Change to a Roosevelt Road bus going east then a something else then a something else. I don't know what he's talking about. Don't think Steve does either. We get off the bus and wait for another one.

Let's get something to eat I say.

Yeah but I got to get home he says.

You got to eat too I say. He don't say nothing back.

Bus comes along. We get on, ask the driver for another transfer. How do we get back to Bronzeville? Driver wants to know where that is. State Street I tell him. This bus don't go to no State Street, it turns at Halsted. That don't mean nothing to me but I don't want the man to think I'm stupid. Oh sure, Halsted. They got anything to eat there?

Best hot dogs in Chicago, man says. Just walk a block south to Maxwell. You can still get back on another bus with your transfers. Just make sure you don't stay off longer than an hour.

We sit on that bus seems like forever. West Side don't look exactly like the South Side but it ain't much to look at neither. Just cars, factories, train tracks and a lot of sorry-looking white folks. We pass County Hospital too so now I can tell Poppa I seen that. He goes there for his diabetes. Says they make him wait all day before a doctor sees him. Says it smells like iodine the whole time.

Finally the driver sings out Halsted Street, exit here for the Maxwell Street Market.

Now we're standing in the street again. I'm so hungry I could eat three hot dogs. But old worry-wart Steve's got that look again. He says How are we going to eat if we ain't got no money? He starts pulling out his pants pockets.

Blessed if he ain't got a little rolled-up bill in his back pocket. Says it was a birthday present from his grandmomma and he went and forgot he put it there.

Well what is it fool I say.

Boy's got ten dollars!

Wow you really are rich I say.

He looks embarrassed.

Well don't feel bad about it I say. Let's find that hot-dog stand.

We start walking. I swear I ain't never seen nothing like this place. There's wagons and carts on the sidewalks, in the streets. Cars couldn't get through if they wanted. And people! Walking everywhere—street, curb, sidewalk, they don't give a care. They squeeze up against each other like they're family. Against me too only I ain't no kin to none of them.

Lots of the men got beards and sideburns curling down their faces. They're white but they look like foreigners. Wearing black coats and hats, don't matter it's June. Some of them wear these little round black things on their heads instead of hats. Sort of like caps only smaller and they ain't got no bills on them. They wear them up on top where the bald spot would be if they were bald but they ain't. Got them caps pinned to their hair with bobby pins. Grown men.

And the stuff! I walk past one of those carts, it's got about a thousand shoes piled on it. Some are hanging by the laces from a broomstick too. Some new some used. Some don't even match. New ones got tags from Marshall Field and Carson Pirie. I ask this one man how he got them shoes from them department stores, he reaches out like he's fixing to hit me.

Another cart, it's full of pots and pans. Same thing —some of them old and full of dents, other ones brand new with store tags. Another cart's got windup toys from Japan. Man's got a tin King Kong on the side of a tin Empire State Building. He sets it on the sidewalk and winds it up, it goes Skree! Skree! Skree! and shinnies up that little old building. Three dollars he says to me. I tell him he's crazy. All right one dollar he says. I start thinking I'm crazy.

We walk along, this colored kid—I mean a *kid*, about same age as Darius—comes up to us and opens his jacket. He's got watches all up and down his skinny arm, wrist to shoulder. Nice ones, some of them. I see a Bulova, a Gruen too. Lots with gold bands like little accordions.

Colored kid don't even look at me. He says to Steve, You look like you might be needing a watch today my young friend. That's what he says, my young friend, he ain't but a couple years older than us. I seen guys like this one on State Street too, getting their watches off the backs of trucks.

But Steve looks interested. I try to pull him away. He goes buying a watch, I don't get no hot dog.

He points to an Ingersoll with a brown leather band. That there watch'll cost you fifty bucks in any jewelry store downtown, cat says. Go into J.P. Stevens and try to buy that watch, you'll see. Give it to you today for just twenty dollars he says.

Ten is all I got Steve says. Oh man!

I call him a damn fool and yank at his arm. He says wait he might want to buy the watch. You ain't buying no watch I say. Come on along before you get us in real trouble.

He catches up with me but I can see he's mad. Why didn't you let me talk to that watch guy? Them watches are stolen I say. How do you know that? Use your head I say—how's that guy going to sell you a fifty-dollar watch for twenty dollars unless it's stolen? Besides, you go blabbing to everyone that you got ten bucks, you ain't going to have ten bucks for very long, place like this. He blushes like some little baby and says he's sorry. Glad of that. He may be ignorant but at least he ain't stupid.

I can smell food real good now.

There's this stand on the corner. It's wood, painted white, built out onto the sidewalk. Didn't know they could build things onto city sidewalks.

I hold onto the counter and go on tiptoes. There's all this meat on the grill, just a-popping and a-hissing, the grease standing out like drops of sweat. Hot dogs. Hamburgers. Some kind of sausage I ain't never seen before, about twice as thick as a hot dog and it's gray, not red. There's a big hot pile of grilled onions too, brown and slick shiny. Makes the water come up in my mouth.

Bunch of white guys behind the counter. This one, he ain't wearing no shirt, all he's got on is his skivvies and a white apron. Got black hair coming out of his armpits. I can see his beer belly too.

What are them there? I point to the gray ones.

Kielbasa, man says. Polish sausage. You want one?

I ain't never heard of no Polish sausage. How much for a hot dog?

Quarter, man says. Come on you're wasting my time.

Steve's jumping up and down trying to get a look

too but he's too short, can't see. Give me a boost he says. He grabs onto the counter and I try to hoist him up under the shoulders but my wrist still hurts and I can't lift him. He goes grabbing at the counter and kicking his feet every which way. Finally he pulls himself high enough for one look before his fingers slip.

He tells me to try one of them Polish sausages.

Naw I'm going to have me a hot dog I say.

My dad says you got to try new things he says.

Well your daddy ain't here and I want a hot dog.

They're kosher he says.

Oh I say. I thought they were hot dogs.

They are dummy he says. Kosher hot dogs.

You mean they're some new kind of hot dog?

Naw he says. We eat them all the time.

What's kosher?

Jewish he says.

What's Jewish?

He gives me a funny look.

They any good?

Sure. My dad says they've killed more Jews than bullets.

What's he mean by that?

I think he's telling a joke he says.

Well are they going to kill me?

Naw he says. Ain't killed me and I must of eaten about a million of them.

You one of them Jews?

Sure he says. Looks surprised. Says, Didn't you know?

How was I supposed to know?

Well your mom must know. She works for my grandpa he says.

Your granddaddy one of them Jews too?

He gives me a look again.

How you supposed to tell when someone's a Jew?

He shrugs. Some of them got hooked noses he says.

You ain't. Your granddaddy ain't.

He shrugs again. Sometimes you can tell by the name he says.

You mean like Feinberg?

Yeah he says. Feinberg Steinberg Greenberg Goldberg.

Man named Goldberg runs the food shop next to the church I say. Gives Momma credit at the end of the month. But he ain't no Jew. He's one of them sheeny men.

Never heard of no sheeny men Steve says. You sure he ain't Jewish?

Naw, everyone calls him a sheeny man. Can't be no Jew.

Well maybe he ain't then Steve says.

He points to a guy on the street, he's wearing a black coat. Looky there he says. See him? He's a Jew.

He don't look like you or your granddaddy nor Mister Goldberg neither.

I think he's some different kind of Jew Steve says.

What kind?

I think he's a Orthodox.

What kind are you?

Reform.

What's the difference?

Reform don't wear no black coats he says.

Are Orthodox hot dogs same as Reform hot dogs?

He says he don't know.

All right I say. Your daddy says to try something new so I'll try one. What are you going to have?

I want one of them Polish sausages he says. He pulls out his ten dollar bill and tries to hand it to the man but he can't reach. Man leans down and grabs it from him.

Man asks do we want sport peppers, onions, sauerkraut? I got to ask him what a sauerkraut is but I don't want to. I tell him just a hot dog please.

Steve says, Let me see them peppers.

Man takes a tong and holds up this skinny evil-looking little thing. Used to be red I think but it's turning green and brown in the vinegar. Steve says yeah, give me mine with peppers and onions and sauerkraut. Trying to act grown-up.

Man hands him a sandwich. It's so big I don't know how he's going to get it into his mouth.

He takes a bite off the end. I ask him how is it. He don't say nothing, just chews. Takes him a long time to swallow. His eyes sort of bug out.

Well? He don't answer. His mouth is full. He just hands me the sandwich and points at it with his finger.

I set down my hot dog and take a bite. Man! It tastes sour and hot and sweet all at once. The bun is nice and soft because it's been in the steam, and the skin on the meat pops when I bite into it. I ain't never tasted nothing so good.

Steve asks do I want to trade.

What, you don't like it?

I hate it he says.

Let me taste the hot dog first I say. I bite into it. Pagh! It's all spicy. Don't taste nothing like an Oscar Mayer. Sure I say, let's trade.

◆　　◆　　◆　　◆　　◆　　◆　　◆

Now we ain't hungry no more so we walk around a little.

There's an old colored guy sitting on the curb playing one of them metal guitars. Got a pop-bottle neck around his little finger, sliding it up and down the strings and singing. Got a tin cup too. He grins up at us and he ain't got his teeth. Least he ain't one of them blind ones like on State Street. Leave this old wine-head alone I say. But Steve just wants to stand there listening like he ain't never heard them country blues before. Maybe he ain't.

Finally I get him to move along. But now he sees this White Sox jacket in one of the store windows. He wants to try it on. I can't talk him out of it. He is one very curious child.

Inside it's dark and shabby. My eyes are used to the sun and I can't see nothing at first. Ain't no electric lights on. Ain't much light coming in from the street neither. There's clothes piled everywhere. Women's, men's, children's, all piled together.

Let's get out of here I say. Ain't nothing in here we want.

Man comes up to us. We're the only people in the store, us and the man. He's one of them Jew people too I guess because he's got long sideburns and one of them little caps on top of his head. He ain't wearing no black overcoat though. Just a sport shirt and slacks.

He tells us to shoo.

No mister I want to try on the White Sox jacket, Steve says.

Man gives him a look, asks does he have any money. Steve nods his head.

Man pulls the jacket out of the window. It's white with thin little black stripes running up and down and it says White Sox in them old church letters. Shiny too like satin. I'd liked to of had it myself.

Steve puts it on and it fits him perfect. He asks the man how much.

Man says twenty dollars. Seems like everything down here is twenty dollars.

Steve says he ain't got no twenty dollars. Man asks how much does he have. Steve pulls it out and start counting.

Put your money away you jackass I tell him. We got to get home.

Man gives me a look like, Shut up. What's your name son he says to Steve.

Steve Feinberg.

Man's face lights up. Oh you're a Jewish boy he says. Secret code sure does work.

Man starts getting all friendly. Wants to know about Steve's momma and poppa, does he have any brothers and sisters, where does he go to school, what grade is he in, all that stuff grownups ask when they're trying to get in good with you.

Steve says he's in the fifth grade. Says he goes to Kenwood School in Hyde Park.

Man's face changes a little. Asks, where does he go to something, sounds like Sinner Gog.

Steve asks him what does he mean.

Man starts looking a little mad. Sinner Gog. Sinner Gog. I swear that's what he's saying.

Now the man starts talking about something else, sounds like Kay Der but he says it K-k-k-Kay Der or Ch-ch-ch-Chay Der or something. I can't make the sound myself. It ain't English I don't think.

Steve don't say nothing. He's looking mighty uncomfortable.

Now the man wants to know has Steve started to read Tow Rah and practice up for his Bar Mits something. Man's getting red in the face.

Then he starts in signifying. I know what you Hyde Park Jews are like he says. You come down to Maxwell Street and pretend to be better than other Jews he says. You play baseball on the Sabbath he says. You don't cover your head in God's presence he says. Your momma and your sister go praying right there with you in the Sinner Gog he says. Y'all pray to God in English. But God don't hear y'all's prayers he says.

The man, he's yelling real loud now. Good thing ain't no one else in the store. I swear I don't know what's wrong with him. He ain't even given Steve a chance to say nothing back. Been me, I'd of told him to shut up, told it to him right to his face.

But Steve just stands there listening like the man's got a right. Man's got his face shoved into Steve's face, bent over and yelling, and Steve's just shrinking up inside that White Sox jacket like he's trying to disappear.

Now the man starts talking some foreign language altogether. He goes spouting off nonstop and I can't make out a word. Lots more of them ch-ch-ch-ch sounds in it. Steve looks like he's going to bust out crying. He tears off that pretty jacket and runs outside.

We get out on the sidewalk, I ask him, what was that all about?

He's crying still. Calm down I tell him. Why'd you let that man insult you?

Steve shakes his head.

What was he so mad about?

Steve shakes his head again.

What's all that Jew stuff? What's a Sinner Gog? What was that talk he was talking?

Hebrew. Yiddish. I don't know.

Oh that Hebrew stuff again I say. Well this time you got to tell me what it is.

The Bible was written in Hebrew.

Oh no I say, I know you're wrong about that. Bible wasn't written in no Hebrew. We got a big one at home and there's dozens more in the church and ain't a one written in nothing but English.

The Old Testament was he says.

Well I say, we mostly read the New Testament. But we got an Old Testament in the front of our Bible too and it's in English just like the rest, so I do not think that you are right.

When Moses came down the mountain with the Ten Commandments they were in Hebrew he says. Look at the picture. Hebrew letters. He says it very positive-like and folds his arms. Least he's stopped his blubbering.

I know the picture he's talking about. Moses, the one with the gray beard, he's got the stone tablets in his arms and they do have funny-looking letters on them. I used to wonder about them letters, come to think of it.

Are the letters on the Ten Commandments the same kind what were on your granddaddy's silver thing?

Yeah he says. Now you know what to look for.

Is Hebrew same as Yiddish?

He shakes his head.

What's the difference?

He says he can't explain it. Then he says he don't know. They sound a lot alike he says. The prayers in the temple are in Hebrew but some of the people talk in Yiddish he says. Them Orthodoxes can talk it he says. His granddaddy can talk it too even though he ain't no Orthodox his own self he says.

What about that other stuff? What's a Sinner Gog? What's a Kay Der? What's a Bar something-or-other?

I don't know he says. His voice starts shaking again. Boy looks miserable.

Well if you don't know you don't know, I say to him. Try not to be so upset about it. I give him a little pat on the shoulder.

That man thinks I'm supposed to know he says.

Rickie's dad asks how come I don't go to Hebrew school. At Aunt Bea's for Friday dinner, I can't say the prayers and she gives me funny looks. Now his lip is quivering.

Don't they teach it to you in Sunday School?

Naw he says. Wish they would. They talk about David Ben-Gurion and make us memorize Give me your tired your poor your huddled masses. The only Hebrew they teach us is the Shuh Mah.

What's that?

You know, he says, then he says the next part real fast, sounded to me like Shuh Mah Yiss Row Ayl, Something Something Something, Ah Doe Noy Eck Cod. Or maybe it was Eck God because it's a prayer. He says the Eck like the guy in the store said Kay Der, ch-ch-ch-ch.

So you can talk that language too I say.

Just that much he says.

So that guy in the store thinks you're ignorant.

Yeah Steve says, and I am. He starts to blubbering again.

Well you know what Jesus says?

He wipes his eyes. What?

Jesus says, Let him who is without sin cast the first stone.

What's that mean?

I think it means you shouldn't go being dicty to other people unless you're perfect yourself.

Steve asks, What's dicty?

Dicty is when you act stuck-up, like you're better than they are.

Steve asks, What else does Jesus say?

If thine enemy smite thee on thy right cheek, turn to him the other also. I don't believe in that one so much. But that's OK. If you don't like one thing Jesus says, He's always got another.

How do you know so much about what Jesus says?

My Poppa is a reverend.

What's a reverend?

A preacher. He has his own church. Don't you know nothing?

Where's this church of his?

Up the street from your granddaddy's movie theater. Across, on the other side.

Ain't no churches in that block Steve says. Just stores.

Yeah, Poppa's church is in a store.

Oh he says, now I recollect going past a church in a store when I came down on the streetcar to the hospital. Think it was called Glory Life in Jesus.

Yeah that's Poppa's church.

Wow he says. So you must know a lot about your religion.

Yeah I say. Too much.

What religion is it?

Holiness. It's called Holiness. We're blessed in the Holy Spirit.

I mean, is it Christianity?

Well of course it is. What do you think it is?

Could be something else he says.

What else is there?

Yeah he says, I guess you're right.

16
Steve

The El

*W*e walk back to where we got off the bus. The sun's going down and there's a breeze like nighttime's coming. We've been gone four or five hours. I've never been gone this long before. They're going to call the police.

I don't see any pay phones.

They're going to kill me.

Sass says Let's get back on the bus.

The driver said it's the wrong one. Didn't you hear him?

He says All right don't get mad. What should we do?

I don't know.

Come on, stop that kicking at the stones. You're the one knows where everything is.

It's not my fault. You and your friends never should of tried to get money from us. None of this would of happened.

Yeah sure, and I suppose it's my fault I'm lost with some stranger white boy.

We sit down on the curb.

OK look up over there I say. Where those tall buildings are. That's the Loop. It's about a mile away. Let's just walk toward it. If we see a pay phone, I'll call Dad and he'll come pick us up. If we don't, then we can get a bus once we get downtown. All the buses end up downtown. State Street is downtown. We can ask where State Street is, then just walk over there and take that bus back to the theater. You can walk home from there.

OK he says. Always wanted to go downtown.

We zigzag toward the buildings. It's real crummy around here, just car repair shops and warehouses. The sidewalks are broken and weeds are growing out of the cracks. There's a drugstore with one of those blue-and-white metal Bell System signs so I go in and try to call again. This time I let it ring ten times like Mom said. Where the heck are they?

We start walking again. Then I spot the ball.

It's lying in the gutter in front of one of these rotten apartment buildings. It's orange rubber. Actually it looks pretty new.

Toss it here he says.

He catches it one hand. He says Can you do that? He tosses it back but I miss.

I can do it though. I just got something in my eye. Anyway I throw better than I catch.

Watch this. I throw it way high so he has to run for it. He catches his foot on the broken cement and nearly falls. The ball rolls out into the street.

But he throws it back even higher. He's pretty good.

Do you know how to play penner?

He says he never heard of it, do you play it with a

ball?

Of course you play it with a ball dummy.

I go over to the side of the building. Luckily it's got a penner, they don't always.

This is the penner.

What?

Where the row of brick sticks out a little from the wall? That's the penner. You have to hit it. Hit the penner with the ball. Like this.

I throw it at the penner but first time I miss so of course it goes down at his feet, rolling on the ground.

Dumb game he says.

No no, I missed the penner. It was just the first time. Watch, I'll hit it this time, and I do. The ball bounces way into the air like it's supposed to. Over his head.

He says, Wow.

Yeah, it's neat when you do it right. Play to eleven?

So I show him how and we play and he beats me.

Don't be mad, he says after.

I'm not mad.

Yeah you are. I can tell he says.

I am not.

Reason you lost, you don't catch right.

Shut up.

No really he says. I'll show you. Go on over there. Now I'm going to throw it to you. Real slow he says. He throws it underhand.

See you did it right, you caught it he says. Now I'm going to throw it again.

Jeez you don't have to throw it all that hard.

I didn't throw it hard at all he says. You closed your

eyes.

Did not.

That's what you're doing wrong he says. The ball comes at your face and you squinch up your eyes. Next time keep them open. Make yourself.

So he throws it again, right at my face, and this time I try real hard and he's right. I want to close them. I can feel them squeezing shut.

See he says, you closed them and you missed. He's not teasing me about it though like Lennie Martin. Heck I'm never going to be as good as Lennie. Why does he have to always rub it in?

All right I'm going to throw it. Right at your face again. This time keep your eyes open wide.

So I take a deep breath and force them to stay open and what do you know?

Pretty good he says. Want to try it again?

I try it a second time. Force my eyes to stay open and catch it, a hard one this time. But this is embarrassing.

He says Don't get mad at yourself that just makes it worse. You'll be closing your eyes again if you do that. Just practice it. Just think about it each time when you catch.

Thanks I say.

You're welcome he says. He gives me a little punch in the arm. I give him a little punch back.

I point to the sun. We better get going.

What are you going to do with the ball?

You can keep it.

You found it.

That's all right. Keep it if you want.

It's pretty nice.

Go on keep it.

OK he says. He sticks it in his pants. Thanks he says. I guess you're all right he says.

◆   ◆   ◆   ◆   ◆   ◆   ◆

We get to the Loop about the time the streetlights blink on. We're at the corner of Van Buren and Wells and he smiles.

Hey here's the El. We're going to be OK now.

But I'm looking up at this thing and I don't know. It's in the middle of the street a whole story off the ground, and right now there's a train going overhead making lots of noise.

I ask him if the El trains ever fall off. I'm thinking about the electric trains, where me and Beth pile up books and set up the track on the books like a roller-coaster. The train never even makes it around one time.

Never fell off where I live he says.

I've never been on the El.

I ain't neither he says. But it stops right at Thirty-Fifth. The Calumet is only a half a block.

Mom says we shouldn't ride on the El. She says it goes through bad neighborhoods.

Oh come on he says. We ain't never going to get home, you keep standing there talking.

I pay the guy two half fares and we go out onto the platform. I walk to the edge of the platform and look for the train coming like I do when we take the Illinois

Central, but this thing has a third rail. It's shiny. With the IC, the power is on the wires overhead. You fall on the third rail and you'll get electrocuted Mom says.

So I go back to the bench to wait.

The train comes up. It says *Ravenswood.* The cars are orange and brown. They're wood, pretty old. The train rocks side to side.

Come on don't be scared, the doors are closing, it's going to be leaving you don't hurry up he says.

We go in the front car. There's almost no one on the train, I guess because it's Sunday and the stores are all closed downtown. The motorman's behind the glass but we can see his dials and stuff. We go right to the front and look out the window.

We're going past empty platforms now. The train stops but nobody gets on. Then it goes around a bend. Buildings on both sides, you can't see anything else. You can't even see down to the sidewalk below. They're like a solid wall.

Man these buildings are tall Sass says.

I can't believe you've never been downtown.

What do I want to go downtown for? Got everything we need on State Street.

You've got to buy things like clothes don't you?

Shoot he says, I got two older brothers. Plenty of clothes for me.

Sometimes we go downtown just to look around I say. I tell him about the parade right after the war ended. I was about seven. There were floats. One looked like a captured German sub, with American soldiers pointing tommy guns at Nazis

I don't need to go downtown to see a parade he says. They've got Bud Billiken Day every year, the parade goes right up South Park Way. They've got big floats and everything, and clowns and marching bands besides. You ever hear Phillips's band? They're better than Benny Goodman.

What's Phillips?

Wendell Phillips High School. Thought you were smart he says.

Yeah well the parade downtown is pretty good too.

There's no one to be taking me downtown he says. Going places costs money and we ain't got much to spare.

Your mom works I say. And your dad gets money from his church.

He says church doesn't pay his dad anything. He says his dad works early shift at U.S. Steel and does church at night.

If it doesn't pay how come he does it?

Heard the call he says. Holy Spirit came in a dream one night dressed in flames and said, Build a church on My rock. Then the Spirit pointed to an empty store on State Street, used to be an incense and oils place with High John the Conqueror and lucky number books in the window.

His dad comes to breakfast with his eyes bugging out. Go throw out all that pagan trash, his dad says, then runs out into the hall in his pajamas. The lady across the hall comes out in her nightgown. His dad says Gal put on your clothes, we're going to build a church on the rock of the Lord. She calls to her husband, Morris I believe James has been touched by the Holy Spirit. Pretty soon everyone's out in the hall carrying on like the Fourth of July. It was a sight he says. I was only five but I still recall it.

Your dad couldn't of ever done that if he was Jewish.

What are you talking about?

When they built the new temple on the lake? They had these dinners, they charged you fifty dollars a plate to go. It took them five or six years to finish it. The steps are granite, so hard it shall resist the tread of generations of Sunday School children to come, symbolizing the eternality of God. That's what Dr. Mann said. That's how he talks.

They had this big talent show at the Piccadilly Theater to raise money for it you know? They rented the whole theater for the night, no movies or anything. My mom and my sister were in it. They played immigrants from Russia and sang this song, *I'm glad I'm not missing the boat*, to the tune of *I wonder who's kissing her now*. It was dumb but they made me go.

He shrugs. Folks are starting churches all the time down in Bronzeville he says. Ain't nothing special.

I ask what they do in his church.

Oh you know, dance and sing and carry on.

You mean people *dance in church*?

Shoot he says. Don't they dance in your church?

I tell him about Dr. Mann in his undertaker suit, going ssshhh to the Sunday School kids.

Well they dance in mine he says. Sing, dance, play the piano, shake the tambourine. The old women get carried away with the Holy Spirit, they start talking in tongues, *layla lullulu lullulu ayala luhluh layahuh*. Church don't make no sense but it's a lot of fun. You ought to come some time.

You think they'll let me in?

He looks confused, like he's not sure.

What's it like in your church?

Boring. And we don't have churches. We have temples.

But they're still churches right?

Now I'm confused.

What was that about a spirit?

You mean the Holy Spirit? Don't Jews have the Holy Spirit?

I never heard of it I tell him.

It's when God comes down and gets inside of you. That's when you get up and dance.

It's not like that at Sinai I say. It's just a lot of responsive readings and *Sh'ma Yisroel*. Nobody dances. Ever.

Heck he says, that's why you ain't heard of the Holy Spirit. He must not come to no Jew church.

◆　　◆　　◆　　◆　　◆　　◆　　◆

We swing left around another bend. There's still a little sun but the buildings are in the way and it's gotten real dark, so dark you can see the blue flashes from the third rail lighting up the sides of the buildings.

Then we turn again, this time to the right, and we're going over a trestle bridge. It's black and covered with soot. Then we're crossing over water. I can see the last bit of sun shining on it, pink and orange.

He asks if that's the lake.

No I say, must be the Chicago River. The lake's *huge*. You can't see the other side. Don't tell me you've never seen the lake either.

Told you I ain't never been out of Bronzeville.

I look at him and I think Jeez, here's this skinny little kid with a bandage on his nose and bloodstains on his shirt, never even saw Lake Michigan. What was I scared of?

I grab his cheek like Aunt Bea does. Why you're just a baby I say, and I squeeze. Witty bitty baby.

He pulls his cheek away. I poke him in the ribs.

Hey baby, if I'd of known about you in the parking lot, I'd of asked if you wanted your bottle. I give him another poke.

So what about the lake? He's trying to change the subject now.

The lake? You could walk to the lake it's so close. Didn't anyone ever tell you there was a lake over there?

So I didn't know about the lake. It's not a crime he says.

Of course not. Pretty soon you'll be a big boy. Maybe mommy and daddy will take you to the lake for a swim. I go kissy-kissy.

All right cut it out he says. He kind of pushes me away. Embarrassed again.

Well I'm glad you're not a sassy little baby anyway I say and give him the raspberry. Then I sweep my arm toward a seat like the butler in those English movies. Do sit down old boy I say.

17
Joseph

The Lion of Judah

This ain't my kingdom. My kingdom's been taken away from me. But it shall be restored.

I only go out on these dark streets so's I can get money to eat. If they knew who I really was. Tell them every chance I get but they just laugh and call me crazy. Crazy Joe.

Wait 'til they see me in my golden robes, wearing my crown. Wait 'til they see that golden scepter. I'll smite them with it, smite all mine enemies. Smite the ones that smile and simper, simper and whimper, whimper and pimper.

Pimper pimps, pimping their pretty peaches. See them every night, standing out on State Street waving at the cars, white folks driving over from Drexel Boulevard. How'd ya like some poontang buddy? Poon poon poon poontang the sinners sing, songs of sin.

But I am pure. I am the Emperor Haile Selassie, King of Abyssinia and Lord of Axum. The singing sinners will praise me, all shall hail me.

Watch. I'll be going down State Street on a golden throne, carriage drawn by stallions. Crowds casting rose petals. Rosie rosie ring around the posie, pocket full of ashes and we all fall down. Then these voices will stop.

Yes. When I am recognized.

Man in the Moon says Joseph, you ain't been reading your Bible. What for do I want to read the Bible? I read it to memory every day in Parchman, every day twenty years just like Momma told me, and much good it did. Read and read yet pay no heed. Marcus standing over me, where was Jesus coming to smite Marcus hip and thigh like the Bible said?

Marcus Parcus Park Your Carcass. You loved me but I never loved you.

You loved my little boy butt, little blue butt, Little Boy Blue Butt. You sang lullabies to my butt. Thought you were winning my heart but I was too smart, I was your tart but I stayed apart. In my heart.

That way I saved the day. Saved the day for the Lion of Judah, Emperor of Africa, black king of the world. I shall be recognized one day. Save that day in your heart.

Shut up Marcus. Don't you go talking to me, never again. You hurt me you bad man. You got no call to hurt a little child. Supposed to be in school, learning the Golden Rule, but you played me for a fool, using your tool. I was too young for that.

Police should've tortured you instead of me. Whispering in my ear. Talking trash behind the sash, say I got to pay them cash. Do what they say or I'll rue the day. Make them shut up, someone.

You can't hurt me no more now Mister Marcus Park Your Carcass. Now I rule, rule Africa with a golden scepter, rule like that other Marcus, Garvey Arvey Arvey, taking the colored back to Africa. Ain't no one going back to Africa 'til I say so. I am Selassie, son of Jah. Can't you see, Marcus? I will call down my armies on your head. Go on back to Parchman with the cooties, you dirty man.

Momma, he hurt me. Momma! Why didn't you never come?

18
Sass

Duane, Ned and Joey Bob

*W*e stop at a station, sign says Chicago Avenue, and three white kids squeeze through before the door closes on them. One of them pushes past Steve, grabs for the straps and starts doing chin-ups. Got a blue cap on his head with that big red C for Cubs.

Bet you can't do this, kid says.

Bet I can says one of his buddies. He reaches up for two straps himself. So tall he ain't even got to jump.

Aw you're cheating Duane, Cubs Cap says.

Hey! W-w-watch this says the third one and tries to shinny up the pole by the door. Face full of freckles.

Bunch of crackers.

We swing around a bend and the train stops again, this sign says Sedgwick. Them white kids let go of the straps and poles and body-slam into the seats across from us.

How long 't-t-til we get there says Freckles.

Ain't too long says the tall one name of Duane. We can take this to Belmont then get on a bus.

Riverview! We're going to Riverview t-t-tonight

says the one with the freckles.

Steve gives me a what's-up look. I give him a shrug. Freckles looks over at us.

Wh-wh-what you guys doing together?

Steve says Huh?

Wh-what are you doing with the colored kid?

Doing? Nothing. We're together Steve says.

He's your *friend*?

Naw I'm his father. What's it to you I say. His mouth pops shut like it's on springs.

You guys going to Riverview too asks the tall one, Duane.

What's Riverview Steve asks him back.

Hey these guys never heard of Riverview Duane says to his buddies. How come you don't know about Riverview?

Steve shrugs.

It's a namusement park. Bi-i-i-ggg one. Lots of rides. Roller-coasters. Ever been on a roller-coaster?

I whisper over to Steve. *You been on a roller-coaster too I suppose.*

No he whispers back. *I never even heard of Riverview.*

I call over to these new guys. Where is it?

Just stay on the train they say. When we get to Belmont, get off and take the bus with us.

Naw we got to get home I say.

All right says the Cubs cap guy. Guess you'll just miss out on the Bobs.

Yeah says the one called Duane, an', an', the Chute-the-Chutes too. You go down this big long water-slide—

reeaaallly long— in a boat. You're going down about ninety miles an hour you know? Faster 'n' faster 'n' faster an' then you hit the water—*ka-splash* He throws out his arms in a splash. Showing us.

I whisper to Steve *You ever been in a boat?* Steve shakes his head.

Hey. How high up is that slide?

Oh jeez must be six stories says the one called Duane.

No ten says the one in the Cubs cap. Got to be right all the time, that one.

The F-F-Flying Turns is my favorite says the freckled one. You g-g-get in these little b-b-bitty cars and they go *UP* the side of the ramp then *DOWN* the side of the ramp then *UP* then *D-D-DOWN—*. Every time he says *up* or *down* he swings his arm through the air. Last time I went on it I threw up he says. Grins.

What you think? I whisper to Steve.

Hey. We're not going there. We got to get home Steve whispers back.

How much money you got left?

Never mind. I said we got to get home.

Yeah. OK.

But them others ain't done with us, not by a long shot. Lemme tell you what else they got at Riverview says Cubs Cap. There's Aladdin's Castle. It's a funhouse, you know? You walk through this barrel—it's a barrel, right? Only it's *big*, big as a room—an' it's *turning around*. He turns circles with his arms. An' you gotta crawl through while it's turning and get to the other side without falling down, right? Except you *do* fall down. He laughs, sounds like a chicken cackling.

An' then they've got this other room, you know? An' the floor's *slanted.* Except it don't *look* slanted. You can't tell, you know? An' then you try to walk to the other side and you *keep slipping backwards!* He cackles again and his face turns red. Starts waving his arms, like he's trying to tell his own self to stop laughing and keep on talking.

An' then, an' then, they got these air holes? In the floor? And there's this guy hiding somewheres, you can't see him? An', an', every time a *girl* walks over one of these *air holes,* the guy presses a button and *blows air up her skirts!* This time he can't make himself stop laughing.

Ooh! Ooh! How about the machine guns? says the tall one, Duane.

Yeah the machine guns. Blatta-blatta-blatta! Pow! Pow! P-P-Pow! The freckled kid makes like he's aiming a machine-gun at us and jerks his body up and down like John Wayne in *Back to Bataan.*

Steve says, They got *real* machine-guns? Guns you can shoot?

Naw they're not r-r-real, they're BB-guns. They're sort of like a big b-b-box, about this long, and he holds his arms out side to side. But it's got a gun barrel. You aim it into the water an' you hit the ducks and b-b-boats, blatta-blatta-blatta! You can see the BB's rolling around inside the glass. Thousands of 'em. Blatta-blatta-blatta!

Wow Steve whispers.

Thought you said you didn't want to go.

Steve sits up straight in his seat. Yeah that's right I
don't. We don't. We can't. We've got to get home. I'll
come back some other time to see the machine guns.
With my dad.

Hey you ought to come with us. Uh you too says
the tall one, Duane, looking over at me. You got transfers?

Yeah.

What's your names?

Steve.

Sass.

Well I'm Duane an' this is Ned—he means the one
wearing the Cubs cap—an' this here is Joey Bob, he's
talking about the one with the freckles and the stutter.

I shake my head. I don't know I say. It sounds
pretty good but we've been out all day. Our folks don't
know where we are.

Where do you live?

By Comiskey Park I say.

Comiskey Park? Them three stranger boys start
howling and punching at each other. Man you are *lost.*
You're *miles* away. You're trying to get to the *South*
Side— but you're on the *North* Side! You get off here,
you'll be at Wrigley Field. *Wrong ballpark.*

*I thought you said the train went to Thirty-Fifth
Street* Steve whispers real loud. He's mad at me this
time for sure.

*It does. I swear. El stops right there—right at Thirty-
Fifth and State.*

Well how'd we get here?

How should I know? Maybe we got on going the

wrong way. I didn't think of that. Did you?

He don't answer. He looks over at the new ones and holds out his hands to them. We'll *never* get home. What are we going to do?

You're going to come with us to Riverview. They start singing *RIV*-ver-view! *RIV*-ver-view! *RIV*-ver-view!

Come on says the Joey Bob one. You'll j-j-just be a little late that's all. Riverview is so neat! Here's B-B-Belmont. Let's get off.

◆   ◆   ◆   ◆   ◆   ◆   ◆

We come up on this place, it's about the biggest thing I've ever seen. Goes to the end of the block in both directions. There's this big arched building thing right in front of us. It's about three stories tall, with fake castle turrets painted yellow and orange, and little flags flying on top with the ends that come to a point, like the ones they sell at the ballpark. There's about a jillion light bulbs blinking on and off like the sign on the Calumet, except they spell out different words,

RIVERVIEW PARK
Laugh Your Troubles Away

And below that sign, another string of blinking light bulbs says

5¢ Night Tonight
5¢ Night Tonight
5¢ Night Tonight

They got about a dozen box offices, not just one like at the Calumet. There's men and women inside making change. They're all white, and ain't none of them smiling the way Momma does when she sells you a ticket. Got a sign over each booth, says **5¢**.

Steve fishes in his pocket for change, two nickels. We start to walk through.

Hey buddy, Duane says, ain't you gonna treat us? You'd of never found your way here without us.

Don't I whisper but too late. Steve lays a quarter on the counter. The quarter slides into a little saucer cut into the wood. I'm thinking must of been a million quarters done landed there before today. The man in the cage waves us all through.

Inside it's like a river of people. Fat men wearing stained straw hats, mommas dragging their crying babies behind them, punks with toothpicks hanging out of their mouths. Out along the edges, guys in white uniforms are picking up gum wrappers and popcorn boxes, they got sticks with nails on the ends.

Smells like sweat, cotton candy, motor oil and burning wires.

I hear a hissing sound but can't tell where it's coming from, and somewhere there's machines pounding so loud it feels like the ground is shaking. There's circus music off in the distance too playing BOOP-loop-loop BOOP-loop-loop. That *Blue Danube Waltz*. The light is yellow and red and orange and green from all the neon signs. Folks are screaming and laughing, moving toward the light like they're moths.

We go past one of them roller-coasters, sign says **Blue Streak**. Let's go on this one Ned says.

Ahh that's for babies Duane says back at him. I'm waiting for the Bobs.

You was chicken to go on the Bobs last time we was here.

I wasn't neither. Anyway I'm going this time.

Hey, the one called Ned says, you want to come with us?

He's talking to Steve. Not me.

Huh?

I mean, mmmm, you know, instead of the colored kid?

Yeah why'n'cha come with us, Duane says to Steve. We'll show you the good rides. We been here before.

Yeah c-c-come with us says Joey Bob, the stuttering one. Let the colored kid go by himself. You'll have a better time with us.

I can't Steve says.

Sure you can.

No. He— he doesn't have any money. I've got all the money.

You mean you're *paying for him too*? You paying his carfare? You buying him food? You eating together?

Well—sure.

How come?

Steve shrugs.

Tell them because I'm your friend I whisper but he don't say it. Just looks embarrassed.

We move on. There's one of them Wheels of Fortune with a guy spinning it around, and another place you can roll a ball into a hole and win a doll, and another one where you hit one of them stuffed animals with a hammer and it pops up another place. Whack-A-Mole. It's better than Maxwell Street.

But old Steve don't seem to think so. First he slips on a Good Humor someone dropped. Then some big guy bumps into him, like to knock him down. Steve says Sorry and the guy don't say nothing back. Then he says he's getting a headache from all the flashing lights. Pushes sweat off his forehead.

What a stupid plan he says. Why'd I go along?

We walk past the Ferris wheel. Goes up higher than a building. It stops just as we come up on it. Stops so fast the seats keep rocking back and forth. Girls are screaming, you can hear them all the way down here on the ground, sounds like a bunch of birds. Their skirts are fluttering up but their faces are just blurs.

Let's get out of here Steve says. I got to get home. Right now. He grabs my arm.

You want to ride on that thing?

Hey didn't you hear me he says. We got to go. Come on

Yeah. You want to ride on that thing?

No I don't want to ride on anything. If I was home right now we'd be eating Sunday dinner, it's usually spaghetti. Aren't you hungry? Let's go. *Please.* He's pulling on my arm again but I shake him off.

Give me a dime then. I'm going on it.

Well you're going to go by yourself.

You wait here for me?

Steve looks up at the Ferris wheel. It's spinning again, and them girls are laughing now. Ain't nothing to be scared of I say.

Steve's looking up at it too. OK just one ride he says. No more rides after that. Then we go straight home.

Right. It's stopped. Come on let's get on before it starts up again.

Steve don't say nothing but he hands the woman his two dimes.

Wheel starts out backward. We get a little ways up and it stops. Chair rocks back and forth.

Look how thin those cables are he whispers. *What if this thing breaks?*

Ain't going to break. Why don't you shut up and stop spoiling it?

Wheel starts up again and this time it makes it almost to the top before it stops. There's a breeze blowing and that makes the chair rock even more. We can see all of Riverview— the Chute-the-Chutes, the Aladdin's Castle, every last one of them roller-coasters.

Steve don't look so good though. He claps his hand on his mouth.

Hey! Don't you puke on me.

He makes a noise, Urp, and his cheeks bulge out.

Aw man! Just keep your mouth shut 'til we get to the bottom OK? He tries but he can't do it. He spits it out over the side but some of it flies back onto his sleeve. Sorry for them folks below us. At least he ain't hungry no more.

Praying for Guidance

I've been praying all afternoon for guidance and I ain't heard no sign.

Yes sister just put them right down there. Put them in a stack. I'll staple them in just a minute.

Jesus help me now. Do I say something? Or just wait, see what happens?

How'd you like a nice cup of coffee Reverend? I was going to fix one for myself anyway. It'd be no trouble, none at all.

When you expect Sister Mattie'll be back? 'Round eight or nine o'clock? Well that's real soon. She might walk in any moment I reckon.

How's your boys doing? That so? Yes Lord he's nearly grown to a man. Mighty hard to talk sense to them when they're that old. Guess you know that though.

Especially with all the sin going on down here every day. Saw a bunch of men shooting dice in an alley just when I walked up to this here church, not no more than an hour ago. Broad daylight they were, no shame at all. And policy! Seems like everywhere you go there's someone is taking bets on numbers. Two drawings a day, every day, Sabbath too. Them runners come right into your kitchenette to pick up your bet if you ask them, morning noon and night. And every sinner in Bronzeville does it, seems like, goes betting their spare change on some lucky number when they should be giving it to the Lord. That's Satan's work, it surely is.

Jesse? No I ain't seen him tonight. Yes sir I'm sure you're right, just out with his friends. Here's that coffee.

Why good evening Sister Mattie. Mighty glad to see you. You care for a cup of coffee too? I just made one for the Reverend. Yes'm I'm sure you're tired after a day's work. You just sit down, take a load off your feet like they say. I'll fetch you a cup too.

You look a little peaked Mattie. Something troubling you?

What kind of commotion?

You say they called the police? Well ma'am I always say movie pictures are the devil's work so it wouldn't surprise me none to hear folks start acting crazy when they see other folks on the screen, kissing and hugging and shooting at one another—.

Wasn't that? What was it then?

Child gone?

Oh Lord sweet Jesus.

What child ma'am? The owner's child? You mean the white folks' child?

No I'm all right. I'm fine, I'm fine. Just feels a little close in here all of a sudden. Think I'll step outside, get me some air. Sure you can come too ma'am. In fact, much obliged.

Yes thanks I'm feeling better already. Just needed to get me some of this cool night air. No nothing's wrong. Just getting old I reckon. What's this about a missing white child?

His grandson? What do they call him?

Dora Barfield, you'd best stop playing right quick and tell this poor woman what you know.

Steve. Yes. And when did they notice he was gone? That long ago eh? So then they just left, went searching for him? Oh I see. What did the police do? Yes yes, guess they got to take their reports first.

Well did they find the child? Oh my.

I can't say it, can't tell her, sinner that I am. Maybe I can help this poor woman some other way. Before things get worse.

Excuse me Sister Mattie. I just recalled a little errand I got to run. I'll be back right quick, half an hour. You just run along back inside.

◆   ◆   ◆   ◆   ◆   ◆   ◆

You mister. Yes you! What you doing hanging out on this corner? You come here. I want to talk to you. Where's your brother?

Not him, your younger brother. Jesse.

Never you mind why I'm asking. Just tell me where I can find Jesse.

Which schoolyard? Raymond? All right Mister Isaiah Nubby Trimble, you just spit out that gum and take me over there. Yes I'm talking about right now. Now march!

Which ones are Jesse's friends? Them there? Call them over. I said bring them over here right now. Don't you go giving me none of your back-talk neither. I took my ruler to you in Sunday School class and I can do it again.

Hey you children, come on over here. Yes you. What's your names?

You called Witchie? What kind of name is that? And Sawbuck? Ain't you got no Christian names? Well Mister Sawbuck, tell me where your friend Jesse Trimble is this evening.

How long since you ain't seen him? All day?

Where would he be? Don't you give me any back-talk young man. Tell me straight out. Come on Isaiah, you're older. See can you make these children talk sense.

Look here now. You boys got to do something. You got to go find Jesse Trimble and bring him back to Glory Life in Jesus Church straight away. It's real important. An emergency. Yes an emergency.

No I can't tell you what's the matter. His momma needs to get him back just as soon as she can. You know where that church is? Over on State Street? All right. I know you know where to find him too so go do it now. Scat!

You too Isaiah. I want you to find that little brother of yours. Go up and down every street in Bronzeville if you got to. Something is wrong sir, real wrong.

No I don't want to tell you nothing about it. And listen here child, I don't want you to go telling no thing to no body your own self neither. That means your own momma and poppa too. Don't you go saying a thing to the Reverend or Miz Mattie, hear? Don't you say a word until you can walk into that church with young Jesse by the arm. Now you scat too.

No-'count children. Sunday night and them out playing in a schoolyard. Should be at home, doing their homework or saying their prayers. These children were back in Mississippi you wouldn't see no carryings-on like this. They'd be in their beds by eight o'clock at night and up at five in the morning. Feed the chickens.

They ain't going to find Jesse though. I know he's off with Steve somewheres. Oh Lord Lord Lord, what am I going to do?

I got to call the Feinbergs. Got to find me a phone and call them. Got to go in one of these here taverns, use their phone and make that call.

Excuse me sir, you got you a coin phone in here? Here's a dollar. I need me some dimes for the phone. *Sinners.*

Miz Feinberg? This here is Dora.

Yes'm. I know already.

Yes'm. I'll be over quick as I can get a bus. I'll explain it all then. You just calm yourself down ma'am. I'm sure he's going to be all right.

◆　　◆　　◆　　◆　　◆　　◆　　◆

Good evening Miz Feinberg, good evening sir. Evening Mister Nate. How you Miz Martha? Sorry folks. Must be awful for you. But trust in the Lord. The Lord is watching over Steve, I'm sure of it. We all just got to pray.

Guess I got to tell you what I know. I think Steve is out somewhere with a colored boy. That's right. Boy name of Jesse Trimble. His mother Mattie works for you Mister Nate.

Yes sir. Same one. Yes sir I know, but if you go on shouting like that I can't explain nothing.

Well. I know about what happened in that parking lot Tuesday night too. Steve told me.

There's more Mister Charles. You ain't going to like this, not one bit.

Day after that stuff happened in the parking lot? Steve went down to Mercy Hospital to visit that colored child.

No ma'am, how can you say that? I'd've never! He did it all by his own self. Got on a streetcar after school and found his own way there. I about fell over when he told me. Went to the hospital, found that child by his very own self. On the streetcar.

Of course I said I had to tell you. But, well, guess I just couldn't think of a way. Didn't want to upset you, you know?

I told Steve he must never do nothing like that again. Tried to tell him how it is between the colored and the white. Don't know was he listening to me or not but I tried. Then he asked me to promise not to tell you what he did, you know, going down to Mercy by his own self and all? Well I figured, OK, it won't come up and no harm done so I'll try to keep my promise to him. But now it's come up.

I'm sorry ma'am. Probably you're going to fire me.

I know that. You just do whatever you got to do ma'am. I know I did a wrong thing. But see, I didn't think it was going to make no trouble because, you know, I never expected he'd go back down there to see that child again.

Yes ma'am. I'm getting to that straight away. Mind if I take a little drink of water? This is kind of hard for me.

Sister Mattie? I mean, Mattie Trimble, the one who works for you Mister Nate? Well I know Mattie. Know her real well. She's the wife of my preacher. Glory Life in Jesus Church, across street from that theater of yours. Preacher is James Trimble, his wife is Mattie Trimble. Your cashier. Same one. Don't go carrying on like that sir, you ain't heard the worst of it yet. There's all kinds of things I got to tell you that you ain't going to believe.

Now Mattie's got three boys. Oldest one is Darius, then there's Isaiah, and the youngest is Jesse.

I'm getting to it sir. Excuse me, I'm just going to take another drink of this here water. Feels like something's stuck in my throat.

Jesse. Like I say, youngest is Jesse. Well. This afternoon I was across street from that theater of yours and I seen young Steve and young Jesse out on the sidewalk, whispering to each other—.

Folks. Folks. Please. *Oh Jesus Lord give me strength. This is the worst moment of my life.* Folks. Calm down.

That's what I'm saying sir. Same one was in the parking lot. Same one was in the hospital. Same one Steve went down to Mercy to visit. Jesse. Jesse Trimble. Mattie Trimble's boy.

Yes, and the same one was in front of the theater talking to Steve. I knew it was him when I clapped eyes on him, didn't matter I was all the way the other side of State Street. Child had those bandages on his nose. And—and—I'd've recognized him anyway because—because—because I teach him in Sunday School.

No sir I don't know what they were talking about. I was on the other side of the street. But I seen them standing together a little ways from the cashier's booth, talking. Was one-thirty, two o'clock maybe. I seen them then I dropped my groceries. When I picked up the food them children were gone. I walked over to that cashier's booth and asked Sister Mattie but she ain't seen them. Said I was imagining it. But I wasn't.

That's the last I seen of them. I think they're still together. Don't ask me why but that's what I think.

Do? You called the police already, right? Police'll find them sure.

What, Jesse? Why he's a good boy sir. He may have a smart mouth but he ain't no bad child. I know that sir. I teach him in Sunday School. He prays to Jesus.

He did what? Oh no! No sir that can't be so. Not Jesse. Was it worth a lot of money? Silver? And you told the police already?

Yes they will. And throw away the key.

Well all I can say is, I've known that child since he was born and I always thought he was OK. But I don't blame you at all Mister Nate. Guess you're right and I'm wrong. Jesse Trimble ... oh Lord. That makes me so sad.

Folks I'd best be going. My place ain't here no more. I got to go back to the church. James and Mattie, they'll be going clean out of their heads when they hear it, but someone's got to tell them too and I guess it's got to be me. Lord God Almighty, don't know how I got into the middle of this.

I'll say goodbye now ma'am. I got a few things in the dining room where I sleep, I'll just gather them up and put them in a paper sack. I know I've given you a lot of grief and heartbreak. You don't even have to pay me for this week ma'am. I wouldn't expect you to, trouble I've caused.

No, bus is fine, I ride it all the time, it ain't no bother.

Oh no sir, that wouldn't be a good idea. Not at all sir. You'd be better off going down to the police station, waiting there. You wouldn't be comfortable, no sir. We're just humble colored folks. It's a storefront church. What would you be wanting to come there for?

◆   ◆   ◆   ◆   ◆   ◆   ◆

You folks wait here in the car OK? Let me go in first.

Mattie? Reverend? How're you all doing?

Is that so? What time is he home usually?

Now don't you worry, I'm sure he's just— uh.

Folks? There's, uh, something I got to tell you. Ruth, excuse us. We'll just go in back for a minute. Folks, you mind?

Um, Mattie, Reverend, it's about Jesse. You see,

actually I wasn't truthful in front of Ruth, God forgive me. I kind of knew Jesse wasn't back yet.

Maybe you all better sit down.

Oh Lord Jesus praise Your glorious name. Pardon me Reverend, don't mean to seem tongue-tied. Just don't know how to begin, that's all.

Well sir, you know I work for white folks. In their home. That's right, taking care of their children and cleaning up.

Well sir, these folks, they're good enough folks. Live in Hyde Park. Jewish folks. Still, they got good hearts. The momma, she's lazy with her kids like some white folks are, you know, but they ain't bad people. Never mind about that sir, that don't concern you.

The daddy, Mister Charles, he works downtown in some office somewhere. But his daddy, Mister Nate, he owns a theater. Picture show. Down here. In Bronzeville. Their name is Feinberg. Man who owns the picture show is Mister Nate. Last name Feinberg. Yes. Same one.

Mattie stop your crying. Hush up child. Let me tell the Reverend the rest of it.

Well now. Mister Nate's got a grandson. That boy is missing too. You ask Mattie here. She's the one told me.

Child's name is Steve. Steve Feinberg. He's the boy I take care of. Swear to God sir.

He's younger than Jesse about a year. Yes sir he comes down to that theater, comes down with his daddy and his granddaddy sometimes. On weekends, like now. Mattie knows him by name, don't you darling?

That's all right sugar, don't you talk. I'll tell him the rest of it.

Reverend? This next is mighty hard for me. You know how Jesse got his self in trouble at the ballpark Tuesday night? Right. Didn't have no business over there bothering them white folks. And the Lord smote him for his sins you might even say.

So the white folks they were begging nickels from? Them white folks were the Feinbergs. Steve told it to me.

Reverend now you must calm yourself. Ain't no call to be carrying on like that. It ain't Christian, pardon my saying so. I know it ain't easy for you and it's a shock and all but you've got to lower your voice. You don't want Ruth and them others hearing you using cuss words like that do you? The most important thing is, we got to find those two children. You shouting and screaming ain't going to help. Besides sir, I ain't done.

Steve, the white boy, he came down to Mercy Wednesday afternoon and visited Jesse in his bed. Got on the streetcar after school and did it all by his own self. I ain't making it up. Steve told me. He couldn't explain why he did it though and I still don't understand.

But anyway, getting to today. After I left church this afternoon, I went over to that little food shop next to Thelma's House of Beauty to buy me some groceries. You know, across from that Calumet Theater. From across street I seen them two boys together, standing out on the sidewalk in front of the theater, whispering. Jesse and Steve.

Then my grocery bag broke and when I looked up

they were gone. I crossed over and told Sister Mattie but she didn't pay it no mind because she ain't seen the white boy herself. So I didn't say no more to no one. Didn't tell Mattie who the white boy was. Didn't say what I knew. Wasn't my business you know? Just went home and read my Bible. Prayed to Jesus to help me figure it all out. But it's been on my mind all day.

Then I come back here this evening and Mattie says the white child, Steve, is gone missing and they've called out the police. I still was afraid to tell Mattie what I knew so I went outside on my own. I sent Isaiah to find Jesse, told Jesse's friends to find Jesse. I expect they're out looking for him still. But they ain't never going to find him because he and Steve are out together. Somewhere. I know it in my bones.

Then I called the Feinbergs.

They—they—I went over to their apartment. In Hyde Park. Couldn't tell them on the phone you know? They're in the same fix as you folks. They're missing their son too. I've been working for them four years. That boy Steve, why, he's as close to me as my own child. Sorry. M-M-Mattie, y'all got another one of them Kleenexes please?

Well, they—they—they said Jesse—Jesse—I'm sorry, I can't go on. Oh Lord Jesus help me now, in Your sweet name Jesus help this poor sinner!

The Feinbergs—they—they—they brought me back down to this here church. And—Oh Jesus Lord God Almighty!—they are—they are—waiting outside in their car right now. They want to come in here. They're just going to have to tell you the rest of it themselves.

Riverview Park

*H*e jumps off the chair even before it stops rocking. He says Let's go on a roller-coaster now and pulls my hand hard but I don't want to. I really don't.

I'm scared. I'm going to call my mom.

Oh man he says you going to start blubbering again? This is fun, and he runs out into the midway trying to drag me behind him. Those other guys, they've just disappeared. I have no idea where they went.

I know what he wants to do now though because we're here. The sign says **B O B S** .

It's huge. It's all wood, a million wooden beams. The other roller-coasters, they've got wire-mesh shields so you can't fly out, but not this one. And it goes *fast*. The cars whip past us and the way the people are screaming, they aren't faking. I'm scared just listening to them.

I don't want to do that I say. I want to go home.

Aw man we got to do it he says. Come on. Just once.

Wait a minute I say because I see a pay phone. I run over and put in a dime and dial. Mom or Dad can tell us how to get home. They're going to be awfully mad though. But it just goes *buzz-pause-buzz-pause*. Nobody home.

I'm afraid to ask any of these Riverview people for help. They all look mean. I can't call the police either. They'll just arrest him.

But he's pulling on my arm again. Come on he says.

The Bobs costs a quarter— fifty cents for both of us. I don't have much left.

◆   ◆   ◆   ◆   ◆   ◆   ◆

Man that was great he says. You know, when it's coming *down*, then it cracks from *one* side to the *other*, and it ain't even hit *bottom* yet? Oooohhh I *really* liked that.

When I close my eyes, all I can see is Mom's face.

Hey he says. You used to talk all the time.

Her face is bigger than the moon.

Want to go on that ride over there?

You said you'd go home after the Ferris wheel.

Aw don't worry we'll get home he says. I could stay here all night. Come on, just one more ride.

We walk some more until we get almost to Aladdin's Castle. It's huge like everything else here. The hugest thing is the genie over the entrance. He's got on a turban and a big black mustache. And an awful smile.

But we don't make it to Aladdin's Castle. Instead we stop at this little stage set up in front of a tent. It's got people sitting on it in chairs—the weirdest people. A woman with a beard and mustache and tattoos all over her body. Another woman so fat she can't even stand up. A guy with skin that's thick like an elephant's. He's covered with warts.

Sass wants to go on to Aladdin's Castle. But I've got to see this.

A guy is talking into a microphone wired to a P.A. Curly gray hair. He talks without ever taking the cigar out of his mouth.

Yes ladies and gentlemen now I'd like to introduce you to the most extraordinary young lady. Step forward Nancy.

She's got on a gold-colored two-piece bathing suit and high-heeled shoes with gold sequins and a gold chain around her neck. Straight blond hair. The Golden Lady.

He talks but she doesn't say anything back. She just sort of glides toward the front of the stage, smiling. Not quite a smile. Almost.

She's beautiful.

Show the people what you can do Nancy. Show these boys here, and he points his cigar at us. Show them your trrrricks Nancy and he winks at us. Bet you ain't never seen nothing like this. Out of the side of his mouth.

What she does next, I can't believe it. She lifts up her right leg, then she grabs it with her right hand like it doesn't even belong to her. She's balancing on one high-heeled shoe but she doesn't lose her balance. Now she pulls up her leg until it's straight up against her side— I mean straight up, toes to the sky— then bends it so her leg is behind her head. Smiling that little half-smile.

I have to catch my breath.

She lets her leg down. Her shoe touches the stage, doesn't make a sound. Now she reaches behind her and goes into a backbend but doesn't stop. She keeps on arching until her body is in an O and her head is poking through her legs. She's sitting on her own head. I can't believe it.

Her body is twisted into a hairpin. That gold chain around her neck, it's almost touching the stage floor. I can see down her front. She doesn't say anything, just keeps smiling. Not really a smile.

I feel so funny. My face is hot and sweaty but I'm cold down below. Down below means *down below*. Where you go to the bathroom.

That guy with the curly hair is talking. How does she do it? How *does* she do it? Well folks there's more inside, much more. Just fifty cents to see the rest of the show. See Nancy do her tricks, *all* her tricks. Step right up, just fifty cents. Yeah you boys can come in too. You got fifty cents?

I try to say something back but I'm choking and I can't talk. The guy isn't paying any attention though, just waving people inside. The guy with the elephant skin gets up to go inside the tent. So does the woman with the beard and the tattoos and the woman who's so fat, though she almost can't get up off the stool. The last one is Nancy. Just before she goes into the tent, she turns around and looks at straight at me with that sort-of smile. My legs feel weak. Maybe she doesn't notice. She turns and goes through the curtain. She's gone.

Mister I've got four quarters. Let us in.

I ain't going in there Sass says. I want to go on the Bobs again.

Come on.

Unh-unh.

All right and I reach into my pants pocket. *Let him go.*

Here's three bucks?

Three bucks? That's a lot of money.

Yeah.

How much you got left?

Never mind. Just come back when you're done on the Bobs.

You sure?

Yeah.

You really sure?

Yeah.

OK— if you're sure. See you in a little while.

◆　　　◆　　　◆　　　◆　　　◆　　　◆　　　◆

I should of gone with him. My mouth tastes like I ate tar. My underpants are rubbing and my crotch is on fire. When I scratch though the skin burns even worse.

I could of stayed with him instead of coming to this show. Taken one more ride on the Bobs, snapped my neck off one more time. Now when I close my eyes I see her *face, not Mom's. Like the carbon arc after you close your eyes, a circle, bright green and red.*

At least when you're on the Bobs, you can't think.

The curly-haired guy has dragged the P.A. inside

and set it up on a corner of the stage. Not much of a stage, just a fake floor a stair-step higher than my chair. Aw right ladeez and gentlemen we're going to get started now. Let's give a hand for our show, give our performers a nice Riverview welcome eh? His cigar has gone out but he's still got it in his mouth. Talking around it.

Meet Tess. His voice is raspy, from those cigars I bet. Tessie come on out. Two-Ton Tess we call her.

It's the fat lady. She has to use a cane. She's just wearing a housedress— probably can't find clothes to fit. Her upper arms are white as paste and they look like sausages. But her hands are tiny.

Careful Tessie, don't sit on that chair, I ain't paid the insurance bill. It's a joke I guess. Everyone else is laughing.

Folks Tessie here weighs five hundred and thirty pounds. She's only five-foot-two. Five-foot-two and eyes of blue. Ain't she gorgeous? The guy next to me sticks his fingers in his mouth and gives a wolf whistle, real loud. I try to whistle too but I don't know how to do it with my fingers. I try to go wheet-wheeyew the regular way but I can't even whistle. My lips are too dry.

He's talking into the microphone again. He's hard to understand on account of so much distortion and that cigar. So tell us Tess how'j'a get so gorgeous? It wasn't them sticky buns I seen you eating for breakfast was it? Say, what's your favorite food anyway?

Pie she says. Banana cream pie. She sounds dead, just dead.

That's great. I just happen to have a big banana cream pie right here. It's all yours Tessie soon's you do one little thing for me.

What's that Mister B? She's taking a deep breath.

Just beg. Can ya get down on your hands and knees and beg? Beg, Tessie—beg like a dog.

She gets up off the chair like a hippo coming out of the water. She leans hard on her cane then drops down onto one knee. She makes a face like something hurts. She's so fat everything probably hurts. She curls her hand in front of her face. Like dog paws.

Rurf. Rurf.

Great Ain't she great folks? How about it for Tess? Tess the Mess! He's waving at us. To applaud I guess.

And here's your pie. But you got to eat it no hands.

Oh my gosh. She's doing it. She's got her hands behind her back and her face in the pie and she's eating it no hands. She's grunting and snuffling. Oh no—she's going to finish it—she *did* finish it except for a spot of pie sticking on the front of her dress. Now she's wiping the cream and banana goo off her face. Her hands— they're like a doll's.

What if I had to do something like that every day?

Go on Tessie, clean yourself up 'cause we got to clear the stage now ... for ... Miss ... Nancy ... Drake!

I can't leave now.

She does the splits ... she sits up ... she's putting her leg behind her head ... both legs ... she's sitting up *with both legs behind her head*. Now she's doing a handstand with her legs *still behind her head*.

I shouldn't be watching this shouldn't be watch-

ing any of this oh gosh oh gosh oh gosh but she's smiling smiling how can she smile when she's upside-down and her whole body is twisted into a knot. How can she?

Shouldn't be shouldn't be she's so beautiful shouldn't be watching. And smiling shouldn't be. How can she shouldn't be how? Smile?

It's over. She's gone. My hands. Look at my hands. They're shaking.

But the curly-haired guy is bringing out the next act before she even gets off the stage. And here he is, the celebrated—the great—the one and only—Fire Man!

He's skinny with a spade beard and a waxed mustache. Dimpy-looking little guy. He's wearing red leotards like Beth wears to ballet except he's so skinny they don't fit right. An *F* sewn on his chest but there's a stitch missing and the corner is drooping over. He's got on a red cape too. What does he think he is, Superman or something?

He reaches into a canvas bag and pulls out three sticks with rags wrapped around the ends. It smells like gasoline. Oh no. He's got a Zippo out of his pocket and he's going to burn the tent down.

Hey careful Fire Man didn'j'a hear what I said about the insurance? The curly-haired guy is winking at us again. Maybe this is just an act.

Now the Fire Man guy is juggling those torches while they're on fire. I'm too close. I can feel the heat on my face. Maybe I can move back a row. Maybe I can get out of here like that other guy who was wolf-whistling, he's heading for the exit, so are the others, I should maybe *but it wouldn't be polite but they're doing it so maybe I could maybe could just move back a few rows maybe. That wouldn't hurt his feelings.*

The curly-haired guy is shouting into the P.A. Hey folks where ya going? Show's just getting started. Fire Man! You're scaring these nice people away.

So he stops juggling those torches. Sticks them in a bucket of sand. He looks annoyed. He's pulling a—.

Oh no.

It's a knife. A dagger. With a cotton wad on the point.

I think I know what's next. I could get up real quietly so they wouldn't notice—.

Well whaddya know, Fire Man's hungry. Lunch time for Fire Man. Folks, what he's gonna do now, nobody else knows how to do this 'cep Fire Man. You won't see this at Ringling Brothers, you won't see it at Clyde Beatty. He's gonna swallow a sword and eat fire at the same time—*Fire Man!*

He's waving again for us to applaud but only one person is clapping. That teenager behind me, he didn't leave either. It's just him and me.

Oh gosh. He lit it. It's starting. I can't watch. He's got his mouth open and the knife is *oh gosh oh no I can't oh.* But he pulls the knife out of his mouth thank gosh. He's holding it up and it's still on fire, waving it around, waving it around and smirking *but it's over I can go now I can—.* Oh no he isn't finished after all *oh don't open your no don't do no oh I can't please.* All the way down his throat.

I think I'm going to puke.

Hey folks how about a big round of applause, *Fire Man!*

It still smells like gasoline and burning mustache hair. That other kid is getting up now. *I could too.*

Hold on young feller best part of the show's about to begin.

Who mister. Me?

Come over here kid, got something to show you. Something you'll like. A new game.

I got to go mister.

Come on kid. Don't be afraid. I ain't gonna bite'cha.

I can't. My friend—.

Naw come on over here to this table. I want to show you something. *His voice doesn't sound so raspy when he isn't using that microphone.*

See this here pea? Well I'm going to set it down on the cloth. The pea is green and the cloth is blue so the pea is really easy to see. Right?

Unh-huh.

You said you see the pea right?

Unh-huh.

Aw right. Now I'm going to cover the pea with this here walnut shell—and now you don't see the pea. Is that right?

Unh-huh.

Now I'm going to lift the shell and there's the pea. Still where it was right?

Unh-huh.

This is fun right?

Unh-huh.

OK. Now here's where things get a little harder.

I've got two more walnuts and I'm going to put them down too. You remember where the pea was right?

There. In the middle. The middle one.

Let's see if you got it. Whaddya know! There it is. Say kid you're pretty good. You sure you never played this game before?

Unh-unh.

I bet if I do it again you won't be able to tell where the pea is. Wanna bet?

Unh-unh.

Aw that's OK. We'll just play for fun. Let's see if you can do it two in a row. I'm just going to put the pea in the middle of the cloth, like this, then I'm going to put a shell over it, like this, and now watch closely 'cause I'm going to move them around, like this. Aw right. Where's the pea?

On the left.

I'll be darned! You did it again. Kid you are *good*. I got to try it a third time. *Nobody* gets it three times in a row. Aw right, we're doing it again a little faster. Make it tougher. You ain't never going to get it this time.

That one.

You sure?

Oh yeah.

How sure?

One hundred per cent.

Sure enough to make a little bet on it?

I don't know how to bet mister. Unless you count marbles. Usually I lose.

But you're sure you know where the pea is. Ain't that what you said?

Mmm-hmm.

A hundred per cent sure, ain't that what you said?

Mmm-hmm.

Well then. Should be worth twenty-five cents to find out if you was right shouldn't it?

But what if I lose?

Kid! How you going to lose? You said you was one hundred per cent sure.

Yeah. I see. OK I guess.

There—put your quarter right there. On the table. I'm going to lift up the shell now and—Golly! I'll be darned! That's amazing! Well here you are young man, here's your quarter. You won it fair and square.

Thanks mister.

Now put down your quarter and we'll do it again.

No I got to go.

Come on kid, one more time. You've already won a quarter. Take a chance.

My friend—.

Your friend will wait.

All right. But just one more quarter. Then I got to go.

Here we go and … here we go and … which one?

The one on the left again.

Daggone! Another quarter! You're cleaning me out tonight.

It's easy mister. All I got to do is watch you real closely. The pea has to be under the same shell every time doesn't it?

Why of course it does son. And you're a very smart lad to perceive that. Tell me, do you do well in school?

Pretty well.

I thought so, I thought so. I can tell about people you know? You work in a place like this, you get to be a real good judge of people. *Real* good. And I could tell about you from the first moment I saw you. A smart boy. Definitely.

Thank you.

Smart. Polite too. *And* a good sport. You are a good sport ain't you?

Um I guess so.

Well then you'll give me a chance to win back my money right? To be fair.

Um. OK but this is the last one.

Put your money down then.

OK.

A quarter? Come on. Good as you are at this game? You keep betting quarters, we'll be here a long long time. How much money you got on you?

Let's see what's in my pocket. Here's the fifty cents I won from you, and the quarter I started with, and two more dollars. And my friend has three dollars.

Yeah well forget about him. Why'n'cha bet one of them dollars.

Unh-unh. I can't.

If you win you'll have three dollars and seventy-five cents. You can go out on the midway and get yourself all the hot dogs and cotton candy you want. How long since you ate? Bet it's a while.

I guess I am kind of hungry.

Come on kid, think of all them hot dogs. Why'n'cha take a chance? Three dollars and seventy-five cents!

If I bet one dollar?

Right. One little dollar. Put it right there on the table.

So I put a dollar on the table and he sets the pea down again. This time though he pulls back his shirt cuffs before he starts, then he wiggles his fingers like he's loosening them up. He puts one of the shells over the pea and starts moving them around, only this time I can't even see his hands they move so fast.

Where's the pea?

I feel like I'm going to go Number Two in my pants. That one.

He lifts up the shell and raises his eyebrow at me. Nope, and puts my dollar in his pocket.

I won't cry. I won't. Not and look like a sissy.

Where ya going?

I lost my dollar.

Nah you didn't lose. You still got a dollar seventy-five. You won fifty cents, you lost a dollar, now what does that add up to? Come on— you said you was good in school— add it up.

It's fifty cents. Mister I got to go.

So you lost fifty cents. So big deal. You know kid, a wise man once said, You got to spend money to make money. You know who that wise man was? It was John D. Rockefeller the Standard Oil guy. *You got to spend money to make money.* And you know who became the richest man in the world? John. D. Rockefeller.

I can't bet again. My friend—if he finds out I lost all the money he'll—.

Look kid, I know it's all you got so I'll make it

interesting. Next time we do it, it's double or nothing.

Huh?

I pay you double if you win. Swear. You could win back everything. When your friend comes back you won't have to say nothing to him. Come on— put down your bet.

OK. I bet these two quarters.

Naw kid, I said *double or nothing*. You can't bet fifty cents on a deal like that.

What? Why?

You got to bet it all. Double or nothing. Means you bet it all and if you win, you double what you already got. Let's see, you got a dollar seventy-five so that's uh three fifty. If you win I pay you three fifty. Plus the dollar seventy-five you got, why, you'll walk out of here with five dollars and twenty-five cents. What'd you come in here with— two twenty-five? You'd have more than twice as much.

I—.

Five and a quarter. A hot dog for you, a hot dog for your little colored pal, cotton candy and root beer too, and all the rides at Riverview. Come on. Come *on*.

He's right. I could win it all back. Double or nothing.

OK here's a dollar and twenty-five, fifty, seventy-five.

All right that's more like it. You ready? Tell me when you're ready. I don't want you telling your buddy you wasn't ready when we started. Say *Go*.

Go. And he starts off nice and slow. I know right where the pea is at first and I'm following it and everything's great and then his hands start moving like lightning again.

Well?

I don't know. *I feel like I'm looking down the side of a cliff.*

Just pick one. *I see him smiling. He thinks I don't but I do.*

You mean guess?

Do whatever you gotta do. But hustle up. I ain't got all night.

I don't want to guess. I don't know which one it's under. Can't we just cancel this one? I'll just take my money off the table. You're still ahead.

Hey k-i-i-ddd. That ain't how this game is played. I'm taking a big risk here. After you win my three-fifty, you'll be rich and I'll be poor. You said you was a good sport didn'j'a? Well fair's fair. Give me the chance I gave you. Now go on— pick.

Unh-unh. No. Give me back my money. Please mister.

You want me to call the cops? Tell them you're trying to cheat me? We got a security force here kid. How'j'a like it if I called one of them in? They're pretty rough mugs. They ain't sposeda but some of them carry guns. Come on, pick.

So I squeeze my eyes closed and try to think how the shells moved around. The pea started out in the middle. Then that shell might have moved to the right. I might have seen that shell move to the right. It's possible I saw that. Very possible. I haven't picked the right shell so far, so the pea should be there this time.

Law of averages.

The right one.

OK let's take a look he says. Oops. Guess not.

When I was seven, Dad got me my first two-wheeler, a Rollfast. He showed me how to ride it but I fell off the first few times. When the horse throws you get back on he said so I got back on and this time I rode it without falling off. Attaboy Dad said.

After that I rode my bike almost every day. I rode it to school, I rode it in the park, I rode it everywhere. They gave me a chain covered with leatherette and a Master combination lock, one of those round ones, and said always lock it you never know and I always did, except. This one time, I rode it to the library. I figured what the heck it's a library no one's going to steal my bike and besides, I'm just going in for a few minutes. But I found a Doctor Dolittle book I never read before and I started reading it. I looked up at the clock and it's an hour later. When I went out, the bike was gone.

I had to go to the police station with Dad. I had to tell the police everything, even about the paint scratches on the crossbar. The police station was really embarrassing. But not the worst. Even losing the bike wasn't. The worst was Dad when I had to tell him I'd let someone steal my first bike, that he'd bought for me. The way I felt when I saw the look in his eyes. That's how I feel right now.

Give me another chance.

With what? You ain't got no more money.

Show me. Show me how you did it.

He smiles again and this time he doesn't try to hide it. Sure sure. Look. I just set the pea here, and he sets down the pea, then put the shell here, and he lays down the shell, then just move them around like this, and he slides them around the table the way he did at first. Slow.

No no! Do it fast! Like you did! I got to see what I did wrong.

Oh you want to see how I did it when you *lost*? Why didn't you say so? You want a *lesson*. Work this scam on your friends and win all *their* money eh? OK I'll show you. Gonna cost you though. You got any more money in there?

Unh-unh.

He sticks his face right into mine. Well then kid, too damn bad for you. Now get out of here before I call a cop.

♦ ♦ ♦ ♦ ♦ ♦ ♦

I have to wait twenty minutes before Sass comes back. My crotch is burning up and now I have to pee too but if I go to the bathroom I could miss him. Doesn't matter though. He isn't going to have any money left.

Here he is. Big grin on his face. Oh cripes.

Man you should of come with me. I went on the Flying Turns and the Wild Mouse and the—.

Did you spend all the money?

Yup. Every bit. Well. I still got a dime.

Give it to me.

Sure. Don't have to shout you know. Where you

running off to?

Pay phone.

Wait up, I'm coming too.

　—Hello?

　Uh, uh—Mom?

　—Who's this?

　Uh, uh, Steve, uh—.

　—What number you calling?

LIVingston 1121.

　—Yeah that's this number. But I ain't nobody's mom.

　Oh. Sorry. 'Bye.

What'd they say? They coming for us?

I've been dialing the wrong phone number all day. I forgot my own phone number.

Why you dumb-ass!

Do you know how to find a phone number when you forget it?

Naw. I ain't never used no pay phone neither.

That was the last of our money.

What you mean?

I lost—it's—I mean I—it's gone. It's just gone.

You only went in that one show. It only cost fifty cents. Should be plenty left.

I know but I—. *This is harder than telling Dad the bike was stolen.*

Gol damn Sam! Wha'd you do with the money?

I gave it—he took—there was this guy—it's—I don't have it any more. I just don't. It's gone.

How are we going to get home?

I'll think of—we could—um, maybe we could walk.

I got to get home. How'm I going to get home, and he pushes me.

I know. Me too. I don't know.

This is your fault. He pushes me again.

I know. I know. I'm sorry, and I don't even push him back.

What about that guy over there? The one was running that show you went into?

I can't talk to him again.

Why not?

I can't tell you.

Well you'd best. You don't, we ain't never getting home. Go on. I'll stand next to you.

Mister—.

Didn't I tell you to go away? I got another show to do.

Mister, look, I know you won fair and square—when I say that I see Sass's eyebrows shoot up—but me and him, we've got to get home. We just need carfare.

Tough titty.

I don't know what he means so I look at Sass. Sass shrugs.

Please mister we don't have any money at all. We don't even know how to get back home. We're lost.

Should of thought about that earlier. He's fiddling with the wires on the P.A. Trying to ignore me.

Sass says Hey mister.

Oh it's your little darkie pal. How'd you get into Riverview anyway bud?

I just paid for him and we walked in.

Why'd *you* pay for *him*?

These questions again. Where will the answers ever come from?

Don't you know there ain't no colored at Riverview?

You mean they aren't *allowed*?

No kid they just *don't come*. Look around. You see any other colored here?

Gee I didn't notice I say. I ask Sass, Did you?

Yeah I noticed Sass says.

Is it a rule?

Naw it ain't no rule the guy says. They probably let this one in because *you* paid.

Look I say. I'll take him out. We'll go. Both of us. We won't make any trouble. We just need carfare. Two dimes is all— half fare, we're both under twelve. And uh could you please tell us how to get back to the South Side?

Go 'way kid. I got work to do, and he starts heading back through the curtain.

Mister please. We'll do anything.

He looks like he's thinking about that. Do anything huh? All right let me do the next show. I'll be back out in a couple minutes.

We wait for it seems like hours until he comes back out, but he looks completely different now. Jolly.

How much money you say you need?

Just carfare.

How'd you like to earn much more, I say *much* more, than that? Eh?

Is this the same man?

How'd you like ... two bucks?

Sass says What we got to do?

Just follow me.

◆　　　◆　　　◆　　　◆　　　◆　　　◆　　　◆

He walks us over to where there's a crowd, young guys, teen-agers. They're laughing and joking around with each other. Packs of Luckies rolled up in the sleeves of their t-shirts. The guy's right about Riverview — all of them are white. There's baseballs stacked along a counter and a sign, **3 for 25¢**. Another sign is hanging overhead. It's got a picture on it of a cannibal. He's got thick red lips and bulging eyes and there's a bone sticking out of his topknot. He's standing over a big black kettle, stirring it with a canoe paddle. There's a white guy in the kettle, tied up with ropes. The words on the sign say

The African Dip

One of the white kids—young men I mean—one of them has a baseball in his hand. He winds up while his buddies are razzing him.

You couldn't hit the broad side of a barn.

Come on Jake let's see what you got.

He tosses at this red-black-and-white cloth bull's-eye but his throw is wild.

Hey pussy! Look at your friends laughing at you now. Ain't you ashamed of yourself puss? Man going to put *you* in this tank and let *me* be throwing the base-balls at *you*.

I look over past the target and I see it's a colored kid. He's sitting on a swing in a sort of a cage that's hanging over a pool of dirty water. The cage is made out of thick braided rope. The colored kid is rocking back and forth on the swing and grinning. His skin is so dark it's a little hard to see him in the shadows.

Teeth and eyeballs.

Hey white boy, you Polish? The polacks always miss me on account of they're so stupid. Come on white boy, give you one more try. Miss me again and I'll know you're Polish, and he laughs at them.

Show that nigger Jake! So the one they're calling Jake picks up another ball and this time he hits the bull's-eye. That makes the swing give way. The colored kid splashes into the water.

Attaboy Jake! Way to go man!

The colored kid is splashing and spluttering and waving his arms while he tries to climb out of the water. He hooks the swing back up and climbs on it again. I swear massa you done dunked this coon he shouts. Then he starts up again with the insults. Water is dripping from his coveralls.

There's three cages side-by-side. The third one is empty. The man with the curly hair bends down and talks into Sass's ear but I'm right next to him so I can hear everything.

You go in that empty one for an hour see? My regular boy'll be back then and you come out. That's all you got to do, just an hour. Two bucks

Sass shakes his head.

All right, suit yourself. Guess you'll just have to walk home.

I look at the man. If we do it, you promise to tell us how to get home?

Tell you anything you want. Only I don't want *you* in the cage son. I want *him*.

I shake my head at Sass. We don't need the money that bad. We'll figure out some other way to get home.

All right make it three bucks. We look at each other again. Make it *five*. And you can come out as soon as my other boy comes back, even if it's less than an hour.

Then you going to tell us how to get back?

Oh that's easy. You just take the El back to the Loop and change onto any train marked *Jackson Park* or *Englewood*.

Sass looks at me. Five bucks he says. I ain't never had that much money in my life. Cash mister?

The man reaches into his pocket. He's got a big roll of bills there, tied with a rubber band. He pulls off a five and waves it in Sass's face. Just get in that tank he says and it's yours.

◆   ◆   ◆   ◆   ◆   ◆   ◆

The man holds up his hand to stop the game and let Sass climb into the one empty cage.

What I got to do mister?

The man jerks his head toward those white kids with the baseballs. Just do what them other boys do. Just insult 'em. Call 'em dumb dagoes, wops, polacks, krauts. That's what they are anyway.

What's dagoes and them others?

Never mind, just do what Marty does, and he points to the colored kid in the next cage over. Sass looks at the colored kid, Marty, at the cage, then back at me. Then he shrugs and hoists himself onto the swing with his good hand. Those white kids are still horsing around, punching each other in the arm and using dirty words. Sometimes they reach in their pants for a quarter and toss a ball. Mostly they miss but sometimes they hit and a swing gives way, dumping one of those colored kids into that scummy water.

My mouth still tastes like puke. My head hurts and it's hard to think on account of the noise—machinery pounding constantly, metal screeching against metal, everyone yelling and shouting. Blue and green neon lights are flashing above the baseball counter and they make these kids look like they're wearing green masks. It's like in the newsreels, where Bob Feller pitches his ninety-four-mile-per-hour fastball and the camera slows it down to make it last five seconds. One of them throws and the ball looks like it's traveling through Log Cabin Syrup. But then it speeds up and smashes the target like a punch in the face. Sass's face. Nancy's face. A face like a lump of silver with letters on it that no one can read. Except maybe God.

I hear a gong and a splash and it's Sass.

Hey nigger get a little wet? Haw! Haw! Haw!

He climbs out with one hand and gets back into the cage somehow. He shakes the water from his street clothes and sits there on that little slat. Shivering.

Hey man whatcha doing? I turn and it's Duane, the tall kid from the El. He's with those other guys, what were their names? Ned with the Cubs cap and Joey Bob with the freckles and the stutter.

Joey Bob points to the cage where Sass is. Hey look! It's the c-c-colored kid.

Ned says Wow. What's he doing inside there?

Who cares? Let's s-s-sink him, and Joey Bob grabs a baseball. Who do I pay the money to? He waves the ball in the air and looks for someone to give the money to.

Gimme some too! They all grab for balls.

Go away! This is m-m-my quarter. You guys d-d-do your own, and he tosses.

Aaahhh you didn't even come close, watch this, and Duane throws. He just misses. He's so tall is why he's got an advantage.

Come on Duane sink him Ned says. He's nudging me in the ribs. Hey watch out you little coon he'll get you next throw. This guy's our best pitcher.

Look at me g-g-guys, I can do it too. Hey you guys really, look at me, watch *me*. All right, now you're *really* going to get it you *j-j-jigaboo!*

But he misses. Ned and Duane punch him and kid him. They're all laughing now, reaching in their pants for more quarters.

Come on, you try it too. Dunk the nigger!

I shake my head.

Come on. You afraid you'll miss?

I don't have any money left.

I'll let you throw one of mine.

I don't want to.

Aah go on sissy, and Ned hands me one of his own balls.

I could say *sticks and stones* but I don't. I don't say anything.

I see someone out of the corner of my eye then, someone I think I know, and it's her. She's dressed in street clothes now. She sees me too—this time I'm sure of it. She stops walking and looks over at me, at the baseball lying in my hand. I look in her eyes. She smiles —well, almost smiles—and I think she nods. At me.

Sissy! Sissy! Sissy!

I've got the baseball in my hand now. I'm squeezing it so hard I can feel the stitches, almost feel down to the inside, through the string wrapping to the hard cork core.

Hard inside, like these teen-agers in their white t-shirts. They're standing around having a great time, using words Mom says never to use. Hard even like these kids, this Duane and Ned and Joey Bob, throwing balls at my friend. They use that word too, that word I must never say, and other words besides— jig jig jig jig whatever it was. Use it like it's nothing. Maybe it is nothing.

And they're kids too, just kids, little kids like me, well maybe a little older, but still. Kids who even look like some of the kids at Kenwood School, white too, might even be Jewish too, who knows, kids from the North Side not the South Side, sure. But still. They said Come with us. Come with us, not your friend, because your friend is not supposed to be your friend somehow, even though he is somehow. Maybe I could be friends with these kids too. Be Sass's friend and their friend too, be friends with both at the same time. Maybe somehow.

Ya gonna throw or not, sissy?

Nancy raises her eyebrows like she expects an answer too, and smiles that smile that only she knows what it means.

So I throw. Better than I thought.

Way to go kid, and someone claps me on the back. You got that nigger good.

Sass's eyes open wide and he disappears. I hear a splash and I see the swing, still rocking, but now it's empty.

◆   ◆   ◆   ◆   ◆   ◆   ◆

I didn't mean it.

He doesn't say anything, just sticks his pinkie into his ear and squeezes out water. He looks like he hates me.

Honest I really didn't mean it. It's just, everyone else was doing it and it looked like—. *Fun? No.*

He looks down the street for a bus. Doesn't want to look at me. I don't care if a bus never comes. I'll stand here for hours if I have to, explaining. Only I don't know how to start.

I'm sorry. Say something.

Thought you were my friend.

I am.

You ain't. You're the same as them others, shouting nigger.

I didn't do that.

Don't matter does it? You threw the ball.

I wish I could un-throw it, make time stop like in the newsreel, run backward. I wish I could grab my own arm while it's reaching for the baseball and pull it back before it throws. I'd tear it off if I could.

It's just, there were all those people doing it too and—.

Shut up. You don't got to explain. He's staring out into the street, the cars, the night. A clock on a bank across street says one-thirty.

I'm sorry I say, but he doesn't answer.

I said, I'm sorry. He folds his arms. *What else does he want me to say?*

Come on. Say something, and I push at him.

He spins around and he's made a fist. The back of his wrist hits me on the side of the head and knocks me off balance. I have to grab at the bus sign to keep from falling.

Hey stop I say but he keeps charging at me. Now he's rabbit-punching at my neck. I try to hold up my hand to keep him from hitting me again, then kick at his shins but I miss. He throws another punch but this time I grab his hand and he falls on me and we both go down on the sidewalk and I guess I hit my head because I see a hot red flash. A red flash and an explosion, like my head is blowing up.

Nigger! Nigger! *What were those words?* You nigger-fucker cocker-sucker coon-jigger! You son of a baster! Damn hell son of a baster! *I'll say them all.* You *shvartze!*

He socks me in the mouth, tastes like wet salt.

Shvartze! Shocher! I sock him back, a solid one, right in the solar plexus, hard as I can. He goes Oof and can't breathe. Tries to talk but he can't. Waves his hands for me to stop. Lies on his side on the sidewalk squirming. Gasping for air. I'm standing over him and my pulse is going pound pound pound in my head. I'm shaking and I can't make myself stop.

Come on! Get up and fight!

He gasps again and shakes his head.

You chicken! You're a sissy chicken nigger *shvartze!*

He sucks in a breath and it sounds like someone gulping water. Does it again, twice. Then he opens his mouth and finally he can talk.

You better stop saying that.

Nigger! *Nigger*! I shout, and start to cry.

The Calumet

*W*e get on the bus. This time I pay, give the man my five-dollar bill and ask for change. I sit down next to a colored woman holding a shopping bag. So there ain't no room for Steve to sit next to me. He sits down across the aisle and tries to say something but I just stare out the window. We get off at the El, climb the stairs, train pulls up, get on the closest car. Ride all the way to the Loop, Wells Street, ain't said nothing for half an hour.

We're standing on the platform waiting for the Jackson Park train, Steve asks what time it is. Knows I ain't got no watch and there ain't a clock in sight.

He says Look I'm sorry. Then he says Here hit me. Make it even. Points to his arm. I shake my head.

I want you to be my friend again he says.

I never was your friend I tell him.

I shouldn't of said those things. I didn't mean them.

Then why did you?

He shakes his head and says, Couldn't you just pretend I didn't? I don't say nothing. Ain't nothing to say.

We get on a Jackson Park train, I look around for

someone to sit next to but there ain't no one on this train at all, it's about two-thirty in the morning. Got to sit next to him though I'd as soon not.

He says, I guess you'll go home when we get off, right? I don't say nothing. He wants to talk, he's going to have to find someone else to talk to.

But then he gets this panicked look and says, I have to go home with you.

I can't take no more of this. Just shut up I holler at him. You're the biggest trouble ever I met. Can't you let me alone?

No no he says. It's so late. I don't have anywhere else to go. I'm sorry I'm sorry I'm so sorry. Looks like he's fixing to start blubbering again.

You ain't going home with me, is all I know.

But I got to he says. Just until morning, then I'll go stand in front of the theater and wait for my grandpa.

I shake my head.

Now he *is* blubbering. OK he says. I'll go stand in front of the theater then. It's just a couple of hours until the sun comes up. I guess I could take a streetcar if I had any money. Could you loan me a dime?

I reach in my pants, give him his dime.

So. So he says again. I'll just go there and wait for— my grandpa or a streetcar or—something. And uh, you'll go home.

Yeah.

And uh, we won't ever uh—.

Yeah.

Um. Would you uh walk me there? I mean, just to make sure I find the theater? I want to tell him no. I want to tell him to just get lost and don't come round me ever again. But then I look at him with them tears and all and he just looks pitiful.

OK I say.

◆　　　◆　　　◆　　　◆　　　◆　　　◆　　　◆

Train stops at Thirty-Fifth and we walk to State Street. It's only half a block. Clock on the Arcade Building, kitty-corner, says three o'clock. We turn the corner and walk over to the front of the theater. He holds out his hand.

Goodbye.

I turn away, start walking up State Street.

Come on he says. At least shake.

Don't want to I say.

We're going to see each other again.

No we ain't. Never.

Yes we are. When the police come.

Aw get off that stuff I say. You've been bullying me all day and all night with it but I ain't taking it no more. You're just full of it. Ain't no police going to come for me, and I start walking again.

Right he says and takes a deep breath. That is, if we could find my grandpa's silver thing. But you know what? I think we can.

What? What crazy stuff you talking about now?

He jerks his thumb toward the theater. Let's look in there.

You're out of your mind I tell him.

I bet he just lost it he says. I bet he lost it in his office. All we got to do is go in there and find it. Then you're in the clear. Come on he says. One last try.

How are we going to get in?

Your mom has a key.

◆　　◆　　◆　　◆　　◆　　◆　　◆

We get to the building, I open the front door and let him in. Hallway smells like fried pork. He asks why there ain't no lights in the hall. Tell him we ain't had hall lights for a year now. We climb upstairs in the dark and I stick my key in the door.

Don't come in, I whisper to him. *You'll hit something and wake them up. I know where everything is. I'll get it out of her bag without turning on the light. You just stay here.*

He stands in the doorway like I told him to do and I listen for Darius snoring but I don't hear nothing. Look around in the light coming in from the street and the cots are empty—no Darius, no Nubby. So I tiptoe over to their room and push open the door a crack. They ain't here neither.

Ain't no one here I whisper.

Can you turn on a light? he whispers back.

I reach up and pull the string and the light comes on.

Jeez he says. It's so small.

What you mean small? We got a bedroom ain't we? That's more than my friends got.

Yeah but there's no kitchen. The stove and the icebox are all in this room. What's that?

Coal stove.

What for?

To keep warm in winter, fool.

You mean no radiators? You got to bring your own coal? Up the stairs?

That or freeze.

I've got my own bedroom he says. And Mom and Dad have one and Beth has one too. He looks embarrassed.

He says Where is everyone?

Must be over at the church I say. Looking for me.

Who lives here?

We all do.

But where?

On them cots. Me and my brothers sleep there. Momma and Poppa get the bedroom. But if they're at the church, she'll be having her keys with her.

Look in the bedroom he says.

It ain't going to be there I say.

I said look in the bedroom. Now. He's got a tone in his voice I ain't never heard before.

I open the bedroom door and turn on the light and glory be, there's her ring of keys, sitting on the nightstand.

We're in luck I say. Let's go.

◆   ◆   ◆   ◆   ◆   ◆   ◆

We get back to the theater but it's too dark so I got to try every key until one works and I open the glass doors. We dast not turn on no lights but we can see a little from the light from the street. There's the candy stand, the hollow post where Mack the usher throws the torn ticket stubs, and the door to the old man's office. Got to try all the keys all over again until one opens the office door. We go inside and he reaches up for the light pull, but I tell him not to pull on it until I shut the door tight. So they can't see no light from the street.

Look in the desk first he says.

We open the top drawer. Some paper clips, a bunch of pencils, a receipts pad with purple carbon paper between the sheets, and a prescription from a dentist.

It ain't there I tell him.

Open the next one he says.

This here drawer is filled with notes and files. We pull them out and spread them on top of his desk, get them out of the way so Steve can reach into the back of the drawer. He feels around, says he don't think there's anything else inside it but he ain't sure. So he pulls out the whole drawer and turns it upside-down on the floor. He's right. Ain't nothing else in it.

He don't even bother opening the bottom drawer, just yanks it out and flips it over onto the floor. What he don't know is there's a glass paperweight inside. It hits the floor and shatters into a million pieces. Into the corners, under the desk, everywhere.

Oh lordy I say.

It's not here he says.

No and we got to put everything back now too. What's going to happen when he finds this glass?

It's *got* to be here he says. We didn't look on this shelf. Come on!

But I hold up my hand. Wait. Thought I heard something.

He listens. You're nuts he says.

No. Listen.

We both hold our breath, don't make a sound, and then he hears it too. It's the sound of the glass outer doors, opening.

King of the Ethiopian Hebrews

Let me see, what time it be, believe it's three, I got to pee.

No one out here. Only time in the whole week, Sunday night past midnight, even the whores gone home. Got all the keys to all the locks. Got State Street to myself. Pee on the wall.

Wait, no, I ain't alone neither. What are them church folks doing with the lights on? Ain't singing tonight like usual. Just standing around talking, big frowns on their faces. And— and— there's some white folks too. What's going on in there? Well, ain't no business of mine. I got my job to do.

Do it right here, here in the rear where there's nothing to fear. Chitterling store. Sweetbreads and beans. All the meat's put away, still smells awful in here. Lock her up quick.

Howdy Miss Thelma, checking up on you too tonight. You got your cash register locked? Don't smell so good in here neither. Ultra Nadinola and lye. Walk around with a sock on your head looking like a fool. None of that conk stuff for me. I am the Emperor, wear my hair long like the lions do.

Goodbye Thelma see you soon, going to visit this saloon. Drink all night 'til dawn's early light. Got them a four o'clock license.

No, no drink for me, I do not partake of intoxicants. Don't you know who I am? Got to stay pure, pure so no cure.

You got no call to say that. I ain't no crazier than you. Got me an honest job. Folks give me good money to stay up all night, watch their businesses. You don't want no crooks stealing your substance do you? Steal your wealth, steal in stealth, wealth and pelf.

Yes thank you, I don't mind a sausage. Tasty. Much obliged. Now I got to go. Good night to you.

Mmm, smells good in here anyway. Karmel Karmel Karmelkorn, take me a box sure as I'm born. They can't sell it tomorrow, ain't fresh no more. Let them spare me this box tonight.

Where is my key, here it be. Lock her up. Click and lock and take a walk, walk on out to the street of dreams, you'll never know how nice it seems or just how much it really means. Rather be in Africa though, sitting on my golden throne, Golden Rule, do unto others 'til you play them the fool.

These glass doors stick every time.

Ah. Dark in here like velvet. Wonderful dark. Darkest place on State Street. I can open my eyes wide and still not see nothing. I know that screen's right up there in front of me all big and white but I can't even see it nohow. Watch the movie in the dark dark dark.

Close my eyes now, make them voices go away. Bad men cussing and spitting, spitting and hitting, hitting and shitting. Just making trouble for themselves. I could see it sure as I'm born and me just eleven years old. Smart little boy. Bend over, you smart little boy, I'll give you something to make you smart.

Wasn't no more trouble after they let Marcus out. They saw the crown on my head at last. Let me out too, just like that. Get on out of here they said. Called me a crazy nigger. Day like any other day. Walk on out, twenty years gone by and it ain't nothing. Ain't nothing to them. Poppa dead, Momma gone, airplanes up in the sky and everyone driving a Ford. Ain't nothing to them, no no.

Walk to Detroit in my prison shoes, talk to Mister Henry Ford, show him the car I invented, Prison Car going to take me far. Ford Ford, you are lord, but I got me a golden sword. Hidden where you can't see it.

Told me can't walk to Detroit. No one walks to Detroit, you got to go where this boxcar takes you. Just get in and shut up. Shut the fuck up or I'll fuck you up. Man in the Moon said no no no. Voice gave him the warning, he should have paid heed, now he's in need because I done the deed. Smote him down, lying across that campfire in Paducah.

Jumped back on the boxcar and hid behind the pallets where the railroad police don't look. And they call me crazy, hunh! It was so dark dark dark when that door slammed, almost like in here, so dark and sweet I didn't mind the clank clank clank. Three days without a drink of water but nothing can harm me. I rule a nation, a people, a world.

Then it got light, so light and bright, white white Whiting it's so delighting, be in Indiana where there ain't no fighting. Two little pickaninnies grinning down from their white white tower. Got the Gold Dust Twins here, sidetracked on a siding in Whiting with the Emperor of All the Africas. Twins got the gold, didn't leave no gold for me.

Twins told it to me, said go to State Street Joseph. Oh go to that home where the colored folk roam and the deer and the antelope play. Just walk down that track and you'll never come back, ain't no one to get in your way.

Movie starting now. From the Hole of Hell to the Golden Throne, starring His Imperial Majesty, Clark Kent and Vivien Leigh. Cast of thousands, slaves to love and passion, slaves in chains, slave children, got to do what the bad nigger wants. Frankly nigger I don't give a damn. I'll kill you Marcus, kill you like I killed that Paducah nigger. Strike you dead with a bolt of lightning from my golden scepter sword.

You couldn't harm me because of my pow pow power. I found out the secret Marcus. Right in front of my eyes. Just stare at the wall and there it is. Little old spider crack in the brick but the Man in the Moon showed me the wedge, opens to a secret path, opens to the Path to the Moon. Now the secret is, you got to stare at it a long time. Dast not blink or that passageway shuts up just like someone poured alum on it.

Stared and stared 'til I couldn't feel my eyes no more. That's when the crack separated and the Path appeared, gold and glowing. Open it any time, force it open with my pow pow power until the golden beam shines through, blinding bright, and I take my seat, ascend the jeweled throne, raise my golden scepter high, bless the multitudes scattering their flowers.

No one else comes through that crack. Not Marcus, not no one. But I would let you through, Momma. Hold me in your bosom right here where it's dark and warm and safe, forever.

What was that?

There. I heard it again. Sounds like scraping. Maybe it's rats.

No. Too loud. Better go look.

Well. Light's on in the office. Where's my golden scepter? Flashlight will do. Got me a robber I do believe.

◆　　◆　　◆　　◆　　◆　　◆　　◆

All right you. You stay right where you are. I got you trapped in there. Don't you move a hair. I'm coming in.

Lord God Almighty. I must be seeing things. Couple of children. Look at this mess you made. What are you doing in here? What's going on?

Why you ain't no older than I was when— when— something happened. What was it? Fell down in a ditch, pitched into a ditch, pitched a perfect game, batted a thousand, batted zero, struck out, went to jail. Went directly to jail.

You two arc going to jail too if you don't tell me what you're doing in here. I am the Emperor of Ethiopia, the great Selassie, lord of the Amhara and the Tigre and the Galla and them Falasha too. I got dungeons of my own, hundreds. Lock up your little butts like they locked up mine.

Oh no no no, Marcus won't hurt you in there. Never let that happen to you boys, don't you worry. Nobody's going to touch your baby blue butts.

Who's he? He's the bad boogie man with the boogie-woogie plan, tried to boogie with my woogie while I'm hiding in the can. Don't you go to no jail now, hear? Bad men in jail. But but but, you're in here stealing and I got got got to send you to jail jail jail, can't make no bail can't get no mail can't tell no tale. Only they didn't say nothing about no kids. Colored and white, ain't it a sight, two little boys sneaking in in the night.

Don't you lie to me. You ain't lost nothing in here. You, white boy, don't tell me you been in this theater before. Ain't no white folks come to this theater excepting maybe the owner.

He's your granddaddy? Bless my soul.

Lost? Silver? Got letters in Hebrew? I am the king of the Hebrews, the Ethiopian Hebrews, the lost tribe, we will find it together my brethren. Take my golden flashlight, get down on your hands and knees, look high look low, look where the rats and the mice don't go. Look in this drawer, put it on the floor, now look some more, pore through a drawer.

I see pencils, I see rings, I don't see no silver things.

So why'd you tell a lie? Why'd you lie to the Emperor?

What about you, Blue Butt? Knew a boy once, looked just like you. Boy name of Joseph. Had a butt of blue but his heart was true. Now he's a king somewhere in Africa. What are you doing here with this white child, Blue Butt? You an Ethiopian Hebrew?

Oh, church across the street. Now I get it. Well, your folks are all over there, some black and some white, looking a fright, crying together at church in the night. Wondered why they were there. Now I can see, makes sense to me, they're looking for babies who're trying to flee. Guess you don't go to jail after all. Get on up. Got to march you off right now. March you off to your mommas and poppas. March you off to Jesus.

◆   ◆   ◆   ◆   ◆   ◆   ◆

You be careful crossing this street, hear? We're in the middle of the block, jay jay jaywalking, ain't no cars but there's lots of bars, and one little church right over there.

Howdy folks, got some children here, some boys. Bad bad boys, didn't make no noise, broke into the theater for some silver toys. Telling me a tale but it ain't no sale, got to put them in jail where they're bound to fail.

I've been in jail too so I know. Long long time ago. Weren't no more than a boy my own self. Had a momma of my own back then. That was when I lived in heaven with the Man in the Moon. Had me a momma in the fields of cotton, things were good 'til they got rotten, sent away, went away, gone to stay.

Them boys are OK, I didn't hurt them none. They're just little boys—little boys someplace they weren't supposed to be. Sure you can have them ma'am. But stop that crying. Please—it hurts to hear it, hurts to hear you cry, cry for a child, meek and mild, sweet little boy but he's been defiled.

You ain't the momma? Why the tears? You're someone's momma, can't fool me. You're the momma of—of—someone I used to know.

Now don't you go hugging on me. Ain't no one hugged me since—since—since ... was a woman once. Big woman just like you, handkerchief on her head too, hugged me day and night. But I ain't seen her since—since ... since a long long time ago, back before Marcus, down in the ditch where the bad thing happened. Three little children, playing by the track, bad thing happened, only two come back. Children just like these here. White boy, black boy, blue boy. I cried on that day too. So many years and now there's no way to get it back, never.

I'll go now. Good night folks. Good night to you too old lady. Give me one more hug.

To Love Mercy

I knew Poppa was going to want to whale the tar out of me. I knew what Momma would be doing too. She'd be crying, saying that old stuff about how come I never do like she tells me. I expected all that. Didn't expect no white folks.

There they are though, right inside our church. I don't recall white folks there before, ever. One with the glasses must be Steve's father. I'm guessing since I only seen him once in my life and that was in the dark. And the lady with the pearls around her neck, she must be Steve's momma.

But that little old granddaddy—now I know I seen him before. Not just that night in the parking lot neither. I seen him a dozen times, hanging around at the Calumet. He's the one is Momma's boss.

Momma says he's always been OK to her but I don't see how that's possible, kind of things he's saying now.

It's hard to make out what they're all talking about, they're raising so much of a fuss. Momma is sitting in one of them little folding chairs moaning and carrying on. She don't even see me at first with her head in her hands. When she finally looks up, old Sister Dora's already gotten to me.

Sister Dora goes down on her knees and, gol-darnedest thing, she scoops me up and Steve too! She goes squeezing us together so we're cheek to cheek like little babies. Sister Dora is hugging us so hard she like to knock out my breath. She's saying Oh sugar child I'm so glad you're OK and I'm thinking, She ain't talking to me.

I try to shake free but she's big and strong and she ain't done with us. This is getting embarrassing, big old lady suffocating me here down on the floor. I just want to get this over with. Take my licking, send me to reform school if they want to, I don't care. Just do it and be done with it. But I see it ain't going to be so easy.

You're going to have to tell these people the truth she's saying, and now I'm sure she's talking to Steve. She's saying, I told them about you coming down on the streetcar, I had to, couldn't keep your secret no more because you let me down, you went and ran off with Jesse. Stuff like that. And she's got tears in her eyes, like she's asking him to forgive her.

Then Steve says back to her, I'm sorry Dora I didn't mean to get you in trouble. Get her in trouble? And how does he go calling her Dora like he's known her all his life? Don't make no sense.

Then the old guy, the granddaddy, him and Poppa get into it. The old guy goes waving his fist in the air and carrying on about that silver thing of his, you'd think it was the Bob Hope diamond. He's saying he's going to put me in the pokey, guess he means jail, and calling me all kind of names.

Make your son give it up he says.

Poppa looks at me. I don't say nothing. I already swore on the Holy Bible, ain't I? What's he want me to do, swear something different?

Old Steve is over to one side raising a ruckus. He didn't he didn't he didn't he's shouting. He's jumping up and down but ain't nobody paying him no mind. He ought to know by now what grownups are like.

See what's in his pockets, old man says.

I turn them out. I still got four dollars and eighty cents from Riverview.

See, the old man says, he pawned it and that's all that's left over.

No no no Steve's yelling, but ain't no point trying to explain things to these folks, least not in the midst of this commotion.

Where'd you get all that money then, Poppa asks.

I don't even open my mouth. They wouldn't believe me nohow. Got a grownup says you're stealing, how you going to prove you ain't? Fact he's white just makes it harder to prove, don't it?

Poppa raises his hand to me. Maybe I ought to just tell them I done it and get this over with, I'm thinking. They'll send me to St. Charles. That ain't so awful. Witchie's brother's been in St. Charles for a year now and Witchie says he'd rather it were him. Got a school but they don't even make his brother go. No school? And three squares a day? Shoot—that'd be OK for a year or two.

Old man don't give me a chance though. All right he says, where's your phone? You can't get him to talk, I'm bringing the cops down here right now.

No no Grandpa he ain't done nothing Steve says. I done it.

At last he figured out how to get their attention. Everyone shuts up.

He didn't take no silver thing Steve says. I took it.

I knew Steve was a dumb-ass but this beats all. *Shut up you fool* I whisper, *this ain't going to make it no better. Shut up yourself* he whispers back.

He says it again. I stole it. And then I lost it. Lost it on the El. So it's gone and you ain't never going to see it again. So you can stop picking on my friend here.

Steve's momma says, Who you calling your friend? Seems she's more worried about the friend part than the I stole it part.

Then the granddaddy says to Steve, Why you trying to protect this little nigger thief? When he says that word, man, everyone goes nuts.

Poppa starts shouting at him, You'd best not talk that way, you'd best shut your fucking mouth. Never heard Poppa use that word before. Never.

Wait James honey wait oh please wait stop. It's Momma. She's on her feet, pulling and tugging at Poppa and the old man too. Shush up James shush up he's my boss you got to shush up honey baby. Mister Feinberg he didn't mean nothing by it, he's got a bad temper but he's a good Christian man, he didn't mean nothing oh please please please. She's crying and laughing at the same time, but mostly crying. I never saw anyone cry and laugh at once. It's something awful scary.

Poppa pushes her away. That vein in his forehead, it's standing out a mile.

He starts in about Jew movie theaters and Jew grocery stores and Jew dry cleaners and a lot of other Jew stuff I didn't know nothing about. Says thirty pieces of silver wasn't enough for the Jews, they had to come down to Bronzeville and take more from the colored. Poppa seems to know more about Jews than he ever let on to me.

Old man ain't sitting still for that though. Says, weren't for Jews, wouldn't be no stores on State Street. Wouldn't be no N-Double-A, wouldn't be no Urban League. Says, weren't for this here Jew, wouldn't be no job for your wife neither. Jews are the best friend the colored man's got he says. About the only friend he says.

Then all them grownups go to shouting at once and I can't make out no more of what any of them are saying. Sister Dora starts to singing hymns. I look at Steve. He looks at me. Let's get on out of here I say. We cut for the screen door and run.

◆   ◆   ◆   ◆   ◆   ◆   ◆

Outside on State Street, the streetlights are still on but the sky's starting to get a little pink. There's a few cars and a few folks going to work. First time I been up all night. Funny I ain't sleepy.

Come on Steve says. I'm going to show you the

lake.

We walk over Thirty-Fifth Street past Michigan, Indiana, South Park Way. I ain't never crossed South Park before except one time to go to the Regal to see Pigmeat Markham, it was Poppa's birthday. We get to this bridge over train tracks, lots of them. There's a sign says Illinois Central and steps going down to a platform. We get to the top of the bridge and that's when I seen it for the first time.

We run that last block to the water. There are big rocks we got to jump over, then we land in the soft sand. Both of us fall down in it and start rolling over, punching each other, horsing around. He gets on top, we roll over, I get on top, we roll over again. He throws a pile of sand at me, I kick it back in his face. He's laughing. I'm laughing too.

Then he says Stop. He holds up a hand and points out over the water.

All that's out there is water and sky and where they meet it's on fire. The clouds are like bars of flame where the sun touches them, then orange, then yellow, then blue and purple on up higher. The edge of the sun where it's coming out of the water is so bright it hurts to look. But I can't take my eyes off it.

We watch until we can't look at it no more. Beautifullest thing I ever seen.

We get up and start walking. It's too hard walking in the sand so we take off our shoes and socks and leave them behind. We go over where the sand is wet and it's easier to walk on, and the waves splash up and cool my toes.

Look he says and he points toward downtown. I can see all them big buildings right across the water, the sun making them like they're set on fire, and they look so close you want to reach out and touch them. But I never saw them from home, even though it's only a mile.

He says What are you going to do now?

I don't know I say. Can't go back to Momma and Poppa like nothing happened.

Me neither he says.

You shouldn't of tried to tell them you stole that silver thing I say.

I just wanted to protect you. He gives me a little smile, shy-like.

You know, that silver thing ain't never going to turn up. He nods.

And he ain't never going to believe it wasn't me who took it.

He nods again. It don't matter he says. I know you didn't take it.

You know the only thing I'm sorry about?

I shake my head.

I'm sorry I never did get to see it. His own grand-daddy made it for him. He was going to give it to me when I got bigger.

Your granddaddy is a mean man I say.

No he ain't Steve says. You don't know him. Then he starts singing this song I ain't never heard before, *Casey would waltz with a strawberry blonde* ...

Why are you singing?

That's what my granddaddy used to sing to me

when I was little. He'd put me up on his knee and sing that song and rock me back and forth. He took me fishing for the first time at the lagoon in Jackson Park. I caught a perch and he showed me how to get it off the hook. He's the one taught me how to catch a ball.

Didn't teach you too good.

Well, so you helped fix it.

We walk on a little more. Sun's up more now and the sky's going from orange to real bright, yellow and white. There's white on the tops of the waves and white birds I ain't never seen circling in the air going skaw! skaw!

How do you know Sister Dora?

She's the maid he says.

What do you mean, maid?

She takes care of us. Cleans house. Makes dinner. Gets me and Beth off to school. Sometimes she sleeps over.

She loves you.

Steve just smiles.

And my momma works for your granddaddy. Ain't that something. Almost like we're kinfolk.

What's kinfolk?

Relations. Cousins. Family.

We walk on a little more. He picks up a shell, looks like a picture in my science book. Here he says. Put it up to your ear. Can you hear the sea?

Naw I say, can't hear nothing.

You're supposed to be able to hear the sea he says. Give me it. He holds it up to his own ear. You're right he says, ain't no sea in there. Why do they tell us stuff like that?

Grownups go telling you all kinds of stuff that ain't true I say.

Yeah he says. Like about us.

I nod.

Would you come see me ever?

Naw. After I went on home, your momma and poppa'd be checking to see what's missing.

He nods, looks sad. You think I could come down and see you?

They ain't going to let you.

I know it he says. They probably won't even let me come to the Calumet again.

Not unless you become colored I say.

He nods again. Yeah he says, I'm figuring that out. You ever wish you were white instead of colored?

I start to laugh. Come on boy, why in the world would I want to be white?

Seems easier.

Wouldn't be for me. I'd have to say goodbye to my friends. I'd have to go to Jew church. You don't even like it so why would I?

Naw you could still be a Christian. I know lots of Christians at school and they're white too.

I look at him. Don't look like he's kidding.

I ask him, Would you want to be a Christian?

Sometimes he says. There's a lot more of them than you think and there's not very many Jews at all. Being Jewish is complicated.

Yeah, same with Christians I say. You got to remember a lot. Only part that's simple is the Golden Rule.

What's it say?

Do unto others as you would have them do unto you.

He thinks about it. It's confusing the first time. I had to think about it a couple minutes too until I figured it out, with all them unto's.

You know what it said on my grandpa's thing? I shake my head.

It said you got to do justice and love mercy. It ain't exactly the same but it's good too. To love mercy.

I look at him standing there and I think about that hurtful thing he did at Riverview. But heck, I ain't perfect. Look at that time I took Grover's ball, the one with Dave Philley's autograph on it. Grover like to killed me if he could but that just made it more fun to keep. Weren't for Poppa's sermon next day I'd still have that ball. Do unto others as you would have them do unto you. After services I gave Grover back his ball. Daggone Jesus sure makes you feel guilty sometimes.

Well I say, what are we going to do?

I just want to know how it's going to be for you. If I ain't never going to see you again.

I been thinking I say. Thinking about getting me a job after school. Get a job delivering *The Defender*. I'm going to get a job, save up lots of money and go back to Riverview.

He smiles. Wish I could come too he says.

I ain't taking no one but Momma and Poppa. Not Nubby, not Darius, just Momma and Poppa. Show them what I saw. Buy them cotton candy and rainbow ice. Go on the Parachute Jump this time. I'll have enough money that we can go on all the rides. Anybody says we got to leave the park because we're colored, I'll just show them my money and tell them to shut up.

He asks me, What about when you get older?

I been thinking about that too I say. Maybe I'll go to DeVry and learn how to fix radios. Lots of folks got radios, don't know how to fix them, but sometimes it's easy. You just stick in a new tube. I'd like it if I could take some man's radio, know which tube and stick it in, then the man got to pay me five bucks and say thanks. Five bucks and he's got to say, Thanks you did a great job on my radio. What about you?

I don't know he says. I'll go back home and go to school, same as always. I'd tell my friends about this but they wouldn't believe it.

Maybe you shouldn't tell them then. It ain't always better. Sometimes it's good to have something that's just yours.

Yeah he says. Mine and yours.

We better go back I say. They'll be looking for us.

We get our shoes and socks and climb back over the rocks. Near the sidewalk, man's waxing his car. He's got the radio on loud, WCFL I think, one of them sports shows. Steve stops.

That's the game he says. They're talking about the game.

What game?

The one last Tuesday night. You should of seen it. Extra innings. First time the White Sox won in weeks.

I say, None of this would of happened if you hadn't gone to that game.

Yeah he says. That would of been too bad.

Yeah. It would of.

Then he says, You want to go to a game some time? I mean, just us?

They'd find out I say.

He shakes his head. No they wouldn't he says. I'd lie.

How much does it cost?

I don't know. My dad pays or my grandpa. I'm just a kid.

I say, Not no more you ain't.

When we get to the train bridge he says, So long.

What do you mean, So long?

You walk back there by yourself he says. I can get home from here.

What are you talking about boy?

I'll take the train he says. I've done it before with my mom. I think I know how. If Mom and Dad are still in the church, just tell them I'll be waiting for them at home. Can you loan me a quarter?

Old Steve, he's just standing there looking more raggedy than ever, with sand on his pants and his hair all messed up. But he's got a big grin on his face.

I reach in my pocket for a quarter. You all take care now I tell him. His grin gets bigger and he sticks out his hand.

You going to shake this time?

Sure, I say.

Afterword

I am white; most of the characters in this novel are black. I grew up in the relatively comfortable, white, heavily Jewish environs of Hyde Park; most of the characters in this novel existed in relative poverty in the all-black neighborhood known variously as the Black Belt or Bronzeville.

In the 1940s, most white Chicagoans knew Bronzeville as a place they didn't want to go at night—nor in daytime, for that matter. But to the black Chicagoans who lived there, it was a warm and welcoming place, full of life and excitement, the center of black culture —Chicago's Harlem.

When I began writing this novel, I thought I had some knowledge of Bronzeville. As a young boy, I hung out at the States Theatre, which my grandfather Nathan Joseph owned and operated for fifty years, located in the very heart of Bronzeville at Thirty-Fifth and State. And from age six to age ten, I was in effect raised by a Bronzevillian, our "maid" Dora Winfield of Sunflower, Mississippi. Her voice is in my bones.

But when I tried to write about Bronzeville, I discovered how little I really knew. I read books, including the classic Black Metropolis by Horace Cayton and St. Clair Drake, and James Grossman's enlightening Land of Hope: Chicago, Black Southerners, and the Great Migration. But books weren't enough. I needed to hear people's voices.

253

By great good luck, I discovered the transcripts and tapes of the Douglas-Grand Boulevard Neighborhood Oral History Project at the Chicago Historical Society. From this 1995 archive come the voices of Timuel D. "Tim" Black, Charles Branham, Junius "Red" Gaten, Marion Hummons, Samuel Stevens and Delores Washington.

By greater luck still, I connected with half a dozen individuals who grew up and lived around Thirty-Fifth and State during the forties and fifties, and interviewed them on tape. Lillie Harston-Thomas and the late Bunny Dallas could have been Jesse Owens Trimble's schoolmates; Enich Hymon and Harvey Lee his younger brothers; Gladys McKinney a young aunt; and William Williams an older uncle. Their generosity in sharing their experiences informs this novel.

These are the voices you are about to hear.

—Frank S. Joseph

Woman sweeping while man delivers milk.

Coming Up North

William M. Williams

[William M. Williams was eighty-six years old when I interviewed him. The following events occurred in Jonestown, Mississippi, when Williams was about seven years old. His father was a sharecropper who worked land owned by "Mr. MacArthur."]

Mr. MacArthur wanted to take the wagon for the next day: My father said no, he could have it after we took the wagon to the [cotton] gin. He got angry, came over to whip my father. That's when the trouble started.

I had a fourteen-year-old brother, I never saw him miss nothing he shot at. Mr. MacArthur struck my father. When he did that, my brother cocked both barrels to blow his head off. My mother knocked the gun up. That's all that saved him [MacArthur].

[MacArthur] went home, got on the phone and started forming a lynch mob. They said they weren't going to do nothing but whip my father, but they were going to lynch my brother. It so happened that one of the people he called, my first cousin, heard the message. She had living quarters behind the main house. They weren't paying her any attention. She went and told her husband, and her husband went to the rest of our boys. They got ready for action.

But my father and brother went into the woods. They went through the woods until they got to my aunt's house [twelve or fifteen miles away]. The mob came to the house looking for my uncle too, but he was up the creek, in the yard, hiding. When they left, he came down the same time my brother and my father walked up.

They told him they wanted to go to the other little town and catch a train. He told them no, no train — they'd have the mob lined up from one little stop to the other, and they'd search the train. So my father and brother walked through the forest and across the fields until they got to the river between them and Helena, Arkansas. A ferry boat goes across there, they called it Trotters Landing, and that's how they got across. Then they caught a train. And when they stopped, they were in Hayti, Missouri. That's where I grew up at.

Gladys McKinney

When we came in [from Louisiana] and I saw the light in the station, I got so excited! I remember the conductor calling out the name [Chicago], and she [my mother] got us all together, all of us standing on the platform, and I saw the light and the people just rustling, hustling and bustling. That's when I saw my aunt, my mother's only living sister, who had sent for us.

She had gotten us a place—a cold-water flat. At that time they didn't have [central] heat. You had a potbelly stove. My brother got burned pretty bad because he banged into it. It sat right in the middle of the floor. And we cooked on it.

The stove used coal. You'd get the coal off the coal truck. Then you'd have the icebox, you had to go catch the iceman, get the block of ice and lift it. The bedrooms weren't heated. She'd leave the door open and the heat from the potbelly stove would heat the bedrooms.

Streets Paved with Gold

Marion Hummons

My uncle wrote and said to come to Chicago because in the North, especially in Chicago, the streets were paved with gold.

Newsboy selling The Chicago Defender, *a leading Negro newspaper.*

Junius "Red" Gaten

You see, life was not easy, but coming from the South where you was burdened down, you were afraid to talk... if you was on the sidewalk white folks come by, you got to get off, get in the mud. Here we had a little freedom. And it meant so much just to be free and to be able to make your own living and spend your money like you see fit. Because you didn't have that when I was a boy down South.

Harvey Lee

Over there by the trains they had coal stoves, but we had steam. I used to have to get up at six in the morning to get some wood, because it's cold in the morning and it's dark. People used to get up in the morning and have their fences be gone.

Enich Hymon

I'd hear stories about people living on the South Side, there is always an electrician in the crowd. Your lights get turned off? There's always somebody who knows how to hook it up to the third rail [of the El]. They had some guys around there that were *good*.

Lillie Harston-Thomas

We would have vegetable dinners a lot. There was more boiling of foods at that time. You'd have cabbage, candied yams, cornbread, that type of thing, and use the meat just to season it. We ate a lot of beans during that time too. Put them in a pot and boiled them with the meat. [Some people might call it] a bean soup; we called them just beans. You'd use bacon as your sea-

soning, or salt pork. Sunday was chicken. Fried, smothered down with gravy, rice, biscuits, vegetables. But
when you speak in terms of having a steak—no.
Chicken was like steak. That was special.

Timuel D. "Tim" Black

[D]uring the Depression ... a thing called kitchenettes began to come up. [A "kitchenette" was an]
apartment [that] would be cut up....Because we couldn't
move around, we had to double up, triple up, in terms
of our housing. And so an apartment like this might
wind up being three apartments rather than one, three
apartments. Although you would pay as much rent as
you would for one apartment, but you couldn't move
anywhere.

The neighborhood was a black metropolis. And
what made it a metropolis because it had everything that
is necessary to survive in a metropolitan area. We had
jobs; we had entertainment; although the housing was
very overcrowded, we had housing.... Although most of
the men worked in places like the steel mill and the
stockyards, but once they came—once they left and came
to the black metropolis, the South Side—they didn't have
to go back out to enjoy themselves.

Marion Hummons

Who's this girl [Lorraine Hansberry], she wrote
Raisin in the Sun? Her father, they had real estate and
everything and he was buying up all of the property. He
was the original one who started cutting up all these
beautiful apartments and making them into kitchenettes, where if you had an apartment with nine rooms,

An alley between tenements.

you'd take the closet and put in a little stove and a sink. Then the Jews began to notice there was money in that, so then they'd buy up the rest of the stuff and they just ruined the whole South Side with these kitchenettes.

But it was the black man, Lorraine Hansberry's daddy, that started that.

Charles Branham

[I]n the Twenties, this area, this Douglas Park/ Grand Boulevard area, was the black business and political capital of America and was so recognized. The reality is that with Oscar DePriest, who became the first black congressman from a northern state; with [anti-lynching and women's rights advocate] Ida B. Wells, who is certainly the most important black woman, I would argue, in the twentieth century; with Jesse Binga, who founded the first state-chartered black bank; with Robert S. Abbott, whose *Chicago Defender* is the greatest black newspaper and certainly was the first national black newspaper; Chicago represented business accomplishment. And so in 1928 when the NAACP gave... its highest award to [cosmetics entrepreneur] Anthony Overton ... it was not so much for Anthony Overton as a recognition of black Chicago as the black business capital of the world.

Junius "Red" Gaten

[S]egregation kept us together. It helped us out during the Depression. Because we had to stay together. ... There wasn't any relief for us. The Catholic Charities went to Catholic people. If you were a Catholic or a black Catholic, you had to be in pretty good shape with the priest for you to get anything. And United Charities was for the white people, and they got whatever they had. We Negroes banded together. You had this house, you had three or four families in it. ... Somebody worked. Somebody had a job or somebody was getting a little something. So you put yourself together and this was the way we made it. And we had a lot of fun doing it. We wasn't fighting or killing one another like you're doing now.

Growing Up

Lillie Harston-Thomas
Your doors were left open. You weren't concerned about somebody coming trying to steal or anything like that ... It was a safe area to come up in.

Enich Hymon
I think I was about eight years old the time I cut school. My father had bought me one of them Daisy BB pistols, so I got that, me and my cousin went back over to Lake Shore Drive and set up bottles. We didn't know that, when we were missing the bottles, we had damaged about thirteen cars. We saw the police coming and my cousin started running. So he's ahead of me, he says, "Man, they're coming this way!"

The officers scared us. They said, "By the time you get out of jail, all your friends will be grown and married and half of them is dead." When I got home that evening, everything was on television, something about juvenile delinquents. "They're coming to get you any time," my family said. "Now, eat all you can, because when you go to jail you ain't going to be eating!" And I never cut school no more.

Bunny Dallas

Back then a kid might say, "Could I watch your car?" I look at it now and it was really a type of extortion, but we didn't know this back then. We used to always wonder why they [whites] would pay us to watch their cars, because nothing would happen to them. And you know what? We would watch those cars!

It was a job. I never felt like any of those [white] people felt threatened or were frightened of us. I guess they just did it because we asked them and they figured, "What the heck."

Enich Hymon

I used to go to Arkansas by myself the last Friday in June. They had the Illinois Central railroad station right there on Twelfth Street. They had what they call Travelers Aid, I had my name right here [points to his chest], designation of where I was going. I started when I was about six years old. I did that every summer. Went back to school the day after Labor Day. One of my parents used to come down to get me every year because I didn't want to come back here.

I did that every year until that guy Emmett Till got killed. Then my parents didn't want me to go down there. But I loved it down there.

Everything down in the South is different. People are more friendly. I always sat in back of the bus driver, and the bus driver would have a conversation with me. Maybe I was just lucky, me being so young, seven, eight, nine, but several times, when I wasn't tall enough to get up to the water fountain, whites held me up to get water.

Lillie Harston-Thomas

I had to be very selective as far as my friends were concerned, and bring them into the house where they could be scrutinized. At one point, we were trying to form a club and one of the boys came over to the house. The minute my brother walked in, he said to my parents, "What is that one doing here?" That boy had been with a group of guys who had jumped on my brother at one point. So I had to pull away from that in a discreet manner. We never wanted our parents to look on us with any disdain. We were very concerned as to what our parents thought of us.

Enich Hymon

At the dances, they patted the boys, so if you had a knife, you gave your girlfriend the knife because they never did search the girls. There'd be a fistfight every now and then.

Sandlot baseball.

Harvey Lee

But we didn't believe in no guns. You get caught with a gun when I was coming up, you definitely were going to jail for a long time.

Discipline

Lillie Harston-Thomas

Dad would only hit you a couple of times, but Mom, she kept it stored. She would tell you, "This is for last week" as she was swinging, then, "This is for the week before last when I told you blah-blah-blah."

Enich Hymon

I was about seven years old. My momma was the treasurer of the church and they were saving money to get the preacher a pulpit. She had a big old can, had two or three dollars in it. I'm slick. I put four or five washers in there for the weight. It ain't dawned on me that eventually they're going to open this can.

I come home one day, there are four ladies sitting around a card table. I saw that can, and I heard my momma shake that can, I heard all those washers hit, Bang! Bang! Bang! She says, "Avi," I say, "Ma'am?", she says, "Bring it to me like you're coming into the world." I'm still slick. I put a spelling book in the back of my pants, you know? So she says, "That ain't the way you came into the world. You didn't have no pants on."

I say, "Momma, all these ladies!" But I had to take off all of my clothes. There was one, her name was Miss Bogessy, she got a ringside seat. She says, "Oh, I never saw no naked boys before." My momma put me in between her legs, wasn't anything but my naked butt is out. And she got to whupping me and she was crying. She says, "You don't lie. This hurts me." She's whupping *me*, and she's talking about this hurting *her*! For a whole month I slept on my stomach because I couldn't sleep on my back.

Gladys McKinney

I was out of high school when I started to date. My mother believed books and boys didn't mix. When I graduated from du Sable, all my friends were going downtown to the Blue Note [jazz club]. I thought I was going to go [but my mother wouldn't let me]. I stood out in front crying. She said, "You can cry all you want to. You stay in my house, I'm your mother, and you're not going."

I didn't get too many whippings. I was the oldest. My younger sister got a lot of whippings though. My mother didn't believe in whipping her children. But when she did, it would last a while. She'd whip you for everything you did, and also everything you did that you thought she forgot.

I had a very good childhood. I felt good about myself when I was coming up. Some of the things I used to see my friends and associates do, I used to wonder why my mother wouldn't let me do, but as I got older, I understood why she held a tight rein over me. When you walked out the door you had to tell her where you were going, leave a telephone number. I guess I picked that up from her. When I was raising my two grandkids, they had to have a telephone number and the name of where they were going to be. And I would always notice what they had on. I told them the reason I did that was, if anything happens to you and the police come to me, I can tell them what you were wearing and give them a general description.

Inside The States Theatre

[My grandfather, Nathan Joseph, owned and operated the States Theatre at 3507 South State Steet. In this novel, the States is the model for the Calumet.]

Bunny Dallas

They would show the double features, the cartoons, *The Perils of Pauline,* on Saturday. As teenagers we would go. Your feet would stick to the floor—it was just plain cement. Gum and candy, people dropping stuff. It was very sparse. You'd go downtown, you got all the plushness, but here the seats were wooden—I don't even think the seats had any padding. The bathrooms—! But this was our neighborhood theater, this was where we went, this is where we spent our money.

Lillie Harston-Thomas

My brother reminded me, "You remember we had to sit on a certain side of the show?" Where we lived, that was our side. Kids from other neighborhoods, they'd sit on the other side–that was their side, this was our side. If you wanted to fight, you'd go over to their side.

Bunny Dallas

I was six years old. I was a free spirit. I went to my aunt and told her I wanted to go to the show. This was, like, twelve noon. She said, "Who are you going to the show with?" I said I'm going with a little girl downstairs, Marie. But Marie was on punishment—she couldn't go anywhere—so I decided to go to the show by myself.

I go to the show, pay my money, and I sit in the middle between these two adult people. I watched this movie all day. I ate popcorn and candy all day. Until twelve o'clock at night.

My aunt sends my cousin to the show about six or seven o'clock because I should have been home. With me sitting between these two adults, my cousin, being a teenager, he half-looked and came back. He told my aunt he didn't see me. I came out of the show twelve o'clock at night—the last show.

And when I came out, my aunt was standing there, shaking. She snatched me—I think my arm was broken. Oh, was she mad! And by this time now I'm sick—my head is hurting from watching this movie and eating all that junk.

Lillie Harston-Thomas

My mom tells a story about going down once to the States Theatre. She seldom went to the show by herself but she went down this once. She was sitting in the back and some guy came and sat right beside her. She felt her skirt being pulled.

She didn't say a word—she just eased her hand into her purse. She had a little knife. She eased into that purse and opened that knife. Next time that guy's hand came over, she never turned around and looked at him, she just put that knife down on his hand. Eventually he had to ease his hand out from under that blade. When he got up, he got up holding his hand, because she had cut him.

Outside Along State Street

Delores Washington

[When she lived at 4725 South Michigan in the Courtway Building,] I remember across the street was the Rosenwald Building. That was where the blacks who had decent jobs lived. What I mean by that, we didn't call them blacks, we called them Negroes. That was where the highfalutin' Negroes lived. And most of them were what were the complexion of what we called high yellow. If you were dark, they wanted to know how did you get into the Rosenwald Building, because you knew they didn't want anybody black in the Rosenwald building. ... If you were a postman or you worked on a railroad or you were a schoolteacher or you had some other kind of job, like downtown in Marshall Field's, Carson's [Carson Pirie Scott; both prestigious department stores] wouldn't hire you unless you were a high yellow.

Harvey Lee

State Street was very busy. There'd be trucks coming down State—that was before they built the [Dan Ryan] Expressway, State Street was the truck route. You know what was right there [at Thirty-Ninth and

Statc]? Was a horse and buggy wagon where they sold watermelons and coal.

Enich Hymon
State Street was beautiful. Lake Meadows [a middle-class high-rise development farther east near Lake Michigan] didn't have anything on us. I was proud to live there.

William M. Williams
There was a guy named "Chicken Man" and he had that chicken do all kinds of tricks and the people would give him money. The people would laugh at him and throw dollar bills in his cup.

Enich Hymon
You remember Casey Jones? He had the chicken who'd drink beer? He'd say, "No dime no show."

This was out on the street, on State Street. And when that guy died, he owned half of King Drive, from Thirty-Fifth over about to Thirty-Seventh. Off his chicken. Give him a dime or a nickel. You just throw him something. He'd pour his chicken a glass of beer—it was a rooster—and he'd dance for you.

You'd see another guy, he'd eat glass. My "play mother" owned the Rainbow Lounge, that was on Thirty-Sixth and State, she'd see him coming, she'd shut the door, because if you didn't stop him he'd eat up all the glass. It was amazing. It didn't scare us. We would go get bottles for him to eat.

Delores Washington

Silvester Washington—he was like Mister Five by Five, you know, like Fats Waller, five feet tall by five feet wide. He had two guns so they called him Two-Gun Pete. He would get to the corner at night, he would say, "I want this corner." Boy, those little Negro boys, they'd get off that corner—they wouldn't give him any backtalk! He wasn't the only police officer—he was just a big black bad Negro cop. He was a bad Negro, OK? He said, "Let me have this corner," and those Negro boys got off that corner. All they had to say was "Two-Gun Pete!" and everybody scattered—gone, no questions asked.

Marion Hummons

You mentioned Two-Gun Pete. I knew his wife and his daughters. He was a very nice looking guy but he was the meanest, cruelest man. He would come down here and say, "Every living ass off the street." And I mean everybody faded. He had no compulsion, no pity, you couldn't say a word to him. He'd beat the people unmercifully. This fellow, a light-skinned guy with really pretty curly hair but he was an alcoholic, he didn't move fast enough so Two-Gun Pete beat the hell out of him. Somebody told his mother. The guy's head was bleeding and everything, and Two-Gun Pete beat that old lady, told her to get away. And that was her son!

The first time I ever saw Two-Gun Pete make a mistake—he let somebody hold the guns. That guy happened to be full of [dope]. He beat the hell out of Two-

Kangaroo court for juveniles.

Gun Pete. Anyway, the fella, whoever he was, he left town, because he would've been a dead duck if he ever came back.

When [Two-Gun Pete] quit [the police force], he got a place down here on Oakwood Boulevard across Cottage Grove, across Drexel, and opened up a tavern, married someone younger than his children. He had a collection of guns. He would always stand with his back to the wall, because he was scared. He had mistreated many people, and people don't forget. But he died—had a heart attack or something—so nobody got a chance to kill him.

Policy, or "The Numbers"

Bunny Dallas

My mother used to play [the illegal lottery known as] policy. My mother used to actually write the "book." Some man would come and collect. She won two hundred dollars one time on a nickel bet. I didn't think it was a vice. I didn't think anything of it.

Enich Hymon

There was this "Jukebox." I think it was the "Jukebox," something, because every policy wheel had a different name—there was the "Jukebox," the "Icebox," the "Five of Diamonds." My grandmomma told me to play it. I would tell her when I had a dream about something, and she would go to the dream book and get it.

I played four cents and I won six hundred-some dollars. I had just made that from the ragman. I was four or five years old.

The runner'd come to your house, come in the morning and evening, and you could bet anything you wanted—two cents. I didn't know it was crooked. I was just four years old. Everybody played it.

Gladys McKinney

I remember policy, because my mother used to write policy. She wrote for the "Windy City." Man used to come and pick up the slips and the money. Back then, you could pay a quarter, fifty cents, and my mom used to write a "book" called the "Windy City."

Back then quite a few people were writing policy. It was like a supplementary income. She wasn't a runner.

Somcone would come pick it up. They would come to her. They'd say, "I want to play fifty cents," or whatever, on the "Windy City," and she would write on a sheet and give them a copy. Then the man, the runner, would come and pick the slips up. Then whoever would win, he'd come back with the winning number and she would call them. This all happened when I was in grammar school.

Timuel D. "Tim" Black

The numbers game was invented by... two fellas, one was Tnan [*sic*] Jones and one was Mush Mouth Johnson... in the eighteen nineties. ... The numbers then became a business which had trained lawyers and accountants. The one that became the biggest, best known were the Jones brothers who had a wheel, which was like a roulette kind of thing, that became known as the "Harlem in the Bronx." ... There was one white guy, Julius Benvenotti, an Italian, who also had a policy wheel. Julius Benvenotti was the only white person who acted like he was a black guy, really, Julius Benvenotti.

[The Jones brothers] decided to take their wealth and leave, and they went to Mexico and lived in Mexico City. But their–their main manager, Ted Rowe..., he took over the business. There was a fella on the West Side who was also [a] numbers king, Big Jim Martin ... and he was run out of business [by white gangsters] because it was very lucrative. And Ted Rowe decided he wasn't going to let anybody run him out of the business. ... One night when he and his chauffeur, or bodyguard, were driving down around Fifty-Second and

King Drive... they were cornered by these white gang-sters. ... Ted Rowe and his bodyguard killed two of these guys. We knew then it was just a matter of time that he would be–that they would catch him. And eventually, about two years, 1953, in a vacant lot across from Bethesda Church... they mowed him down.

That effectively wiped out control [by] the blacks. But what was the reaction of the black community to that? They began to not play the numbers any more. Without being told, they began to not play the numbers. The admiration that they had for these self-made mil-lionaires and the kind of interest that they had because it was almost a social as well as a luck affair, that you would go to a policy station–a policy station was like a bookie–and you had tellers right there. And you could also talk with your neighbors and your friends while you were putting in your numbers.

Night Life

Delores Washington

There was a dance hall called the Peps that I wasn't allowed to go to, but I went. You had to walk up some dark dingy steps, and when you got to the top of the steps they'd pat you down to see whether you had a gun or knife on you. They would pat you down, but the music was good. You'd dance and dance. And the boys would stand around the wall like they probably do now, looking at the girls. Then, boys wore suits and they had their hats cocked to the side, walking around looking cool.

You could go to the show for ten cents. Can you

imagine going to the show for ten cents? Can you imagine going to see a stage show with Cab Callaway and paying twenty-five cents? And the Regal Theater was just beautiful—I saw Cab Callaway, Lionel Hampton, all the big stars, we could see them for twenty-five cents. The Met was on one side of the street, on South Park, and the Regal was on the other, and the shows would be all lit up.

And in the summertime, people would be out on South Park. They'd sleep out on the [grassy median] strip all night and nobody would bother you. And then too, they had radios in those days, and we'd listen to those shows—"Let's Pretend," "The Shadow," and on Saturday nights people would hear "I Love a Mystery" and just sit there and be quiet and listen to that spooky stuff coming on with the lights out. The most famous of all were "Amos 'n' Andy," even though they were played by white actors. In the summertime, you could walk down South Park and hear everybody playing "Amos 'n' Andy" on the radio.

Gladys McKinney

When I was coming up, for big entertainment, Sixty-Third Street was the highlight for us. They had every kind of blues, nightclubs. Mostly they'd have some little combo or band though. I didn't remember seeing any stars. I used to go downtown to see Nat King Cole, Duke Ellington, Count Basie, down at the Opera House.

Back when I was coming up, it was rare to see a black young teenager sitting in the Opera House for a concert. There were not too many blacks going to the Opera House. At that time, when blacks went downtown to a hotel, they might have been there working as waitresses or waiters.

I really didn't run into a lot of racial problems, though. Chicago was so big that you could go places and you didn't have to come in contact with that if you didn't want to. Just like it is today.

Blues at the Maxwell Street flea market.

The Church

Timuel D. "Tim" Black

There was some people who went to church on Sunday morning and they didn't come back home until late in the evening. They'd stay at church all day, not just praying and listening to the preacher, but because there were a lot of activities in the church ... [S]ome of us were on church baseball teams and basketball teams and football teams. ... And then it was a place for education, like when people would come to Chicago from the South, the church was one of the places where they might go to get information about where to go look for a job, to learn to read better. ...

Sunday morning we would get up early. My mother would cook, cook, cook. And we would have great big Sunday morning breakfasts. We might have smothered pork chops, smothered chicken, rice or grits, and rice and grits. ... Great big beautiful biscuits, and we would eat and eat and eat, and then we would set off for church. ...

[M]y father worked in the steel mill or the stockyard, whichever he happened to be. They worked twelve hours a day, six days a week. But ... on Sunday, that was our day. And he'd just give himself to that day.

Gladys McKinney

We were raised up in the church—Monumental Baptist Church, Thirty-Ninth and Cottage Grove. We went to church morning, noon and night—snow, rain, there wasn't no excuse. We'd go there for Sunday School, we'd stay there for B.Y.P.U. [a youth group].

We'd stay there all day. See, we'd go to Sunday School, then after Sunday School was the time for the regular worship service, then after the worship service they would feed us there, then we'd stay there B.Y.P.U. If we left, we had to come back. And if you didn't go to church on Sunday, you didn't have no activity—you

Gospel service.

couldn't go to the show.

I enjoyed it. It was a ritual, something she required of us. [But] you couldn't wake up and say, "I'm not going to Sunday School." You had to be sick.

Lillie Harston-Thomas

Storefront churches reminded me more of the down-home churches, down South. I sang with the junior choir. We were always going to different churches, singing. I was in high school and I think we went down South for a funeral. The storefront church had bare floors, and the congregation would go into those hymns, and all you could hear [she stamps her foot in rhythm on the floor] on those wooden floors. I was sitting there thinking, "Oh, God, is this floor going to hold up?"

Foes ...

Junius "Red" Gaten

Life was not easy here. They [whites] didn't want you over here. We had a church move from Thirty-Fifth and Dearborn called Ebenezer Baptist Church. ... They moved over there; the white folks bombed it, tore it up, knocked all the front out. ... Beverly AME Church, they bombed in 1924 and set it afire, burned our church down. Said we were making whiskey in there, because they didn't want us over here on Grand Boulevard.

Samuel Stevens

I knew Jack Johnson. He was heavyweight champion. He was married to a Caucasian lady. When he got out of prison, they voted that nobody over forty could fight again. So they tried to disbar him from that. I remember he fought [white boxer] Jim Jeffries and they gave the title to Jim Jeffries. We had a lot of good fighters at that time. Harry Wills was one of them, and Sam McVeigh—oh, there were a lot of good colored prizefighters. But they wouldn't allow them to fight the whites until Joe Louis came along. Then Joe Louis came along and he won the title—the Brown Bomber. I remember him very well. He didn't come into [my drug] store. He was around Thirty-Fifth Street and by that time I was around Sixty-First Street.

Bunny Dallas

I guess I was wearing rose-colored glasses all of my life but I was never made to feel—discriminated against. Except once. And you know when that was? I had just graduated high school and I was looking in the newspaper for a job. At the Stevens Building, downtown on State Street, it listed file clerks. I walked up to the receptionist's desk and saw all these ladies around. I told her what I was there for. She said, "Oh, I'm sorry, we don't cater to Negro clientele."

I almost collapsed. I could just barely turn and head for the elevators. Tears just rolled down my eyes. I really don't look at [skin] color like a lot of people do. I had heard of this, outside of your community, but I had never run into it—and if I did I was too blind to see it. It didn't taint me or scar me or anything because I was seventeen or eighteen years old, it was just that— what I'd heard was true!

Enich Hymon

You weren't allowed in Bridgeport [the white ethnic neighborhood west of Comiskey Park]. Right now, behind the old Comiskey Park? We [blacks] better not go there, and that's a public facility of the City of Chicago—they have a swimming pool over there. But we used to come over there and everybody learned how to drive, in the parking lot, off season.

One time, I was eleven or twelve years old, a brick comes through the window. We come back on Cottage Grove, about four carloads of us, and we see four or five [white] guys under the lights. The more you walk, the more people come out of the bushes. You know Mack's Truck Company, it's still over there on Thirty-Third? I elevated myself up on a [truck undercarriage] and I stayed there until daybreak.

They [whites] caught a couple of friends of mine and took them to Thirty-Fifth and Lowe [in Bridge-port] and they let them go, I think about eleven or twelve o'clock at night. They knew my friends would have to walk through Bridgeport at that time to get back on Cottage Grove. But I was slick—I stayed under that truck. One of those eighteen-wheelers. I was greasy as hell when I got home, and I did get a whipping. When I told my mom and dad what happened, they didn't want to believe it. My old man said, "What were you doing over there?" I was just following the crowd.

Gladys McKinney

Now the Tivoli [a grand movie palace that] used to be at Sixty-Third and Cottage Grove—we used to sit in the balcony. I'll never forget, I was in high school, had to be about fourteen, fifteen, maybe sixteen [around 1945]. I went there one day and I refused to go up in the balcony. They said they were going to put me out. I said, "You can put me out but I'm going to be right back." There were seven or eight of us. We weren't disorderly or anything, we just refused to go up in the balcony. Finally, they saw we were determined and they let us sit downstairs. And didn't nobody bother us.

My friends told me, "Don't do it." But when I was coming up, I wouldn't say I was militant–civil rights activities didn't come until the Sixties–but I was the type of child who would try, just to see what the outcome would be. I'd say, "Whatever happens, I'm in God's hands."

Junius "Red" Gaten

In our community at Thirty-First and Indiana ..., Walter Power's restaurant was there. They wouldn't serve Negroes. So some of the hustling boys asked me, said, say, Red, say, we want to borrow your horse and wagon. ... They threw some bricks through the window and that's how we got in the–broke the glass out the windows. And that's how they opened and let us eat. ... I serviced all seven of Power's restaurants. I could eat in them. I delivered ice to them all.

Gladys McKinney

The two high schools we went to were du Sable and Phillips. Back then, blacks weren't going to Hyde Park High. When a black went to Hyde Park High back then, that was the cream of the crop. To go to Hyde Park High School, you had to live in Hyde Park or use somebody's address. They would call and verify that you stayed there. That's the way it was back then, yeah. That happened. They would call and you'd say, "Oh yeah, that's my niece."

Lillie Harston-Thomas

We would get on the streetcar on Sunday sometimes and just ride. It was a form of entertainment. We did not get off because we did not know the different areas and because it was just something for us to do. We knew we were going into strange areas, so we weren't that adventurous. Our parents never told us you can't go this far or that far, but we knew. We couldn't go west past Comiskey Park because they'd want to jump on us because of our color.

Bunny Dallas

My dad would have been a Stokeley Carmichael if he hadn't been born in that time. He'd get to preaching, how the white man—and he didn't make any distinction—he did this and he did that. Sometimes we'd be sitting in the living room talking about something else and he would bring it up, especially if he had a couple of drinks. He would make comments like, "I don't like nothing white. I don't even like a white shirt." That crazy stuff. But he got along well with his people that he worked with. He worked with a lot of immigrants.

He did manual labor work. When he was down South, before he married my mom, he was an insurance salesman. He only had an eighth grade education but he was very well read. When he came here, you just can't come up with an eighth grade education and get certain jobs. I think Dad thought the world cheated him, that he deserved more than he had.

My father was a very fair-skinned man. In fact when he worked up North, he used to—remember them old-time caps men used to wear, refugee men?—my dad dressed like that. He would buy all of his clothes from Maxwell Street, because it was cheap.

He would come home sometime and tell my mother, "Goddammit, that 'hunkie' come *sprechen Sie Deutsche* at me."

He didn't say "honkie," like they do now. It was "hunkie," like "bohunk" [derogatory slang for a native of Bohemia], and that's what he called it. Momma would say, "Well, you dress just like them."

Delores Washington

Life was slow and easy going in those days. It wasn't like, "Oh, I gotta be doing this and I'd better be doing that." We knew it was prejudiced—we knew they weren't going to hire you downtown in a store unless you were very high yellow, we knew that—but we were proud just to be allowed to get on the bus to go downtown. We knew you couldn't go across the boundaries of certain neighborhoods, but that didn't bother me because I guess I went to all-black schools, went to all-black high schools. When it really started hitting me about the races was when I went to junior college, which was Wilson—began to realize, "Oh, white kids go here." ...

[After her family and other blacks moved into previously all-white Englewood], gradually the whites moved out of the neighborhood. And that's really what tears down the neighborhood. See, those homes weren't that glamorous. They were just average homes, like in Cicero or Bridgeport—just simple homes, nothing fancy. But [whites] kept up their streets—they swept their streets, kept the papers off, the yards were all neat, so you thought when you were moving there, you were moving somewhere nice. You were! But then when we [blacks] started migrating there, it started deteriorating.

The blacks in the city of Chicago in the thirties, forties and fifties, they had pride. When they started moving out of the neighborhood and the sixties came along, blacks with pride seem to decrease. That's when they started saying, "Oh, I'm black, we can do this, we can do that," you know? Civil rights came in. The prominent blacks, the stable blacks, moved out of the neighborhood.

... and Friends

Marion Hummons
I don't think [the Depression] really affected us too much. You see, you had these Jews who had these mom-and-pop stores. Today you hear some of these black people, they hate the Jews, but you see, they are young. They might have been babies during the Depression. They don't know anything about these Jewish people who owned the mom-and-pop stores. They [Jews] used to give the fathers jobs, and any other old produce that got stale but you could still cook. If it hadn't been for these Jews, the Negroes would have starved to death.

Samuel Stevens

I came to Chicago [around 1927]. I started to work for a Jewish fellow named Max at Thirty-First and Vernon. He wouldn't let you run the register, but you could wait on the customers. The Jewish people have always been great friends and benefactors to colored people. Colored people had to get credit. Nobody else would offer credit, but the Jewish people would always give you credit. What the blacks say about the Jews now, they say just for the lack of knowledge. They've been the biggest help to blacks, the Jewish were.

Black safety inspector, the supervisor of his white coworker at International Harvester.

Bunny Dallas

Most of them [white merchants] were Jewish. That's what a lot of blacks don't understand. The Jewish storekeepers would give credit. A&P [supermarkets] wouldn't give you any credit. Then they [Jewish storekeepers] would knock up this price a little bit and that one a little bit—that's to cover the people who moved out of the neighborhood and wouldn't pay them. My mom, Saturday mornings she would get up and say, "I want me some strip steaks. Go to the little store on the corner and tell Mr. So-And-So give me ten strip steaks," or twelve, depending on if my aunts or different ones were coming over. And I would go and he would put it in the book.

And What Happened Next?

Charles Branham

The restrictive covenants were a series of pseudo agreements—"pseudo" I say because they were later declared unconstitutional by the Supreme Court. ...

What happened is that community institutions, the church, Commonwealth Edison, and some of the major business, even scouting organizations, canvassed neighborhoods or used the church as a mechanism for going around the neighborhoods, getting them to sign an agreement that they would not sell or rent their homes or their apartments to blacks. ... Once seventy-five or eighty percent of a specific community agreed, it was assumed that the entire community was covered by a restrictive covenant. That means that nobody, whether they signed the agreement or not, was going to sell their property to a black family. And throughout the twenties and thirties ... Chicago was protected from racial integration by restrictive covenants. ... [I]t was not until 1948 [that the Supreme Court] finally came down that restrictive covenants were unconstitutional. ...

In point of fact, restrictive covenants ended in 1948 and you really have not seen a significant increase in racial integration in Chicago until probably the late seventies or early eighties. Why? Fear of violence. Blacks have been afraid for several generations, in fact, to go into certain neighborhoods. ...

Black movement has been block by block, often faced with violent resistance, sometimes with gangs, sometimes with organized attempts to prevent blacks from moving into certain houses on certain blocks. So the end of restrictive covenants had very little effect on the integration of black Chicago.

◆   ◆   ◆   ◆   ◆   ◆   ◆

Starting in the fifties, "urban renewal" began depopulating Bronzeville. Small businesses like the States Theatre closed for lack of patrons. The Robert Taylor Homes, the world's largest public-housing project when it was built, opened for business in 1962; it quickly became synonymous with crime and social breakdown. In 1998 the Chicago Housing Authority began demolishing the Taylor Homes. By that time, though, the rest of Bronzeville had been pretty much urban-renewed to the ground. Today, demand for affordable close-in housing is sparking a revival in the neighborhood. Encouraged by organizations such as The Black Metropolis Convention & Tourism Council, developers are renovating what housing stock still remains standing. Yuppies, buppies and dinks are moving in. Market forces may yet accomplish what fifty years of social policies could not.

# # #

All photos courtesy of Wayne S. Miller, from his book *Chicago's South Side, 1946-1948*, University of California Press, 2000; except the newsboy with *The Daily Defender* on p 257, courtesy The New Press, from the book *Bronzeville, Black Chicago in Pictures 1941-1943.* ©2003.

About the Author

Frank Joseph cut his teeth as a writer at the City News Bureau of Chicago, a noted training-ground for journalists. He worked at The Associated Press, covering the Democratic National Convention street disorders, the Detroit riot, Dr. Martin Luther King's march into Cicero, Illinois, and almost every ghetto uprising and incident of urban violence that defined the turbulent mid-sixties in Chicago. Joseph was an editor with *The Washington Post* during the Watergate years, and in 1982, he founded Key Communications Group Inc., a specialized-information publishing company. This is his first novel. He and his wife, Carol Jason, a sculptor and artist, met in Chicago and now live in Chevy Chase, Maryland; they are the parents of Shawn and Sam.